OBX

DAVID DEAN

DEDICATION

For Josh. Keep on trucking, son.

"Water is the boss the land must obey." - Anonymous

CHAPTER 1

For the first time in her life, Kathy Kirkland was afraid.

The young, athletic blonde lived each day without fear, especially when soaking in the coastal waters of her native North Carolina. The ocean had always seemed like home, but this humid August night the lukewarm Atlantic swirling around her ankles and sticky breeze on her face were only adding to her anxiety.

Taking a long drag off of what was left of her joint, she tipped her head back and closed her eyes, trying to relax.

For the third time since wading into the water, Kathy heard a soft, faraway voice tugging at the corners of her consciousness.

The toke caught in her throat — coughing violently, she dropped the joint into the water, stumbling slightly, shuffling her bare feet through a minefield of pointy, painful seashells. She opened her eyes, glancing nervously left and right, seeing nothing in the moonless, hazy summer night.

Kathy stared down at the black water now lapping against her calves. Where were her sandals? Concentrating hard, a rush of images blurred together. Flirting with the bartender. Cuervo shots. A brunette passing the joint in the bathroom. Starting to feel dizzy. Stumbling out of the bar and walking across the beach road toward the dark ocean.

Tossing her sandals over her shoulders as she skipped happily into the rolling waves.

So that's where my sandals went.

Suddenly, she heard the voice again, louder this time. She couldn't make out what it was saying or where it was coming from.

Kathy spun from side to side, searching frantically, wiping her long stringy hair from her face. All of the movement forced a series of coughs in her throat; bending at the waist to catch her breath, she felt water lap against her chest, soaking her knit tank top.

She snapped straight-up in the water, almost losing her balance again, stretching her arms out to her sides to catch herself, the jumble of colorful images rushed from Kathy's rambling train of thought, pushed out by the sound of crashing waves all around her.

I'm waist deep in water.

In the first moment of clarity Kathy had since starting her partying, Kathy realized she was alone, in the middle of the night, in the ocean.

"Okayokayokay, calm down," she muttered to herself. Trying to get a grip on her situation, Kathy could feel waves pushing against the lower part of her chest and hear more breaking several feet behind her. Panic growing, she took another deep breath of the heavy, humid air, trying to locate some lights from waterfront houses and the beach road.

All she saw was blackness.

Kathy heard the far away voice again, clearer this time; it was a man's voice, louder than before, yelling to her. "Turn around! You're walking into the ocean!" it warned. Kathy took another breath and clumsily moved her feet, turning her body around. Waves were now pushing at her back instead of her chest and surging up to her armpits. Focusing hard, she could see some blurry lights peeking through the dark and hear waves breaking in front of her.

"Movemovemove," Kathy mumbled, willing her body to move forward, feeling the ocean recede to her thighs, then calves. Water began rushing back over her feet, toe to heel, pulling hard out to sea behind her.

A heavy wave broke over her lower back, surprising Kathy and sending her hard face-first into shallow water. The wave receded, rolling her a few times away from the beach. She began pulling herself up to her knees and crawling forward, coughing, and spitting sour seawater out of her mouth and trying to catch her breath. A whooshing sound rushed at her from behind; another heavy wave knocked her underwater, rolling her out to sea as it receded. Kathy pushed herself up and broke the surface, gasping for more of the chewy, salty air; another wave crashed over her, rolling her onto her back.

She couldn't figure out where the surface was.

Holding her breath underwater, Kathy started to vomit into her mouth. The receding current was dragging her across the rocky, seashell-ridden bottom into deeper water. Head swimming, heart pounding, Kathy was unable to stop herself from sliding.

She flailed her arms frantically and tossed her head up to where she thought the surface was. Instead, she hit the back of her head hard on the sand and shells, seeing stars. A muffled crash from above told Kathy she was completely underwater. She felt herself being pulled faster out to sea, feet-first.

She listened hard for the voice again, but heard only the muffled crash of waves.

Then, nothing at all.

In her dream, Kathy was on the swing set in the backyard of her childhood home, a young girl again, kicking her feet back and leaning forward, then kicking her arms straight and leaning way back to get as high as she could go. She could see two blurry figures coming out the back of her house, although she couldn't see their faces. Probably mom and dad, coming to get her for dinner. Kathy stopped kicking and leaning, and felt her swing slowing down. She looked down at her feet just skimming the top of the grass, feeling the soft blades sneak in the slits of her sandals and tickle her toes.

Someone grabbed Kathy from behind, yanking her down off the swing.

Shaking, coughing, spitting, Kathy awoke half on her back, half on her side up on the beach. She endured dry heaves, spit up seawater, and started wiping sand-filled hair from her face.

Somebody grabbed hold of her from behind, trying to prop her up. Kathy began flailing her arms in panic, unsure of her surroundings; she felt her left hand hit something, like someone's face, and she clawed at it, trying to look up. She sort-of saw the shape of someone's face, but it was blurry, like the faces of the people in her dream.

Suddenly, Kathy felt the most excruciating, piercing pain on the top of her head she'd ever felt before. She felt herself fall out of the person's hands — falling, falling, falling, blackness closing in all around her, the sounds of the ocean, the grass beneath her feet on the swing set, everything fading into nothingness.

Kathy Kirkland would never wake again.

Floating along slowly in a sea of rush hour traffic, Robbie Cartwright thought the morning light reflecting off the cars looked a little like sunshine dancing on water.

The peaceful moment brought a brief smile to the round face of the 300-pound, six-foot North Carolina native.

A look at his watch and the smile was gone.

The head of the Raleigh office of the North Carolina State Bureau of Investigation cringed at the thought of getting to work later than 7:30. Robbie had some 30-plus people under his command, and was always sure to set a good example, especially getting to work early.

A slew of disturbing late afternoon calls and e-mails he'd received at the office the day before did not put him in the mood to be late this Thursday morning.

Still, another smile crept onto Robbie's face as a 30-something yuppie next to him in a Volkswagen frantically rolled up his windows and wiped his brow with his sleeve, desperate for air conditioned relief from the stifling August heat. Robbie checked himself in his rearview mirror; not a bead of sweat on his 50-year-old slowly balding head, despite his windows being wide open to welcome in the muggy southern air.

Twenty minutes later, he was out of his car and moving spryly toward the front of the SBI office, a five-story red brick structure that used to house offices for a tobacco company just a few blocks from the State Capitol. Its historic looks were offset inside the front doors by high-tech security devices, surveillance cameras, and numerous guards filling the large lobby. Passing through some metal detectors, Robbie headed at a quick step through the lobby, past a set of double elevators to some stairs.

The fat man flew up the steps hardly breaking a sweat, emerging on the third floor at the same quick pace, blowing into the hallway outside the SBI administrative office and then striding through the front door of the lobby with confidence. "Mornin' Kelly," he said in a strong, friendly voice. The 40-something brunette receptionist waved happily, unable to return the greeting due to a mouthful of warm Krispy Kreme donut.

Robbie kept moving, past the main lobby, past a break room toward the end of the hall. He nodded at two young male agents — Finneli with his slick-black hair thin, hipster looks, and Walsh, a handsome 30-something college quarterback type -- who stood talking among themselves, interrupting their conversation to mumble greetings to their boss.

Striding into his glass-walled office at the end of the hall, Robbie busied himself with turning on his computer. As he moved back across his office, shrugging off his sport coat and hanging it on the rack behind his door, he caught snippets of the agents' conversation.

"Finished up the Patterson case," Finneli, the more ambitious of the two said.

"Oh yeah? That's the, uh, the drug trafficking in Durham, right?" Robbie heard Walsh reply.

"Yeah, we seized a carload of pot and some pills outside the house."

"Where outside the house?" a female voice interrupted.

For the first time in his busy day, Robbie stopped. He stepped away from his coat rack and peered around the corner of his doorway. Across from the two agents, on the side of the break room in his line of sight, Robbie saw the source of the female voice.

Michael Francis. She was stirring a cup of coffee, leaning her slender, athletic five-eight frame against a counter, shapely legs casually crossed beneath a knee-length black skirt, neither boasting nor hiding her knockout good looks.

"Sorry, what?" Finneli asked incredulously. Robbie saw Michael's flawless face light up in a disarming smile, her green eyes widening below a long wisp of auburn hair that had found its way out from the confines of a ponytail.

"I'm sorry, I heard you talking about an evidence seizure at a crime scene. Was the car outside the house in the street or the driveway?" she asked sweetly.

Robbie heard an awkward pause, followed by a curt, "It was in the street. One of the perps said it was his car."

Quickly, Michael volleyed back, "Was it?"

More silence.

"Yeah, it was. I asked him if it was his car, he said yes.

He even had the keys."

Robbie saw Michael turn from Finneli and shoot a hopeful gaze over at Walsh, who just glared back at her. Looking dejectedly down at her coffee cup, fumbling with it absent-mindedly and placing it on the counter, Michael closed her eyes, as if trying to select her words carefully.

Robbie thought he saw her left eye twitch.

"I'm just curious, see, because if the car was in the street and the car isn't registered to the perp--"

"--let the professionals who've been around here for a while work the details after the fact, Agent Francis," Finneli hissed. "That's how it's done. The real show doesn't run by the book. Then again, you probably wouldn't know that, seeing how you haven't been the primary on anything since you've been down here."

Robbie grimaced as he saw Michael hang her head, staring at her feet.

"Agent Francis, could you come in here please?" Robbie called out over his shoulder as he moved behind his desk.

Robbie saw her take one last glance at her two peers as she strode quickly through his doorway, buttoning her suit jacket along the way.

"Shut the door please," he said. "Making lots of friends today, Agent Francis?"

Michael closed the door, turned and clasped her hands behind her back, smiling sweetly.

Robbie smiled.

Collecting herself. I like that.

"Please have a seat, I wanna talk about somethin' you might find interesting. Now, I received several calls and a couple e-mails yesterday from the regional SBI office out east in Rocky Mount," he said, leaning back in his well-worn brown leather desk chair. It was hot in the office; as in his car, Robbie shunned air conditioning. Despite the overbearing North Carolina August heat and humidity, he relied instead on a slowly turning ceiling fan.

He watched for Michael to start fidgeting in the sticky heat.

Nothing.

"The office there got a call about a possible murder, said they got a special request to have it investigated at the highest level."

Michael slid forward in her seat. "Where exactly? Any details from local law enforcement?"

Robbie leaned forward in his chair and crossed his arms on his desk. "Well now, it's interesting you ask that, Agent Francis, because that's the curious thing about this case. The local law enforcement did not call the SBI."

Michael knitted her brow. "The local LE didn't call, sir? Then who did?"

Robbie smiled, leaning forward to grab a manila folder on his desk. He slid it across to Michael.

"A very insistent woman named Amy Miller with the Dare County Chamber of Commerce called the SBI on her own. She said the locals were dragging their feet trying to find out what happened to a young lady in Nags Head. You know where Nags Head is, Agent Francis?"

"Down where Route 64 ends at the coast?" Michael answered, taking the folder and opening it to review the contents. "Out by Kitty Hawk, where the Wright brothers flew. It's a town in a chain of barrier islands running up to the Virginia border, right?"

"Right. Outer Banks. Tourism central for eastern North Carolina, some seven million visitors each year, thereabouts," Robbie said in an over-accentuated southern drawl. "Those folks out there got hit real hard by a hurricane or two a few years back, especially Dare County which has the beaches. Governor soaked up all the recovery money to balance the damn budget. As a trade-off, the state legislators out there been carryin' a lotta clout with the Governor and the state legislature here in Raleigh. Ever heard of State Senator Skip Pennington?"

"Sure," Michael answered. "He's from that area, always

popping up on the talk shows. Vocal critic of the Governor from within his own party. Wants to develop infrastructure, bridges, that sort of thing to help the tourism trade, the environmentalists hate him. Seems like he's looking to go to D.C. just about any day now, run for Senator Fairley's seat, rub elbows with the big boys."

"Lotta folks know Skip Pennington, Agent Francis, including Amy Miller. She dropped his name quite frequently when she called. Also, lotta folks hate him," Robbie interrupted. "He's one powerful mother, U.S. Senate wannabe or not. Needless to say, the Dare County Chamber of Commerce has a whole lotta say when it comes to utilizing state resources like the SBI thanks to people like Pennington, and what Amy Miller says goes as far as we're concerned." He stared straight at Michael. She leafed through the papers in her hand, skimming them.

After a minute or so, she looked up at Robbie and brushed a wisp of hair away from her face.

"Sir, if they're still dragging their feet why would we get involved now?"

"Look at the victim's employment history."

After sifting through some papers, Michael said, "She worked in Senator Pennington's office."

Robbie got up from his chair and walked over to the window behind his desk, gazing down at the busy street below.

"You been in North Carolina how long?"

"Almost a year now," Michael replied.

"So you missed Hurricane Floyd a while back," Robbie said, still looking out the window. "We felt him all the way here in Raleigh – high winds, lots of rain, flooding. A real bastard. They start with a tropical depression in the Atlantic, Agent Francis. Within days, they can either peter-out or ramp up quick and turn into a tropical storm. At that point, they start headin' north-northwest real quick. When timin's right, summer through October, they can build up steam and hit the Carolina coast, usually Outer

Banks, in no time flat. Flooding and winds wipe everything out that ain't tied down, then everybody rebuilds."

He turned to Michael, his face scrunching into a serious scowl of concern. "These folks out there, lots of 'em got their businesses, homes wiped out. If enough of those types of folks scream long and loud enough, Skip Pennington does what they want. And if he don't get what they want, well the good Senator can come down here, wave his hand, and poof, the Raleigh SBI office as we know it is no more."

"Sir," Michael almost interrupted, "I'm still wondering; why didn't the locals or even someone from Senator Pennington's office request SBI assistance? Why'd the request come from the Chamber of Commerce, that just seems--"

"--odd," Robbie finished her sentence. He walked around his desk and sat on the corner nearest Michael, lowering his voice and leaning in close. "What's missing from that report?"

Michael took a minute to sift through more papers. Looking up at Robbie, she asked, "Where's the crime scene information?"

Robbie nodded. "Agent Francis, we've got 23 agents here, and only one of 'em ain't from the Tar Heel State with 15 cousins who know what color socks Skip Pennington wears when he gets up in the mornin'. You wanna guess which one?"

Michael tried to smile, and looked back down at the papers in her hand.

"We need to do our part as asked, due diligence, that's just fine. But I ain't been doin' this job this long ta' let some good ol' boy do a half-assed job to cover the ass of one of his second cousins, you know what I mean? This murder's already a couple of days old. I need you to get out there tomorrow, poke around, and get back here with some information. If -- and this is a big if -- there is somethin' funky goin' on out there with the locals, you report it back to me, you hear? Directly to me, and we can move on it at a later date. But remember, this is the most powerful government official in the state of North Carolina we're talkin' about here, so mind your p's and q's."

"You do want me to solve the case, right?" Michael quipped.

"We need to do our part, be ethical and prudent," Robbie replied harshly, adding, "And I want it done right, sure. But only if something's there — don't go lookin' for trouble, if you know what I mean." The big man got up, moved back behind his desk and busied himself with paperwork, waiting for his visitor to leave.

"Sir, why didn't you just tell the Rocky Mount SBI office to take care of it themselves?"

Turning and smiling, Robbie laughed. "Already did, Agent Francis. They wouldn't touch this with a ten-foot pole. My position within the bureau precludes me from simply ignoring this. It falls in our lap, like it or not."

♦♦♦

After spending the day researching Senator Pennington, the murder file, and other information about her new case Michael headed back to her home in the suburbs. Pulling up in front of her two story brick colonial, she turned off the engine and sat silently in her Subaru wagon for a good fifteen minutes thinking about the challenge before her.

The thoughts made her uneasy.

A young woman was murdered in a vacation hot spot, with connections to a high-powered politician seeking higher office. A curiously rushed, half-assed investigation by local authorities, judging by the files.

And the worst part; upon further investigation, Michael had discovered multiple missing persons cases in the Outer Banks over several years, with victims closely matching the physical description of the murdered girl.

No bodies. No arrests. Just young girls gone missing.

Michael watched through the family room windows while her two oldest daughters sat in front of the television; her youngest, still at a friend's house down the street. What if one of them had gone missing? Or worse? Would she be able to find them, to protect them?

Would Brian?

Doubtful, she thought. The thought of her husband filled her with a mix of disgust, anger and guilt.

Here it was 6:30, and she was just getting home from work. As bad as she felt about that, she got angry remembering that Brian usually didn't get home until eight, nine, some nights ten o'clock, even though his shift was supposed to end at 6:00. Such was the life of a beat cop.

Or someone who did everything possible to avoid coming home.

The end of the summer was supposed to be the return to a sought-after season of routine for Michael Francis, the first repetition of back-to-school that would finally bring a feeling of normalcy to her mid-30's lifestyle after relocating from the frozen tundra of Buffalo, New York late last fall.

Brian was another story.

The move was tough on him, despite his finding a job in the Raleigh Police Department. It seemed nothing was good enough, and Brian's dissatisfaction with their new life had affected their relationship. Although not abusive in the physical or verbal sense, it had become neglect in a more terrifying way: they never talked, were hardly ever in the same room during the day for more than five minutes, and came to bed at different times to go straight to sleep.

Then there was the night of June fifth.

Michael closed her eyes and held them shut, willing herself not to cry. After some calming breaths, she opened them as if waking from a dream, realizing that it wasn't June fifth anymore.

A rush of guilt almost overwhelmed her.

Soon she was able to get herself together and found herself standing at her front door, with two beautiful daughters inside who had to be told that their mother was leaving first thing in the morning for a week or more to work a case. After the trauma of this news subsided, Michael knew she would have to do it all over again when her daughter Anna came home.

Michael started feeling the guilt rushing back. She began to get sick to her stomach.

Her left eye started to twitch.

CHAPTER 2

The unwanted dream kept rushing back over Amy Miller in waves, teasing with the possibility of a happy ending this time.

In her mind's eye the 30-something redhead was back in her Cabriolet early Tuesday morning, driving with the top down on the main thoroughfare between the first and second rows of beach houses in Nags Head, smack dab in the center of the Outer Banks. Stopping at a red light, the real estate broker closed her eyes and breathed-in the sweet smell of the nearby ocean just a hundred yards away.

Opening her eyes Amy shifted her gaze between houses to find the most unobstructed view of the water, in a smallish lot next to the two-story vacation home at 3042 Beach Road. Her eyes were quickly drawn from the lot to the cedar-shingled home's upside-down "For Rent" sign dangling precariously above the empty carport as well as the unit's unhinged screen door, slowly moving back and forth in the slight breeze, revealing a darkened foyer. Amy hoped that some stupid kids hadn't broken into the vacant home overnight and trashed the place; as it was one of her units, she'd have to get it fixed before the next renters arrived.

Turning across the street and pulling into 3042's driveway, she got out and stepped quickly up the flight of sand-tainted wooden stairs to the front screen swinging freely on its hinges. Amy tried the latch on the knob, but it wasn't fitting right. The inner door, wide open, caught in the wind and creaked softly, beckoning her inside.

She walked in, looking around the empty foyer, then closed the door securely behind her.

As she did, she heard suction from the doorframe, signaling an airtight fit. That told the experienced vacation rental professional that all the windows in the home were closed. She stood silently for a minute in the dark alcove beyond the door, listening. She heard nothing.

But she smelled something. A heavy, odorous stench.

Amy stepped into an empty bedroom to her right, and sniffed; the smell wasn't coming from in there.

She ducked her head into the other two bedrooms and a bathroom; the scent was definitely coming from somewhere else, a stopped-up toilet perhaps.

From upstairs.

Amy made her way up the narrow, dark stairwell into the kitchen area where the stench got stronger. The family room was across from her as she stood at the top of the stairs, at the far end of a 25-foot open space, separated from the kitchen area by a dining room. A set of glass sliders was directly across from her, on the far side of the family room, curtains drawn to block the glorious morning sunshine. Nice unit, she thought, her eyes following the sliders over to a huge flagstone fireplace and a bare hardwood floor.

That's where she saw the body.

Her heart began to race. She could feel her stomach start to churn.

Facing her, lying propped-up against one side of the fireplace, was a naked young woman, face blue and somewhat bloated, head half-crushed, with what looked like dozens of stab wounds all over her chest. Her head was resting partly on her shoulder, tilted up on its side toward Amy. One of her lifeless eyes was wide open, halfway popped out, dangling from its socket.

A foreign hissing. Violent gurgling. Amy's coffee maker snapped her out of the dream that ended as it always did, and back into the reality of Friday morning. Rubbing tears out of her eyes, she started to feel bile form in the back of her throat again, just like Tuesday morning, and leaned forward over her kitchen sink, holding herself up with stiff, trembling arms. She closed her eyes again, took a deep breath, and felt the warm summer sun on her face through a set of wide bay windows. It felt like an old friend giving a hug.

Amy wondered how long the feeling would last.

For now, she just leaned there by the window, taking in all the sunshine she could get.

Outside, across the street, the driver of a white SUV with tinted windows watched Amy through binoculars with a mix of anger and glee. Once its prey moved away from the kitchen window, the SUV purred gently to life, pulled away from the curb and floated up Beach Road.

◆ ◆ ◆

Michael Francis stood outside the grey steel SBI supply room door, looking up into a video camera mounted on the ceiling. She unclipped her ID badge from her lapel and held it up next to her face. The camera lens whirred and moved, and a loud buzz preceded the door lock clicking open. Michael pushed through and made her way into a small 8' x 12' air-conditioned waiting area.

As the thick metal door clanged shut behind her, Michael turned to face a cache of weapons locked into place on the wall behind a fence of iron bars. Simple shotguns, M-16s, Berettas -- whatever the gun of choice, the supply room had it in stock.

Officer Mike Reynolds, a somewhat portly, older southerner with a well-worn brown face shot Michael a friendly smile from behind the bars, the tips of his thin mustache turning upward like a secondary grin. Michael was overwhelmed by the scent of Reynolds' lifelong attachment to cigarettes, the tobacco stench permeating the entire supply area. Why they let this man sneak cigarettes in the back of the armory by all that ammunition was a mystery, Michael thought.

"Agent Francis, how we doin' today?" Reynolds asked in a husky voice, walking over to a small opening in the wall of iron that constituted a service window.

"Great, Mike. Down here at the butt crack of dawn for a trip to the beach."

"Don't know if we have any umbrellas or coolers handy," the officer chuckled, taking Michael's requisition form through a service window in the middle of the wall of bars. He took a minute to go over his visitor's list.

Reynolds leaned forward, his forearms on the countertop behind the service window. "This list don't read like no fun day at the beach to me," he softly chided. Michael just nodded and smiled. "Blue Star?" Reynolds asked, adding, "not Luminol?"

"Nah, Luminol deteriorates the DNA in blood. Blue Star keeps the DNA intact," Michael replied.

Reynolds raised an eyebrow. "You, uh, goin' somewhere you expect to find a lot of blood?"

Michael smiled and shrugged. "Hey, you never know."

As Reynolds turned to walk back deeper into the supply room, Michael felt a sudden rush of anxiety.

"Mike, ah, you know, I think I might want to change what I put down weapons-wise," Michael yelled back clumsily. Reynolds came back up front with a box of supplies and stared at her blankly.

"Changed your mind, huh?" he said curiously.

"Changed my mind. Along with the extra ammo for my

service piece, I think I'm gonna also get--" Michael paused, looking at the wall of weapons, "--a pump-action."

Reynolds turned to unlock a shotgun from its place on the wall. Under his breath, he asked, "Shotgun, huh? You are just investigating a murder, right?"

"Just get me the damn shotgun," Michael ordered rather than asked, turning away and pretending to check her requisition list. She didn't want him to see the slight twitch she had started to notice just above her left eye. Her heart was racing, like she'd gotten away with something she shouldn't have. She swallowed hard, forcing the twitch to disappear.

She hoped Reynolds would think the shotgun was extra security.

Michael knew better.

♦ ♦ ♦

Another hot August day at the beach had begun, but the muggy, saturated air was gone, thanks to some stiffening ocean winds. The strains of a Creed heavy metal ballad blared from the open cockpit of the bright yellow Jeep Wrangler as it followed early morning traffic on Beach Road. A crusty old out-of-towner with Virginia plates glared in his rearview mirror and his passenger even turned her gray-haired head around to look directly out her back window at the vehicle with the offending music.

Rocking-out behind the wheel of his Jeep, Sergeant Toby Jones smiled and wondered: if his vehicle didn't have Dare County Police plastered all over it and police lights atop his roll bar, would the old fogies have shot some expletives his way?

The tanned and buff law officer switched on his rollers. Squealing its tires, the Jeep swerved angrily around the old folks' car still sitting at the red light, Officer Jones' long blonde ponytail flapping over his headrest.

At his height of cool, Officer Jones fumbled the clutch

going into second gear and ground his gears with a sickening grinding. He glanced out the corner of his eye and saw the old man grinning.

Jones zipped through the intersection, his lights flashing for another 500 feet until he hit another red light. He made sure the elderly car was nowhere in sight as he meekly cut his lights off.

"Eesh, you're such a dink. Serves you right," the 26-year-old chastised himself in the rearview mirror, shaking his head and laughing.

As his gaze left the mirror and moved up the street to his destination of 3042 Beach Road, the officer's mood took a turn as he spotted his Sasquatch of a boss rolling up crime scene tape around the perimeter of the front yard.

"Oh, crap," he sighed.

He hit his rollers again and sped through the intersection, off the road, and over the yard, catching his back left tire on part of the drainage ditch as he rolled over the corner of the driveway. He cut the lights and engine and jumped out, buttoning-up his uniform as he quickly made his way over to his commander.

"Some entrance, Jonesy," Police Chief Curtis C. Anderson mocked. Officer Jones finished buttoning his uniform shirt and snatched off his glasses, squinting his baby blues as he walked determinedly towards Anderson, asking incredulously, "Chief, what're you doing? It took me three hours to secure this area Tuesday, by myself, thank you very much, while keeping the locals away!"

Chief Anderson turned to face his underling. He stared down through his mirrored aviator glasses at his young underling and smiled, his close-cropped mid-forties hair adding to his 1950's-style hard-ass appearance. At six-foot-six and a muscular 275 pounds, Anderson looked like a pro wrestler in a police uniform. His size and demeanor had intimidated many men larger than the muscular Jones.

"Crime scene's been taken care of, Jonesy," Anderson said matter-of-factly in his taint of a southern accent.

"Coroner's report is in, we're getting into the case. House is clean, got an ID on the deceased, took pictures, the whole nine yards."

Officer Jones looked up, mouth open in stunned silence, as Anderson resumed walking and rolling the tape. "Whoa, Chief, the house is clean? No biohazard crew to dust it good, look for DNA? I mean ... you sure we got it all?"

Anderson stopped short and spun around, glaring down into the face of his sergeant. "Yeah, I got it, Jonesy. Thanks for your concern," he said, briefly forcing a condescending smile for a moment before continuing to move along, rolling-up more tape. Jones caught up to him again. "No, no, I didn't mean -- I mean, I'm just wondering what to tell people," he fumbled apologetically.

"Tell anyone whatever you want. Had to rush on this one, my boy," Anderson shouted over his shoulder. "Next-of-kin have been notified, we're prepping the body for shipment to the funeral home in Raleigh. Everything's cool." He stopped, turned, and walking forcefully into Officer Jones' personal space. "We got businesses here don't need tourists driving past police tape. And you know as well as I do that the girl worked in Senator Pennington's office. I don't need any pressure from out-of-towners on this one, I want it tied-up quick. You understand? No fucking distractions," he cussed, turning and walking back to a section of yellow tape along a dune fence.

Unsure of what to do next, Officer Jones ran his hand down the length of his pony tail and looked back at the beach house. "Yeah, I uh, I didn't know the crime scene was cleared. I'm not so sure they're gonna like that."

Anderson violently ripped the last bit of yellow tape from the fence and turned back toward his underling. "Not sure who's gonna like what?" the hulking figure shot back in an ever-increasing angry tone, a length of the yellow tape punctuating his point as it snapped in the wind.

Jones took a step back to gather himself. "Well, I mean, that's kinda what I came over to tell you, Chief. State Bureau of Investigation in Raleigh, they're sending some people over to check things out. The girl, you know she ... she worked for Senator Pennington, right? Well, you know he's tight with the Chamber, and, well, Amy Miller call—"

"--don't tell me MILLER found a way to rope in the freaking S-B-I?!" Anderson screamed, marching toward Jones. He snapped off his aviators and burned his deep brown eyes into his sergeant's skull, his face flush red with rage.

"Well, she, uh, she called around to the regional office I think, and someone told her because it was Pennington's staffer they needed to contact Raleigh. The guy runnin' the show there, he's sendin' some of his people or something. I was told to meet them at the station today around noon."

"Bullshit!" Anderson barked, turning and putting his sunglasses back on slowly, taking a deep breath, trying to calm down. "That's such ... this whole thing is bullshit. You meet them," he said, turning back to Jones, shaking an index finger in his face. "You meet those goddamn agents, you do not let them talk to Miller, you bring them to me when they get here – as soon as they get here, dickweed. I'll tell them what we've got and get them on their fucking way."

Anderson turned and headed over to his white crew cab police truck, slamming the door hard as he wedged his massive frame behind the wheel. Jones followed him over and asked through the open driver's side window, "Chief where you gonna be? You want me to call you if they get in early?"

"Yeah, fine, I'll be at the morgue talking to Lane," Anderson mumbled, peeling-out backwards, cutting-off traffic, then slamming into gear and gunning his engine down Beach Road.

Shaking his head, Jones turned to walk into the beach house to make sure all the doors and windows were locked. As he did so, he brought his hand up to his face and looked at the sunglasses he had been holding.

One side of the glasses was crushed. His hand was drenched in sweat, and there were deep indents in his palm and fingers.

Friggin' Anderson, he thought.

He owes me $125 for these.

♦ ♦ ♦

Robbie Cartwright marched determinedly toward the lobby stairs inside the Raleigh SBI building, looking forward to his morning climb. For the extra-large Robbie, the daily exercise, prescribed long ago by his doctor and drilled into his head by his wife, was keeping his heart pumping. After all, his age was the only thing advancing faster than his waistline, thanks to all the eastern Carolina vinegar-laden barbecue and hush puppies wolfed-down at the local buffet joints.

Robbie never sweated going up the stairs. To him, sweating meant nerves, and nerves meant being unsure about something.

That rare agent who kept up on the stairs, who avoided the sweating, breathing heavily, or even chastising Big Robbie for not taking the elevator in the first place, that was always someone with a little something special.

Michael Francis had taken a trip or two up the stairs with Big Robbie in her first few months on the job.

She climbed the stairs with him on her third day, with Michael cheerfully engaging Robbie in conversation about family life, how great Raleigh was, etc., without missing a beat. Hell, she even held the door for Robbie at the top of the stairs. From then on, Robbie was always watching her out of the corner of his eye, watching how she interacted with her peers, lawyers, administrative types, local officials. He was at once impressed with her, yet worried about her. She never seemed to fit in with her peers at the SBI—

especially the born and bred southerners—and Robbie, to keep morale high, had been hesitant about showing his approval to a yankee at so early in her stay in Raleigh by giving her the lead on a case. Still, something about her made Michael Francis seem like a keeper.

Which is one of the reasons Robbie had sent her to Nags Head.

He needed to keep her confidence from sinking too low, had to throw her a bone so she could take some time and develop into the agent Robbie thought she could be. The Nags Head case should be a long-termer, as the early reports held no great hopes for a clear-cut solution. Robbie's crew needed to make an immediate appearance to make things look good then refocus attention when appropriate after any publicity had died-down.

Sounded like a perfect job for Michael Francis. New to the scene, she most likely wouldn't make any progress right away, but would work hard to make a good impression with her first real case and get enough details to help with a deeper investigation at a later date. Robbie didn't want any of his inbred agents simply caving to political influences and burying the case; a girl had died, for goodness sake, and she deserved a real investigation. Still, the case needed to be handled with kid gloves, balancing effort with political gamesmanship.

Especially with Skip Pennington involved.

Speak of the devil.

Robbie caught sight of Bart Taylor, Senator Pennington's young and overly enthusiastic legislative director, ending a conversation by the elevators and heading over with a pasted-on smile a bit too large for a Friday morning.

"Agent Cartwright! Bart Taylor. We met at Clyde Parker's fundraiser this past March," he blabbered, reaching out his right hand as he closed-in on the big man. His strong cologne enveloped Robbie as he approached, his full head of blow-dried straight brown hair giving the air of someone who tried really hard to look good, half Breck Girl, half politician. The combination of scent and sight was too much for Robbie so early in the morning. Forcing a small grin, Robbie came to a stop and raised both arms to show they were too full to shake hands; the left side carrying a briefcase, the right side a Bojangles breakfast bag. Taylor waited a half-second, sizing things up; Robbie put down his briefcase, switched hands with the Bojangles bag, and opened the stairwell door, offering a half-friendly, "Mornin." Taylor followed close on his heels.

As the two men entered the steamy, stagnant red brick stairwell, Taylor did not wait for an invitation to chat. "Agent Cartwright, the senator asked me to stop-by to thank you for helping out in Nags Head with this unfortunate incident with our staffer. I don't have to tell you the repercussions an unsolved murder floating around would have on the economy of the Outer Banks, and the senator is very interested in helping to continue to build his constituents' economy."

His voice trailed off to take a breath as the men climbed at a brisk pace.

"Well, that sure was nice of Skip to send you down here to thank me, but it certainly was not necessary," Robbie said in a slow drawl.

"Yes, well, we want to do everything we can to help in the investigation, get some people lined-up to help. The senator was wondering if he knew the agents you sent, if any of them had east Carolina connections that might be, ahh, concerns?"

Robbie stopped on the second landing and turned to look quizzically at the fast-talking unaccented yuppie. "Skip wants to help with the investigation, does he?" Robbie declared rather than asked.

Taylor, sweating a bit in the stuffy hallway, wiped some off his forehead, brushing back some stringy brown hair that had fallen out of place. "That's part of his job, as he sees it."

"Well now, I'm not sure I see it that way. You tell Skip thanks, and I'll call him personally when I get my agents report back," Robbie said, turning to continue upstairs, hoping Taylor wouldn't follow.

"You said agents, as in plural; did you send a whole team? Are we going to have to worry about a swarm of agents descending on a quiet beach community?"

More than a little angry, Robbie stopped three steps short of the third floor landing, turned, and stuck his hand carrying the now-greasy Bojangles bag in Taylor's face, index finger pointed squarely between the young man's narrow eyes.

"You know what, Mr. Taylor? Part of me wants to tell you my investigation is none of your damn business. Part of me wants to call your boss and tell him you're a real pain in the ass, harassing one of the Senator's staunchest supporters early in the mornin' on what should be a nice, relaxin' Friday. But I figure to give you the benefit of the doubt, so listen up. I have no time for questions about a case I have no information on. When the report comes in, I'll let your office know."

Undeterred, the legislative hack stashed his smile, furrowed his brow, and stepped around big Robbie, sprinting the last three steps to the landing and grabbing the handle of the door to the third-floor lobby. Looking forcefully at Robbie, he wheezed, "Look, I don't want to make anything out of this that it doesn't have to be. You know the senator. And believe me, the senator knows you." Taylor paused for effect before continuing. "He sent me here with some questions and expects me to come back with some answers. If you don't have the time to help me out now, I'm sure he'll find some time in his busy schedule to come down here himself, if he has to."

A look of resignation crawled across Robbie's angry face.

Propping open the door and brandishing a sickening

lobbyist smile, Taylor closed the deal. "I'm hoping you could spare just a few minutes before you get too far into your day? I'm just gonna need to know who you're sendin' and chat with them for a few minutes to make sure we're all on the same page with the details of the investigation. For the senator, of course. Then I may need to use your office to make a few calls. But that's it," he said, his smile widening.

"Sorry friend, my agent's likely gone already."

"Ah. Too bad. Regardless, I'm sure the senator would like to know who exactly has this extraordinarily sensitive case in their hands," Taylor said softly, yet firmly.

Robbie took his gaze off Taylor and looked straight ahead and walked into the lobby, Taylor close on his heels. "Kelly," he called to the receptionist as he passed with his first appointment of the day, get this young man all the details on Agent Francis' case, her logistics and contact info."

Stopping and turning, Robbie added under his breath, "And hold my calls please, darlin'. Gonna be a rough one."

As Michael Francis snapped the pump-action shotgun into its rack in the trunk of her borrowed standard-issue navy blue Crown Victoria, she felt a sense of empowerment wash over her. Stepping back, she reviewed the contents of her trunk: shotgun, shells, extra ammo for her service piece, first-aid kit, cans of Blue Star, light sticks, crime scene kit, case of bottled water, extra blankets. She slammed the trunk shut and stepped around to the driver's side, unlocking the back door and placing her suitcase, shoulder-strap briefcase, and duffel bag onto the seat. Shutting that door, she took one last look around the parking lot and felt under her left shoulder for her holster and piece. All set.

Sliding in behind the wheel of the Crown Vic, Michael

located the radio, air conditioning, and cigarette lighter into which she then plugged her cell phone charger. She adjusted the seat, rear and side mirrors, pausing before turning on the ignition. The sudden realization that she was leaving her three daughters for a week sent a pang of Catholic mother guilt straight into her gut. Still, they were all strong girls, the two oldest more than sure enough about themselves to take care of things.

Then there was Brian.

Michael wasn't so much worried about Brian handling himself as she was about him handling her leaving without telling him. This was the first time since things started getting really bad two months ago that she had left home for any extended period of time. When their relationship started its fast-forward free-fall, Michael had begun spending more and more time at work, later nights in front of her computer, and some office time on weekends. The girls were not handling things well at first. They'd come around recently, though, with the help of friends in the neighborhood and at school.

Michael remembered one night she got home late and found her 14-year-old Megan curled up in the corner of her bedroom, crying. Michael had tried to talk to her. "Giving up on someone because they're going through a rough time means you're giving up on yourself helping that person. You and your sisters need to help Daddy and me make things right by believing that...well, that we can make things right."

"What if you can't?" Megan worried, voice trembling through tears.

Michael couldn't answer her daughter that night.

Snapping back to reality, Michael straightened herself in her seat and caught a glimpse of herself in the rearview mirror. She had to focus on her job, on this case, she told her reflection.

She had to make things right.

One way or the other, she thought.

Michael leaned back in her seat in a quiet moment of contemplation. After a few calming breaths, she threw open the door and reached down beside her seat and reached for the trunk latch.

Scurrying out of the car, she walked back and grabbed the half-open trunk, lifting it up the rest of the way and staring at the shotgun in its rack. Michael stood and stared in silence for a couple minutes until she noticed butterflies in her stomach. Waiting for her eye to start twitching, she was pleasantly surprised at its stillness.

Michael slammed the trunk shut, leaned forward with both hands on the rear of the car, and closed her eyes. After taking a few deep breaths she straightened up and walked back to the driver's side, got behind the wheel and slammed the door shut.

Michael furrowed her brow, started the car and moved out of the parking lot into the early morning traffic. Her hands tightened on the wheel, and adrenaline began to surge through her body as Michael pushed everything out of her mind except the fact that she had to get moving.

"Wherever I'm headed, I'm on my way," she sighed.

CHAPTER 3

The bespeckled, middle-aged medical examiner was used to talking out loud to himself in the dimly lit, windowless morgue in the basement of the Dare County Hospital, just as he was used to the usual causes of death up and down the Outer Banks. "This is still the same sleepy part of the world you grew up in, you sixth-generation beach bum. This is your home. This is your life. This is normal," his voice echoed off the steel walls as he slipped on his lab coat and walked over to the examination table.

Chris looked down at the body of Kathy Kirkland.

"Normal," he sighed.

The girl was in her mid-twenties, dirty blonde shoulder-length hair, blue eyes, athletic. His index finger and thumb propped the dead girl's right eye open. As he pulled his hand away, her eye remained open, like she was watching him. It surprised and embarrassed Chris, who instinctively looked around to see if anybody else saw it. Of course not, he thought, he was all alone. He reached down and gently closed the eye shut, running the back of his hand gently across her cheek.

Chris took a few minutes looking over the girl's chart, hung it on a hook over the steel gurney before him, and proceeded to position his flexi-lamp to shine on the corpse's chest. He grabbed a digital audio recorder out of his white lab coat pocket, clicked it on, and started talking in hushed, unemotional tones.

"Stab wound at the top inside section of the stomach cavity, where the instrument was roughly driven into her body and removed. Multiple similar stab wounds, no specific pattern."

Ugly cuts, Chris thought as he looked at the haphazard, angry wounds around the stomach and chest. Totally different from the work of a professional surgeon, or even a seafood chef or a fisherman who are used to cutting things open.

"Coulda been anybody," he editorialized, adding, "That's what everybody will say, anyways." He did a double take at the recorder in his hand, wondering if he had actually spoken out loud. He clicked it off.

He looked back at the top of her head, which was a mess. The girl was already dead from a blunt trauma to the head before she was stabbed. Before he could examine her any further the doors to the morgue slammed open.

"Lane, you got our girl there?" Chief Anderson barked as he burst into the morgue, startling the M.E.

"Jesus Mary and Joseph," Chris said, flipping his glasses up onto his thinning red hair and rubbing his scratchy red eyes before looking at the interloper. "Yes, Chief. I was just examining her wounds again."

"Four, five hours plus Tuesday, more on Wednesday, then again yesterday, now you're at it one more time? Christ, you fallin' for this girl or what? And since when are you growing a beard? You're looking pretty ratty."

Chris averted his eyes from the Chief, absent-mindedly rubbing the scruff on the left side of his face. Anderson stepped next to him, looked down at the girl, then nudged him with his elbow and drooled under his breath,

"Wouldn't blame you, buddy. She's pretty sweet."

"Excuse me," Chris said harshly, moving away from Anderson and zipping up Kathy Kirkland's black body bag and pushing the wheeled examination table over to a storage drawer.

"We've got your autopsy, let's get everything signed-off and get this poor girl back to her momma in Raleigh," Anderson barked.

Shutting the drawer into place with a loud clang, Chris turned to face Anderson with a quizzical look. "You want to give her up so soon, Chief? My report was preliminary. We need to confirm the toxicology at the lab in Raleigh. That won't happen most likely until next Monday or Tuesday at the earliest."

"Yeah, well, I think you've already done all there is to do. There's no reason to keep her here any longer while we wait on the toxicology, we can get her results with her back in Raleigh just as well as we could with her here. Hell Chris, I don't want her here, the business community sure don't want her here, the tourists don't want her here. I'm sure your uncle, our great state senator, wants her back to her family ASAP. Think about it, Lane, do we wait until the TV hounds catch the scent and descend on this place and shove a microphone up your ass, that what you want?"

"Chief, this is a murder—"

"—nobody said this is a murder," Anderson cut him off. "Not yet, anyhow. Look, we've got all the clues we're gonna get from the body, there's no reason to keep-her-around," Anderson strung the last three words out for emphasis while jamming his index finger toward the girl's drawer in the wall. Lowering his voice, he added, "This isn't like the last time. I hope you've let that go by now."

An uneasy silence fell between the two men. Anderson stepped forward slowly, grasping Chris' right shoulder with the palm of his massive hand and casting an authoritative glance downward. "Look, let me level with you. This girl worked for Skip Pennington. She comes from a strong family in Raleigh, you know what I mean? I don't want any delays with this coming back to haunt me professionally."

Anderson moved his face closer to Chris', continuing in a hushed voice. "I know you think I'm a prick for saying that, but it's the truth. You can either help me out or not, that's your call. I'd just ask you to think about her family, and what I said about the media coming. It's Yin and Yang, my friend, good with the bad. You know it's right to send her home to her family, I know I'm a prick for not wanting to catch any heat for getting video of her body being transported out to a hearse on the evening news. Let's do what's best for everyone. We've kept this quiet as long as we can. There's nothing else you can do for her now; we'll take it from here."

Chris thought hard for a moment, looking flustered. "Alright," he finally said, lifting his tired gaze up to meet Anderson's. "I'll call an orderly to get her out of here by close of business."

Anderson shook Chris' hand, smiled, and turned to walk solemnly out of the lab.

At the door, Anderson stopped and turned back. "Oh, Lane," he asked politely, "any reason we can't get her outta here by noon?"

♦ ♦ ♦

The happy, upbeat rhythm of Cheeseburger in Paradise lightened Michael's mood as she drove. About two and a half hours into her trip, she was having trouble bringing herself to think about her task at hand as she worried about the three daughters she had left behind. Michael had learned that traveling to and from a crime scene, you were not to think about the case if something else was on your mind. If you didn't have a computer screen, witness, paper trail or dead body in front of you and you weren't at a crime scene, and something was going on in your personal life, you should think of something else, preferably positive and upbeat.

Motoring along to Jimmy Buffet seemed to fit the bill.

Michael slowed down a bit as Highway 64 East narrowed from four lanes to a two-lane state road about 40 miles West of Manteo, the gateway to Nags Head and the Outer Banks. Traffic was thin, surprising for a Friday with nice weather; Michael had figured everybody would be heading to the beach. She was in a part of North Carolina she had never been before. Far from the traffic, energy, and middle-class lifestyles of Raleigh/Durham/Chapel Hill, hog farms and fields of cotton and tobacco whizzed by Michael's car windows, as did single-story claptrap houses with nary an air conditioner in sight. She cringed at the thought of living in this steamy, humid climate without central air, and felt herself getting hot and sweaty just thinking about it. She reached down to the dash to turn up the air.

Michael's entire body was slammed forward awkwardly by a sudden impact from behind. As her foot and leg shot forward, she hit the accelerator briefly; the jerking motion of the car jolted her, and she struggled to set herself right while keeping the wheel from steering into the oncoming lane. Luckily, there was nobody coming the other way on 64, and she had crossed the center line only slightly, thanks to the size and suspension of the Crown Vic.

Heart pounding, eyes darting from the road ahead to her rearview mirror to her side mirrors, Michael immediately assessed the situation: her car had been hit from behind only seconds earlier, she was still going straight on 64, and her foot was off the accelerator and the car was slowing.

With a loud bang the vehicle behind rammed her again, sending her flying straight forward down the road. She held the wheel tightly and straight and glanced in her mirror to see if a tractor trailer was out of control or if a car's brakes were going out or something. Instead, she saw a dirty, dark late-model pickup truck with tinted windows bearing down on her.

Just before the pickup hit Michael floored the Crown Vic. Its engine roared and lurched into its special overdrive gear, installed especially for high-speed criminal chases. Looking into her mirror, she saw the distance between her and the pickup immediately widen, until the truck looked as if it were going backwards.

She realized the truck was slowing down. She did the same, still glancing in the mirror.

She saw the truck spin left and pull a U-turn.

Michael looked ahead to see if any cars were coming in the opposite lane. None were. She slammed on her brakes and executed a nearly flawless 180, switching both feet at once to the brake, then taking one off and onto the accelerator, just like they taught her at the academy.

She surprised herself at her efficiency.

Michael sped up to a cloud of dust and smoke billowing behind the truck from where it spun into the dirt shoulder after making its turn. Without knowing how far the truck was in front of the cloud, Michael sped full-speed into it, glancing briefly at her speedometer which read 45-50-55-60-65-70. Suddenly, she rear-ended the fleeing pickup with a solid smack. Michael's arms stiffened on the wheel, and she gritted her teeth and switched her foot to the brake. The two vehicles separated momentarily, then the Crown Vic hit the truck again as it weaved and shuddered, losing acceleration quickly. The Crown Vic pressed against its rear bumper, getting tangled up in it, and pushing it along the highway.

The squealing of brakes came from the truck; the driver was applying his brakes. Dust and smoke began obscuring Michael's view of the vehicle in front of her; she moved her left foot onto her brake pedal, willing her car to slow down. The truck in front of her jimmied right then shot left, across the center lane and into oncoming traffic.

A loud bang blasted Michael's ears and a cloud of flames, smoke, metal, and glass flew a few feet outside her side window as the pickup was hit head-on by a tractor-trailer.

The pop/crunch zipped past Michael's left ear as the Crown Vic lurched forward, skidding, and the truck and trailer sped past the other way. Michael put all her weight on her brakes, keeping the wheel straight, and the Crown Vic skidded some 50 feet before coming to a stop.

A squeal of brakes and the unmistakable sound of downshifting told Michael that the driver of the rig was still in control. She checked for traffic in the oncoming lane – there was a minivan about 500 yards ahead that was stopping – then Michael turned the Crown Vic around and sped up to the rear of the rig.

Slamming the car into park, Michael kicked open the door and leapt onto the highway with the ignition still running. She glanced forward but could only see the tractor trailer with a lot of flames and smoke in the front.

Michael started to feel light-headed.

Move, she told herself.

Get the rear door open ... grab the shoulder holster ... pull out the service revolver ... assess the threat ...

Michael held the gun in her right hand above her head with her elbow bent at a ninety-degree angle, pointing the gun at the sky. Crouching, she moved cautiously to the front of the rig, and saw that the driver was quickly climbing out of the cab.

"Get out! Get back! Across the road!" Michael began yelling in an authoritative tone.

Her head started spinning as she yelled.

The unkempt truck driver's eyes widened as he saw Michael's gun, then stumbled past her at a brisk pace toward Michael's car.

The explosion that came next rocked the pickup truck from under the engine block of the tractor trailer, tossing the huge rig's front end a couple feet into the air. Michael tried to recoil into a defensive stance but was knocked on her ass by the explosion.

Grimacing as she hit the ground, Michael felt her grip on her revolver loosen momentarily. She bit her tongue hard to avoid blacking-out. Propping herself up onto her elbows, she tightened her grip. Michael could feel the intense heat of flames singeing her skin and bits and pieces of metal and plastic shooting her way, some of it hitting her. She heard loud clangs as pieces of metal hit the pavement around her.

As the noise of falling objects and roaring flames seemed to slow down a bit, Michael looked hard at the flaming mass of metal about 30 feet in front of her. She squinted her eyes, trying to see if there was any chance of the pickup's driver being alive. All she saw of the truck was burning parts; the pickup's cab was nearly impossible to make out, as half of it was under the rig in a twisted mass of burning steel and plastic. As she peered ahead into the flames, Michael's eyes caught a shadow sneaking under the engine block of the tractor trailer.

Fuel. The impact and pickup explosion had ruptured the rig's fuel lines.

Run, Michael yelled silently at herself.

RUN!

Somehow, she got to her knees, spun around, jumped up and started sprinting across the road back toward her car and the driver of the rig. As she did, the entire front cab of the tractor trailer exploded, up into the air and to the right, away from where she was, as if flipped up and over by some huge invisible hand. The shock wave knocked her off her feet again, and she tumbled onto her right shoulder and over onto her back, curling up into the fetal position.

Michael saw stars and started to black out.

Before she could, the tractor trailer driver was pulling her to her feet and off into the grass off the road next to her car.

Michael, kneeling in a crouch, gagged a bit, and putting her arm on the trucker's shoulder, coughed out, "My gun;

did you see it? State Bureau of Investigation."

"Sorry ma'am, I didn't see no gun."

A preppy-looking man in his early forties, with John Lennon glasses, reached the two of them from the minivan.

"Sir, did you see a gun anywhere?" Michael asked him from a half-prone position, bent over with her hands on her knees, head swimming and pounding at the same time.

"I saw you drop something when you were running. I think it went over there," the man said, pointing about ten feet up the gully.

Michael half-ran, half-stumbled over to the weeded area and began frantically swinging her hands in the grass, searching for the gun. A glint of steel caught her eye, and the dark barrel of the gun presented itself to her.

Just the barrel. The rest of the gun had snapped off somewhere, disassembled itself upon impact.

Straightening her body and lifting her head to the sky, she closed her eyes and shook her head, then turned to walk back to reassert herself in her official capacity to the two men, one of whom was already on his cell phone, most likely calling local authorities or state troopers.

At least, Michael thought, she wouldn't be worrying about her daughters for a while.

◆◆◆

"Officer Francis, you have a call from your daughter," squawked the dispatcher on the other end of the two-way radio in Brian Francis' police cruiser. "Put her through," the mildly annoyed 38-year-old father answered, choking down the last bite of a ham and cheese sandwich.

"You might want to keep your cell phone on," Brian's 14-year-old daughter Megan chided.

"You couldn't wait 'til I was home?"

"Well, I have no fucking idea when you're gonna be home, right, so I figured at least I can find you at work."

"Hey hey hey!" Brian yelled. "Watch the language!"

"Whatever. Look, Mom's gone to the beach on like an important case or something, I wanna make sure when you're gonna be home tonight. You know, so Anna won't worry or anything."

"What? Where's Mom?" the words tumbled off Brian's lips before his daughter finished.

"Oh, Jesus, please tell me you at least know that she's on an assignment. You didn't know that, did you?"

No, I didn't know that, Brian thought. His wife hadn't told him about her case. He had no idea that she was going out of town.

"Dad, you didn't know, did you!?"

"No, Meg, I guess I didn't know."

"I can't believe you didn't KNOW!" his daughter screamed.

Brian felt his blood rushing to his face. He closed his eyes and took a quick breath. "Look, I'm not supposed to be home until nine or so, but I can stop home mid-afternoon when Anna gets off the bus and stay a while before getting back to work. Who's watching her after school?"

"Mom said to go next door to the McCairn's house after she drops off her stuff," Megan said, adding, "You know what? Don't rush home on our account. We've got it under control, okay? I figured you wouldn't be home. Don't try to – "

"--Megan, look, I can get off a little early if I – "

"--Dad, just forget it, okay? Everything's fine. You don't have to be the hero. I'm sorry I bothered you."

She hung up on him.

Brian stared at the cars passing by in the street across the parking lot. Everyone seemed to be going somewhere important. Yet here he sat, waiting for something to happen.

His blood was boiling. He was tired of waiting.

He hit the ignition, revved the engine and pulled out

onto the street, hitting the sirens and lights to clear the way.

◆ ◆ ◆

It had been about 20 minutes since the young man who had stumbled across Agent Michael Francis' automobile accident had called 9-1-1 for assistance. A fire truck and ambulance had arrived moments before. Most of the original fire from the pickup truck and tractor trailer had either petered-out or been sprayed-out with fire extinguishers some local volunteer firefighters arriving in pickup trucks.

"Agent Francis?" a stranger asked in an inquisitive, respectful voice from underneath an oversized, beat-up old firefighter helmet.

"Yes, that's me," Michael replied, producing her SBI identification badge. As the firefighter took a close look at it, he removed his helmet to reveal an older, weathered face underneath a wild mess of thinning brown hair.

"My name's Boyle Sinclair, I'm local law enforcement around here, work outta Bulah," the 45-year-old southerner offered in greeting, along with an open hand after returning Michael's ID. She accepted his handshake with hesitant gratitude, casting a quizzical glance at the firefighter helmet in his hand. Catching her look, Boyle said, "Oh, uh, we kinda wear all sorts of hats around here."

That made Michael smile.

"Look, Agent Francis, I got an earful from one of the volunteers over there, but I'd like to talk to you one-on-one about what happened and why you're here. You two gentlemen, you'll have individual firefighters taking your statements. Do either of you require medical attention?" Boyle asked the yuppie and the driver of the tractor trailer. Both shook their heads and looked lonely as Boyle put a friendly hand on Michael's shoulder to steer her away.

"Now, the two stories of those fellas there make sense,

so I don't have any questions about the physical events, just..." Sinclair's voice trailed off as he looked downward, removing his helmet and rubbing sweat from the back of his neck as the two slowly walked down the closed-off highway past the wreckage of the pickup truck.

Michael couldn't tell if Sinclair was mulling something over or if he was feeling her out, waiting for her to tip him off to something.

"Chief, Sheriff, whatever your title is, thanks for coming by, I appreciate your questions, really. I certainly want to talk with any local law enforcement, but I'm on a case and need to get to Nags Head as soon as possible."

Sinclair looked up at her, and a scowl seemed to cross his face.

"What's the rush?" he somewhat accused. Crossing his arms across his chest, he glared at Michael. "You, uh, did take part in a traffic fatality. You do realize that?"

Michael just stared back.

Agitated, Sinclair turned and walked determinedly toward one of his firefighters near the wreckage of the pickup truck 25 feet away. He motioned toward something on the ground, and the firefighter picked up an object from a pile of wreckage and handed it over. Sinclair turned quickly and strode back to Michael.

When he was no more than two feet from her, Sinclair stopped, and brought a charred license plate up in front of his chest, displaying it before Michael with both hands on either end so she could read the number.

It was a North Carolina tag, personalized plate, ARTMAN.

"That truck in your accident," he said, "that was Arthur Jackson's pickup. He's the local mechanic. I knew him, he's got three kids."

Michael felt a wave of nausea hit as she looked from the plate into Sinclair's eyes. She brought her left hand up to cover her mouth.

"Three little girls."

Michael spun away, walked over to the side of the road, bent over, and threw up.

Letting her be for a moment, Sinclair walked slowly forward and placed a reassuring hand on Michael's right shoulder. "I'm wondering, did you know him at all?"

Michael half turned to face Sinclair and shook her head no, straining to say, "No, I did not," between throat-clearing coughs.

"Sheriff!" a firefighter mulling through the tall grass beside the wreckage yelled. "Found a cell phone! All burned up."

"That yours?" Sinclair asked Michael.

"Likely, yes, it was in my shirt pocket but it isn't anymore," she mumbled.

"Alright," Sinclair said, turning back to Michael and helping her stand up straight. "You want to use my phone to call your family, tell 'em you're alright?"

Spewing out what was left in her mouth, Michael thought about that. Part of her did want to call home, tell her daughters. Not Brian, though. Definitely not Brian.

She stood up straight and wiped her mouth, breathing in a deep, cleansing breath.

Stay strong, she thought. You don't need to worry anybody. You've got this.

Her left eye started twitching. She rubbed her eye to make it stop.

"I'm good, need to get collected and on to Nags Head, if my vehicle's alright. Just have your office call my office, ask for Agent Robbie Cartwright, here's the main number," she said matter-of-fact, digging a business card out of her I.D. wallet.

Sinclair put his hands on his hips and raised both eyebrows before accepting the card. He shook his head, then turned to walk over to the rest of his crew to survey the damage.

Sinclair's gut told him there was nothing nefarious going on with this SBI agent wandering around in his neck of the woods. It didn't seem she knew Art or was investigating him. Either that or she was extremely cool under pressure. First of all, Art's last name was Swanson, not Jackson, and he didn't have any kids. He wasn't even married. He was a loser of a man, a mechanic by trade who spent most of his time growing pot out on his parents' land behind his beat-up old trailer. The Sheriff knew him because he'd busted him numerous times and cited him for possession, but every time he'd get some judge to keep him locked up to teach Art a lesson, Art would mysteriously get let off. Sinclair figured the local loser had some strong political ties somewhere.

Kinda weird about that, Boyle had always thought. He looked over at the burned-out truck, looked back to the SBI agent, and frowned. If the Francis woman wasn't in town investigating Art, and had no clue who he was, and if the yuppie's eyewitness account of the accident was true, why the hell was Art trying to run her off the road?

If in fact that was Art in the truck.

Boyle had a lot of questions. He could feel a real bad headache coming on.

"Gonna be a rough one," he mumbled.

◆ ◆ ◆

"Robbie Cartwright's office," Bart Taylor answered his host's phone on the first ring.

"This is the Bulah Sheriff's Office, I'm trying to reach Agent Cartwright," the man on the other end of the phone said.

"He stepped out, not sure when he'll be back; I'm the agent in charge, is there a message?"

"Yes sir. Could you please tell him we've been in contact with one of his agents, Agent Francis, she was in an automobile accident."

Taylor's pulse began to race. "Is the agent okay?" he asked.

"Yessir. She's requested to be released from the scene, I'm told, pending a statement. She gave us instructions to call Agent Cartwright, please tell him that an officer will call him back within the hour with an update."

"No problem, absolutely, I'll get him this information ASAP," Taylor replied, hanging up. Blood rushing to his face, adrenaline pumping, Taylor took a breath to calm himself, ran his hands through his slicked-back hair, smoothing it down, then straightened his tie. He stuffed the rest of Michael Francis' personnel file and notes about her latest assignment to Nags Head into his briefcase and hurriedly slammed it shut.

He closed his eyes, rolled his head around to crack his neck a few times and moaned.

As he did, Robbie Cartwright swung open the door and shot an irritated look at Taylor.

"Thanks for waitin'," Robbie said grudgingly, grabbing his sport coat from the rack on the other side of his door. "You ready? Or do you need any more information on any more of my agents?"

"Ready in a minute, can I make one more call?" Taylor said.

Robbie shrugged. "Long as you're buyin'," he said, turning to walk out.

"I hope you're hungry; I can feel my appetite kickin' in!" Taylor yelled after him, picking the receiver up and dialing.

CHAPTER 4

Amy had never liked Chief Anderson. He reminded her way too much of a roid-rage pro wrestler, both in attitude and looks. A real weasel-face, angry-at-the-world-all-the-time S.O.B. It was hard to tell if that was his police training, an overprotective pride in his community, or if he was just a hard-ass prick.

She stuck with hard-ass prick just to play the odds.

Amy remembered Toby Jones was the first one to respond to the scene after her 9-1-1 call. He'd spent the first couple of minutes running around, securing the crime scene, then spent a good five minutes just holding her as she cried. Amy had seen Anderson glare at his sergeant as he walked past with two state troopers who had come to help out. Anderson never even said anything to her when he arrived on the scene.

"Amy, it's gonna be fine, girl. You just hang on, okay?" Toby had reassured her, just before Anderson had yelled from inside the house, "Sergeant! You going to join us today or no?" Toby had given Amy a knowing look if to say *see, I knew that was coming*.

Amy remembered that had made her smile.

After a good hour, Anderson had come out of the house and leaned-up against Toby's Jeep, right next to Amy. Crossing his arms, he'd spoken to her in a soft, even tone as he looked out past the house toward the ocean. "Mizz Miller, we're going to need to talk to you about what happened here. I'm going to have one of those troopers come with me and you and we're gonna go down to the station together and take a statement. You understand?" She had nodded her head. "Now, there's nothing to worry about. You just happened to walk-in on a horrible scene in there. We're going to get you in touch with a counselor in New Bern I know of if you need it. Don't worry about your job; I can call in for you, get you paid leave for a while. I know this house is your listing, so I'll contact another realtor with your company, and we'll get everything all cleaned up. You don't have to do anything."

Amy remembered feeling as if a gear had slipped in her mind when she heard the tail-end of the Chief's monologue. "Cleaned up? What are you talking about?"

"Well, it's pretty messy, but we're going to do our business and then clean it up. You know, scrub the floor, get rid of any—you know—spots, that kind of thing," Anderson had said.

Amy remembered talking without thinking.

That's when she remembered the conversation sliding downhill.

"Chief, with all due respect, what are you talking about? You have no idea who did this – should you be cleaning everything up already? What about getting some outside help, the FBI, crime lab professionals?"

"Now listen up buttercup, I appreciate your unsolicited advice, truly I do," Anderson said sarcastically, turning to face Amy, unwrapping his arms and pointing a finger in her face as his tone turned rough. "Unless you have some experience in crime solving, leave this to us. Nobody needs a mess like this getting out, drawing attention. Especially nobody in the business community, which you should care about, since you're supposed to be their advocate." With that, Anderson had walked away, back toward the front door.

Amy flashed back from the horrific images from earlier that week to her present situation, sitting in her car, staring at the Dare County Public Safety Building across the street.

Chief Anderson, Sergeant Jones, and their visitors from the Raleigh SBI office didn't know it yet, but they had an appointment with her.

◆◆◆

Brian Francis sat in his Raleigh police cruiser in front of 120 Hidden Pine Way in the Raleigh suburb of Apex. He stared at the unkempt lawn and hedges, the dead leaves from last fall sticking out of the gutters. When was the last time he had done yard work? He couldn't remember.

A stranger in his own home, which was how Brian had been feeling for the past – good Lord, had it been six months? Nine? More and more time away from home; keeping tabs on his daughters like he was on a stakeout. He had seen all three grow a little older adjusting to their new environment in the south. He was proud of them for finding their niche. He was up to date on all their lives.

Not so with Michael.

Brian's wife had completely tuned him out last year, when the blow-ups had withered into not talking at all. He tried sleeping on the couch downstairs, but that proved grossly uncomfortable and screwed up the kids' mornings. So he and Michael had opted for a new futon in the den. At least Michael had; Brian had come home one night and there it sat, still in its plastic wrap.

He stared up at what used to be his bedroom window, running his fingers through his think blonde hair while trying to remember the last time he slept in their bed.

Definitely not since that night in June.

Brian's mind quickly ran away from that memory and toward his current situation. Michael's trip out east had totally surprised him; not that his estranged wife kept him up-to-date with her work schedule, but her leaving town without telling giving him a heads-up about the kids' situation was very strange. What if Megan hadn't called him at work? When would he have found out Michael was gone? After she had returned?

Brian felt like something was not right, but he couldn't put his finger on it. In the academy, they had taught about following one's instincts to a logical conclusion. Brian called it his Spidey Sense.

It was tingling now.

Not quite like an emergency, just that maybe he was caught off-guard by the suddenness of her trip, and that would explain his feeling of uncertainty. Still, he felt the need to at least contact her, to maybe call ahead to wherever she was going and talk to authorities there to find out what was happening. He needed a little control over the situation. Like a good detective, even though he was just a beat cop, Brian was going to search for clues to get his ducks in a row. He was going to check their home office before heading back to the Raleigh police station to check-out for the night. Brian thought he'd just take a quick look through Michael's computer files, her closet to see what she was bringing, how long she was staying, without the girls home to see him snooping around.

He didn't want any more surprises.

He took a deep breath, then got out of the cruiser, slammed the door and walked across the front lawn toward the front door. A dog was barking like crazy; Brian recognized it as Max, the McCairn's enormous German shepherd next door. The dog sounded like it was inside the house, which put Brian somewhat on edge. His feeling of apprehension grew as he felt like he was sneaking around his own family, wondering if the neighbors were watching this wayward father and husband slink into his own home to check up on his wife behind her back. As he did, he turned his head to the right over to the Jacobson's house, saw nobody peering out the front windows, and then turned his attention back to the homestead.

That's when he saw movement inside a second floor bedroom window.

Brian stopped in his tracks. It was the middle of the day, early afternoon; the girls would still be in school. Michael was traveling east. Yet he saw something move across the window inside the office. They had no pets. It had to be a person.

Brian snapped open the holster on his belt and withdrew his service piece. He brought it up in front of his face with both hands, and flung his athletic six-foot frame up the steps, his left side to the butt of the door frame.

Max kept barking. Aside from the dog, Brian didn't hear any other noises. No cars on the street, nothing.

Brian's pulse was racing, and he could feel himself reacting instead of thinking before he moved. His military experience was kicking-in; he felt like he was sneaking up on an Iraqi mud hut on the outskirts of a hot zone. Brian closed his eyes to calm himself. He took a few deep breaths. He counted three Mississippis, then reached for the door handle. He pressed his thumb down on the latch.

It clicked open. Jesus, the house was unlocked and somebody was inside.

Brian's heart pounded and his head swam. What was he doing? Maybe it was one of the girls or a neighbor; he reached down and lifted up the corner of the front mat, and saw the spare house key still there. Only he and Michael had keys, save the spare; whoever was in the house wasn't supposed to be there. Should he call out? No, that was dumb. He'd just keep his safety on, and surprise the intruder, shocking them by his mere presence in uniform.

Max kept up his barking.

48

Decision time.

Brian slowly pushed open the door with his left hand, holding the semi-automatic in his right hand, double-clicking on the safety with his thumb. The door moved silently open, and Brian poked his head around the corner to peek inside.

As the door continued to swing open, it reached the end of its destination, slowed a bit, then creaked a horrible, loud creak.

Brain had to move quickly. He darted inside, to the right past the stairs in the foyer and into the formal living room. He swung his body around to the left, pushing his back up against the wall. He counted three Mississippis again, then swung back into the foyer, gun drawn out in front of him with both hands. He swung its barrel across his field of vision, into the adjoining family room, up the stairs to the second-floor landing, then shut the front door with his left hand. As it clicked shut, he fumbled for a moment for the lock, then drew the deadbolt shut.

He was now locked in with the intruder.

Brian thought quickly – the only other door outside on this level was the sliders to the back deck via the formal dining room, which was at the other end of the formal living room. Between the two rooms was a short hallway to the right that led to his first-floor office, where he and Michael used to keep their spare guns.

He wondered if the intruder had found them.

Moving fast, keeping his ears open for the sounds of movement upstairs, Brian darted through the living room and into the dining room. He ran to the sliders, and saw that the lock was depressed and the safety bar was set against the wall. The intruder had not entered this way.

He had come through the front door, and he hadn't knocked it down. Did he pick the lock? Did he use the spare key, then place it back under the mat?

Did he have a key of his own?

Brian threw his body, back first, against the dining

room wall next to the office hallway. He had to know if the intruder was armed, if he had found their guns. He threw himself against the opposite wall in the hallway, then slid to the doorway to the office.

He jerked his head into the doorway quickly, took a quick glance, then jerked it back again. Brian spun into the doorway, gun drawn, and crisscrossed his field of vision with the barrel, side to side and up and down. He looked quickly under the desk. He then backed into the room and across the doorway to the closet. He kept his gun drawn on the door, grabbed the handle, and yanked it open.

A whoosh of air and ruffling winter coats was all that greeted Brian Francis. No maniac jumping out. Shit. He almost wished there had been. He tossed aside the coats and saw their gun safe sitting on the floor; he yanked at the handle, and it was still locked. Just then, Brian heard a noise from outside, the gunning of an engine. Was it a getaway car starting down the street? Too powerful, more likely a truck.

Or a bus. A school bus.

Dammit. Brian looked down at his watch. It was 12:45 in the afternoon! What the hell was a school bus doing dropping off kids?

He ran to the office window and looked outside. Sure enough, eight-year-old Anna had gotten off the bus and was saying goodbye to one of her friends, making her way across the front lawn.

What is she doing home?

Brian heard footsteps running over his head. The intruder was in the bedroom.

Running toward the stairs. The stairs that led to the front door.

To where Anna would soon be.

Before he could think, Brian felt himself clicking off the safety on his gun.

Bolting out of the office and into the short hallway, he heard the unmistakable sound of footsteps bounding down the stairs. He ran into the dining room, then across the threshold into the living room. He banged into a coffee table, sending a plant and some oversized hard-cover books to the floor as he yelped in pain, half-stumbled, and looked up into the foyer.

He saw a black male with close-cropped hair, dressed in jeans and jean jacket, fumbling with the lock.

In what felt to Brian like slow motion, he watched the man turn, wide-eyed, and look straight at him with a look of fear and surprise. The man's gaze turned to the gun in Brian's hand, then the man reached under his left arm, drawing a revolver of his own.

This guy's gonna shoot me in my own home, Brian thought. The scene suddenly sped-up to real time, almost overwhelming him.

Brian drew his piece up in his right hand, and still stumbling forward, squeezed an off-balance shot into the foyer. He heard the man shout, then saw him back into the family room on the other side of the foyer. Brian stumbled into the front wall of the living room, and as he threw out his left hand to catch himself before his body hit, it went straight through the front window with a loud crash. A shot rang out, and Brian caught a glimpse of the man in the family room standing in firing position. Brian threw his right arm in the general direction of the family room and squeezed-off two shots, pulling his left arm back out of the window and throwing himself backwards and down onto the living room floor, out of range of the intruder. The intruder fired back three times blindly into the living room.

Brian rolled over on his left arm, cried out in pain, forcing himself into a crouching position. He ran, crouched-down, straight into the foyer and threw himself against the front door, bringing his right arm up for a sweep of the family room as he did so. He saw a blur of the intruder as he moved out of the other side of the family room into the kitchen. Brian squeezed off a shot which blew apart a side of the entrance frame between the kitchen and family room.

He heard the intruder fumbling with a doorknob. The door to the garage. Brian heard it click open and footsteps as the man ran outside.

There was a whirring mechanical sound. The garage door opener.

Brian tried to unlock the front door with his bloody left hand, yelped in pain, and heard a girl's scream.

His daughter was right outside the front steps.

"ANNA, GET DOWN!" Brian shouted as loud as he could as he moved into the family room. He ran to the first of two front windows, and with his left foot kicked at the glass frame. The window smashed outward, and Brian knelt down, whacked at the glass with his gun to clear a space, and leaned his upper body out of the window. He could see the intruder bolting down the driveway, gun in hand, about 30 feet away.

Suddenly, still running, the intruder turned, his attention drawn by the breaking window.

He was facing the house and Anna.

He was bringing his gun around, trying to aim it.

Brian was surprised to find himself pulling the trigger on his gun. He pulled it again. And again.

Neighbors somewhere, perhaps across the street, were screaming. Brakes squealed as the bus, halfway down the street, skidded to a stop. Brian saw the intruder crumple to the asphalt face-first.

He pulled himself back inside the window, jamming his gun into his belt. He managed to unlock the front door with his right hand, his left dangling uselessly, bleeding. His daughter was lying face-down on the front stoop, behind the wooden railing and security bushes. She had her hands over her ears.

Brian ran and picked her up with his right hand, putting his bloody left arm behind his back where she couldn't see it. Anna, whimpering, scrambled to her feet and threw her arms around her father. "DADDY!" she yelled and then began to cry hysterically.

"Shhh, baby, it's okay. It's okay," Brian said. On one knee, he strained his neck to see over the bushes. The intruder wasn't moving. Brian could see a pool of blood forming by the man's head. In the distance, he heard multiple sirens drawing near.

"What in the hell is going on," he muttered, burying his head in the top of his daughter's hair.

CHAPTER 5

It was quiet in the waiting room of the Dare County Public Safety building. Insulation in the new facility kept out the noise from the busy four-lane Route 12 on the West side of the building, not to mention the less-traveled Dare Street outside the front doors. Amy Miller was alone in the cool, quiet 12-seat room, leafing through her third People magazine while waiting for the arrival of the agents from the Raleigh office of the State Bureau of Investigation.

She was told the agents would arrive at noon; here it was almost 1:15, and still no sign of any outsiders. That really didn't surprise Amy any. Folks from Raleigh who weren't regular visitors to coastal Carolina often misjudged the heavy traffic summertime Fridays brought. She had counted on 1:00; still, Amy thought she should be here to get hold of the agents before Chief Anderson. She wanted to see the look on his face when she strolled-in, flanked by three or four dark-suited heavy hitters from the state capitol. That was the only way to legitimize her presence at the preliminary investigation hearing, she figured. Anderson was a definite chauvinist pig, and there was no way he was going to let her get any closer to this investigation than as a witness to a crime scene. If she got the outsiders to bring her in as someone important, however, that was different.

There was no music piped into the waiting room, only a television set with the sound off on a shelf in one corner near the ceiling, where the side wall met the glass-enclosed front desk area. Amy lifted her gaze from her magazines to a clock next to the T.V. The afternoon soaps had given way to a brief half-hour newscast; no major events had flashed upon the screen in 30 minutes of news, but now there was something going on with the weather. She caught a glimpse of the local weatherman looking quite serious in front of a map of the southeast, and pointing to a circle of white clouds off the coast of Florida. After gesturing with his hands in a sweeping motion up toward the coast of North Carolina, he clasped them in front of his waist, nodded his head knowingly, and then was replaced by the station logo and the words *Tonight at Six* before some soap opera made its reappearance.

"Amy," Sergeant Jones said from a propped-open door near the empty receptionist desk. "No word. Still waitin' to hear."

Amy smiled and nodded, then turned her gaze back to the TV set and saw a man in a hospital bed with bandages wrapped around head talking to a provocatively dressed young woman with bad hair. She went back to her magazine.

The click of the front door knob and whoosh of air startled Amy. A pang of guilt ran through her body; the whole reason she was here was to greet the SBI agents at the door, and she had let her guard down while they arrived behind her back! She sprang to her feet and unconsciously wiped her hands down the front of her blouse and skirt to smooth out any wrinkles, and turned to the figure walking through the door to her left.

Chief Anderson caught Amy's antics and smiled wryly,

taking off his sunglasses and purposely placing them neatly in his front shirt pocket while the door whooshed shut behind him.

"Don't get up on my account, Mizz Miller," Anderson said with a dose of contempt. Amy had figured he questioned her femininity from the first day they met, when his overbearing flirtations fell on deaf lesbian ears.

"Hello Chief," she replied dryly. "Don't suppose you've heard from the SBI?"

Anderson stopped halfway across the waiting room floor, turning to address Amy with a hands-on-hips defiant stance. "I appreciate your concern, but you know how them Raleigh folks are. I'd put money on that agent not arriving for some time."

Amy's heart sunk. "Agent?" she said with a sense of urgency.

Anderson's grin grew a bit wider. "Well, yeah. What, one's not enough for you, Mizz Miller? How many you want for this unsolved mystery? Six? Twelve? Twenty? You want CNN to show up with a camera crew in tow?"

"Wouldn't hurt," came Amy's snippy reply. She closed her eyes and pursed her lips as she silently berated herself for stepping out of the detached professional personality she had carefully crafted for this occasion.

Too late.

"Well, I do hope your confidence in our little-bitty backwater law enforcement office is not shaken now, is it, Mizz Miller?" Anderson's condescending tone seemed to worsen as he moved three steps toward Amy until he was a foot in front of her face, glowering down at her. She could smell his Drakkar Noir drifting up from his neck, mixing with the Redman chewing tobacco seeping out through his toothy grin.

Anderson lowered his voice. "Here I thought we were gonna get along real nice now, Mizz Miller. Hell, you don't have to be here; you're lucky you're gonna get to talk to this agent at all."

"Look, Chief, I have a right to be here. And let's not forget our little chat in your office the other day. We made a deal; no going to the press on my part, no shutting me out on yours." Amy surprised herself with her aggressive reply. The grin on Anderson's face disappeared. He stood, unmoved, still looming above her. Amy stammered, "I expect you...us, to be professional about this." She sat back down in her seat, grabbed her magazine, and slowly, carefully opened it as if looking for where she left off.

Anderson regarded her for a moment, then laughed and clapped his hands once, turning and walking away. "Alright, girl, we'll see about that. We'll see."

As the reception area door shut behind Anderson, Amy looked up from her magazine and stuck her tongue out at the Chief, took a deep breath, and tried to calm her racing heart.

◆ ◆ ◆

"Brian, that's about all we'll need," his boss, Sergeant Tomlinson, repeated for the second time.

"Got it," Brian muttered, still clutching his daughter's book bag.

Anna stood off to the side of the front walkway with her older sister Mary, who was helping to straighten her shoulder-length hair. The oldest of the girls, Megan, was in transit. Both older girls had gotten the news that there was an emergency at home with Daddy but everyone was okay. All three girls had been released from school early, as Friday afternoon was the first teachers' work day of the school year.

What a greeting for Anna, Brian thought to himself, watching his girls hug and talk to each other. Even though Brian had never run Anna through any emergency drills aside from exiting the house when the fire alarm went off, he had nonetheless warned her, as he did with all his girls, to do exactly as he said if he was yelling at her and she didn't know why. Anna had remembered to do as he said, dropping to her belly in the grass and covering her head.

Brian's guilt and pain mixed with pride in Anna's decision making. He walked toward his daughters past a few uniformed policemen who were patting him on his back, reassuring him that everything was going to be okay. "Girls," he said, "I want you to go next door to Aunt Sue's and wait for Megan to come over, and then I'll be back later."

"You going somewhere?" Mary asked.

"I've got to go down to the station house to take care of this and get hold of your mother."

The remnants of the Francis family embraced, their neighbor Sue McCairn came over to collect the girls and go wait for Megan, and Brian walked over to Sergeant Tomlinson's car. He slid into the passenger seat, and both men were momentarily silent as the car pulled slowly out of the driveway, past the scattered groups of waving policemen, and out the street to the connector highway that would take them into Raleigh.

"No contact with her at all?" Brian asked dejectedly.

"Nothing. Her cell phone must be out or off," the Sergeant answered, adding, "You gonna keep trying her?"

"Not right now. Maybe she'll call when she gets where she's going."

Michael Francis pressed the accelerator of the beaten-up Crown Victoria almost to the floor. Rattling from the engine didn't seem to increase at all over what was already pretty loud. Definitely something loose there. She checked her speedometer; 45, 47, 49, almost up to 50 miles per hour. The spare tire she had slapped on the front left side said she shouldn't go any faster than that lest it blow out. And Michael had had enough of fantastic automobile accidents not only for today but for a lifetime.

She started to think back only an hour and a half ago, to the pickup truck ramming her from behind, her giving chase, and the horrific head-on with the tractor trailer. When her memory conjured-up the site of the fire, she blinked her eyes rapidly and forced the thought from her mind.

Her eye began to twitch once more.

"Come on, Mikey," she said to herself. "Focus." The words rang in her ears as her mind filled with images from second grade, back home in Buffalo. She was eight years old, playing fall soccer. She was the only really talented girl out of three on a pretty decent team full of aggressive young boys. With only two losses, they seemed destined to make the rec league playoffs.

One game in particular muscled its way into Michael's mind. The bigger Stars were dominating her Panthers, 2-0. It was the end of the second quarter, and every Panther, Michael included, had flubbed the ball, been faked out of their shoes, and beaten to the offensive zone ever rush downfield.

Michael plopped down dejectedly on the grass on the sideline and popped-open the top of her thermos, downing a little cool water and pouring a lot more over her sticky-sweaty short auburn hair. As the water dripped off her head and down in front of her face, Michael looked to the right where her coach had all the boys gathered together in a circle, berating them about this and that, while the two other girls on the team wandered back and forth behind Michael, alternately sipping water and looking randomly at the game being played on the field next to theirs.

"Hey Mikey," her father said from over to her left. Carl Bisette's reassuring tone was welcomed with a smile. Hands in pocket, sorry-it-turned-out-like-this sympathetic smile crisscrossing his still youthful 45-year-old face, Michael's dad stood there, his tall lanky frame towering above her. A slight wind ruffled his thinning brown hair as he regarded the coach and the boys on the team. Nodding toward the group, her dad said, "Don't pay any attention to them. They're douchebags." Michael smiled as she saw a couple of soccer moms sitting nearby in folding chairs glare at her father's coarse language.

Carl Bisette kneeled down next to his daughter, looked down at the ground, and pulled up a few blades of grass, regarding them as he spoke. "Listen Mikey, don't get too mad at yourself. Sometimes you play good, sometimes you play bad, but you always try your hardest. That's just the way it is."

"Yeah, but Dad, it's hard to keep trying when you try to play good but you keep playing bad."

Her father puzzled for a moment, flicked the grass into the wind, looked at his daughter and said, "So I guess you have to make a decision."

He stood up and put his hands back in his pockets. Michael looked up at her father; he wasn't telling her what to do, he was telling her she needed to decide whether to give up or not. Looking up at her father's strong face framed against the ash colored upstate New York sky, a sense of confidence came over Michael. She popped up onto her feet, tossed her thermos, and walked over to the scorer's table to check in for the second half.

"Hey Mikey," her Dad called to her. Turning to see him standing on the sidelines, she heard him say, "Focus."

Back on Route 64, Michael snapped back to reality and lifted her hand on the wheel to check her speedometer. As she lowered her hand back on the wheel, she paused for a moment and turned her arm over, looking at her left wrist.

The scars had healed long ago. She hadn't thought about them since she was a teen, in the hospital recovering.

Her father's death had rocked her hard. Cut her to the bone.

Murdered. A cop on the job.

Just like her.

Suddenly, Michael felt naked, trapped, caught.

She felt like she did the night of June fifth.

Shake it off, Mikey, you've got a job to do, she told herself.

Thirty-one years ago Michael had told herself the same thing, focused, and run herself silly in the second half of her soccer game, scoring twice and setting up another goal in a 5-3 loss. At the end of the game, she collapsed to her knees and cried, her father running to scoop her up in his arms. She left everything she had on that field.

Now, she needed to summon that strength again.

Her father wouldn't be there to scoop her up when she was done.

CHAPTER 6

Amy Miller was tired of waiting. It was 1:35 p.m., and the agent from Raleigh's SBI office was over an hour late now. Although the Chief had practically gloated about weekend traffic, it shouldn't be too bad, what with the bypass built in the last decade. Although she didn't think anything nefarious was going on, Amy was sure Chief Anderson knew more about the delay than he was letting on.

The door to the police station swung opened, and for a moment Amy felt a rush of adrenaline, wondering if the agent had finally arrived. Instead, she saw the confused face of Margot Tenneson, the well-meaning grandmotherly type who worked as receptionist at Peterson and Associates, the development firm that Kathy Kirkland had been using as an office.

When Margot saw Amy, her face brightened as though she was in a foreign land and had recognized Amy across a crowded room. Fumbling with the door, Margot crossed over to Amy, nervously babbling, "Well hello, Amy! Fancy meetin' you here. I'm not sure if this is where I should go..." Her voice trailed off as she looked toward the receptionist area across the room. She slowly glided over and rang the "press for service" buzzer on the wall beside the glass. In seconds, Sergeant Jones appeared, smiled, and clicked a switch and leaned forward to talk into a microphone. "Hey there Miss Margot. What can I do for ya'?"

Margot took a step back, looking even more confused, her eyes darting around the glass in front of her, looking for an opening in the partition to reply to the deputy.

Her answer came in the form of Toby playfully tapping the glass in front of her and pointing to a six-inch round metallic circle that looked very much like a dish drain.

Laughing to ease her embarrassment, Margot leaned forward and spoke into the circle. "Thank you Toby. Umm, I'm not really sure if I should be here, but I thought you should know that Kathy Kirkland didn't come into work yesterday or today. I called her place, but she didn't answer. I'm a little concerned, what with her being here all by herself."

Toby looked stunned. "Margot, Chief Anderson hasn't spoken with you?"

Margot blinked her eyes, the full effect of the deputy's words not yet hitting her. "No. Why?"

"Margot, step over to the door please," Toby said. A buzzer sounded, and he held the door open and ushered Margot through to the back office. As he did, Toby shot a look of concern to Amy who, now standing defiantly with hands on hips, could only stare back with mouth agape.

Nobody had told Kathy Kirkland's employer she was missing, Amy thought.

They were covering it up.

She suddenly felt sick. She walked across the room and stepped through the double set of doors leading outside and stood on the front porch of the Public Safety Building, pulling her cell phone out of her purse. Dialing the number from memory, Amy paced in the stiff wind as she waited for an answer on the other end.

"Senator Skip Pennington's office, Raleigh office, how may I help you?" came the cheery young girl's reply.

"Yes, hi, this is Amy Miller calling for Senator Pennington. Is he in?"

"Hold one moment, let me transfer you real quick," the girl replied. Amy began to chew a fingernail before she heard a man's voice on the other end of the line.

"Bart Taylor here, how may I help you?"

♦ ♦ ♦

"Where's Doctor Lane? This ready to go?" Brad, the young orderly motioned to the zipped body bag on the gurney in the middle of the exam room. The nursing assistant who had finished prepping the body for transfer nodded. "He signed off on it earlier," she said, helping the orderly push the gurney to the extra-large elevator.

After filling out paperwork at the rear nurses station Brad hung a clipboard on the end of Kathy Kirkland's gurney and stole away for a combination bathroom break and soda purchase before the long drive to Raleigh. After a good 20 minutes of prep time he finally pushed Kathy's gurney through some automatic doors that opened into a loading zone with the hospital's older backup ambulance – which doubled for a hearse, in addition to many other uses – that would transport her back home.

Kathy's escort got some help loading her into the ambulance, then hopped into the driver's seat, shut the door, and started the engine to get the air conditioning going. Sitting there, he grabbed a clipboard and double-checked the three sheets of paper it contained, making sure everything was signed-off and he had his directions and arrival time in Raleigh set.

Soon he put the ambulance in gear and followed the driveway around the back of the hospital and out the front entrance straight onto Route 12 West, turning right into steady traffic.

Not far behind, a white SUV with tinted windows pulled out of the hospital parking lot and followed in the same direction.

♦♦♦

Michael Francis was coming up on the bridge spanning the wide, glorious Alligator River separating Roanoke Island, the gateway to the Outer Banks, from the mainland. As she took in the sights and saw signs for the island, a fleeting memory of a passage somewhere about the missing inhabitants of Roanoke Island came to the forefront of Michael's mind. If she recalled the story correctly, Roanoke Island was one of the first colonial outposts of English settlers. A thriving small community, all at once the settlers disappeared without a trace. Investigations found no signs of a struggle, nor any signs of the people packing-up and getting ready to leave. It was as if they had simply disappeared from the face of the earth.

I wonder why they left such a beautiful place, Michael thought. Maybe it wasn't their idea to leave.

The ride over the bridge was soothing, even after all she had been through this morning. The crystal-blue water of the river shimmered on either side of her car as Michael cruised over numerous fishing boats, small and large, bobbing in somewhat heavy surf blown by a stiff breeze. Many of the men and women dropping lines in the water seemed young, many not much older than, say, 30. What did these people do for a living? Doesn't anybody work out here on the coast, she thought?

The minute or so drive over the expansive bridge came to an end at the tip of Roanoke Island. The part of the island nearest the bridge was still undeveloped, with great pine forests and lush marshes casting an otherworldly spell over their new visitor. The highway traversed these forested areas for a good ten minutes before Michael's car crossed another smaller bridge over another stretch of water and onto Roanoke Island proper. She began to see brown tourist signs directing folks to the various plays and exhibits celebrating the missing colonists.

Imagine that, people celebrating missing persons. A curious smile crossed her face.

Traffic began to slow down once Michael entered Manteo, the community of note on the island. Enormous Live Oaks blew their leaves from an expansive canopy over the road, and impeccably maintained lawns on either side with splashes of color from southern bushes and ornamental trees Michael didn't recognize let the visitor know there was some money in Manteo. Once Michael got into the touristy business district, the lawns became less well-kept, and beach-themed restaurants began popping-up.

After a few minutes of stop-and-go traffic, the road widened and then split into two directions, one of which led under a large highway sign for the Outer Banks. Michael sat at the red light at the highway split and began to fix her clothes and hair, shifting in her seat in part to shake the exhaustion from her bones after her long and eventful drive. Gaggles of smiling families walked past her on the sidewalk to her right, walking to and fro between gift shops and restaurants with black and white lighthouses on their signs. When the light turned green, she pressed on the gas and headed toward the bottom of a tall bridge, which then led up over a magnificent body of water -- Roanoke Sound, judging by the signs -- with dozens of incredibly expensive fishing tour boats docked at an upper-crust condo development to her left, and unfettered marshes that seemed to go on forever to her right. A few water skiers and personal watercraft zoomed back and forth in the sound, jumping some of the wind-whipped whitecaps, and as Michael crested the bridge she saw rather large sand dunes to her left in the distance, with brightly colored hang gliders lazily floating down their slopes. Out of the corner of her eye, Michael caught sight of parasailers being towed behind motorboats. Ahead of her, on both sides of the highway at the end of the bridge, were tourist shops and restaurants. She still couldn't see the ocean, though, which by all rights should be straight ahead of her in the distance, beyond the breathtaking scene surrounding her.

It had to be there, though, she thought. She just couldn't see it.

Michael's attention snapped back from the child-like sense of awe at the beauty around her when she heard a soft electronic "dinging" coming from her dashboard. Looking down, she saw her gas tank was nearing empty. Now at the end of the bridge, Michael looked right and then left, spotting an Exxon gasoline sign on top of an expansive thatched-roof tourist spot named Eddy's Crab Shack.

Putting on her blinker and slowing to a stop in the middle of the highway, Michael waited as a cherry red convertible and ambulance passed her going the other way, then she began to make her left-hand turn into the gas station. Three hard, quick horn blasts by a white SUV caught Michael before she could complete the turn; she had been temporarily distracted by the ambulance and would have smashed into the SUV had the driver not laid on his horn. She braked, shook her head in disgust, checked more carefully to make sure she wasn't about to cut anyone off, then crossed traffic.

Once in the parking lot, Michael had a fleeting thought about the possibility of the ambulance making a run out to the scene of her earlier accident.

That passing thought made Michael realize the distractions of the natural beauty of the drive had her almost completely forgetting about almost dying earlier. Cutting her engine, Michael put her game face on, took a deep breath, and prepared to get on with what she was trained to do.

"Focus, Mikey," she said aloud.

CHAPTER 7

Brian Francis sat at the edge of his wife's office chair, rummaging through piles of paperwork on her desk. Everyone at the SBI office in Raleigh knew Brian and nobody had a problem with him coming in to look for something his wife had asked him to pick-up.

That was the story he gave them, anyway.

The last place Brian Francis wanted to be was skulking around his wife's office digging through her files. He had three daughters at a friend's house worrying about their father who just shot a man to death in their driveway. He had an estranged wife travelling to the coast on a moment's notice without leaving any details.

Brian still pined for his wife, despite their emotional distance after that tragic night earlier in the summer, just weeks ago. She had always been his crutch, his best friend; she had trusted him completely and he had trusted her with feelings he hadn't shared with anyone, not even with his extensive immediate family back home in Buffalo.

Their relationship had completely fallen apart. He and Michael had argued on and off, but not really addressed the situation. They went forward ignoring each other, not sleeping together, eventually leading to Brian moving out, failing to discuss the "new normal" with the girls. It was as if the five of them all knew their family was in a holding pattern, the girls fearfully waiting for the final straw to force their father to file for divorce. Instead, things progressed to a working environment of bliss-less ignorance.

Brian hated it.

He started to get choked-up. Wiping his eyes and clearing his throat, Brian kept digging through his wife's files. There had to be something tying-in one of her cases to the intruder.

After all, it wasn't a random break-in.

Tomlinson had called him with info on the shooter. He had a record, but not one Brian was expecting.

Instead of a rap sheet, the intruder had a military record.

Cooper, Michael J., was a former United States Marine stationed at Camp Lejeune in the southeast corner of North Carolina.

Brian had shot and killed a fellow veteran.

Shaking the painful thought out if the forefront of his mind, Brian focused back on the task at hand. Most of the information on Michael's desk was from old files, some of it more recent than others. It had been about a month since Michael had been on a case. The last one was more of a paper chase than a serious investigation, revolving around a Durham, N.C. city councilor who misappropriated some loan funds. Still, Michael had tied everything up neatly in just over three weeks, impressing the primary on the case and especially her new boss.

Brian liked Robbie Cartwright, and not just because he had no designs on stealing Michael away from him as they went through their difficulties. Robbie struck Brian as more of a father figure who looked out for the men and women under his care. He had a stellar background and was well-liked in political circles. If you were a friend of big Robbie Cartwright, you were alright.

Still, Brian thought Robbie would react negatively to one of his agent's spouses rifling through one of his offices. That's why Brian worked fast; he had heard that the big man had stepped out to an off-site meeting, and that seemed like the perfect time to do a preliminary search of his wife's cases to see if the man in their house had been connected to the SBI or a case in some way.

Brian's initial thought was that there might be a leak in the SBI office that may have given sensitive information away to one of Michael's suspects. The suspect may in turn have tried to put a hit out on her, or maybe rifle through her stuff at home to scare her off the case or to find some pertinent information.

Michael's Durham case didn't seem to match that profile.

If they hadn't had been fighting and not talking for the better part of a year, maybe Brian wouldn't have had to come down to her office. Michael more than likely would have told him of any big cases or any problems with suspects or nasty people. Unfortunately, they were distant strangers at home and he knew next to nothing about what his wife was doing. Brian found out most of his updated information about Michael via their three daughters, pumping them for information. Well, his two oldest daughters actually gave it to him most of the time, trying desperately to maintain his interest in their family while he floated around aimlessly, trying to find his way.

They would be proud of him for coming to look through her desk. It showed he still cared about his family.

Brian's focus on his sudden epiphany was broken by the ringing of his cell phone.

"He's coming inside," Brian's lookout, Sergeant Tomlinson, said anxiously.

Quickly piling Michael's paperwork back onto her desk, Brian stood up and began to make his way out of her office and toward the back stairs to avoid Robbie.

Suddenly, the phone in Michael's office rang. Brian paused, thinking about picking it up, out of sheer frustration and curiosity. He stood, frozen, indecisive. The phone slowly rang two more times, then the phone mail system kicked-in and it stopped ringing. Angry at himself for not answering it, Brian turned and hurriedly left the office.

On the other end of the line, Michael Francis punched in numbers on the gas station phone to check her messages, of which there were none. As she did so, she thought briefly about calling home to check the messages there. Never mind that, she thought. Brian would be home in a couple of hours and take care of anything out of the ordinary.

Besides, what's the worst that could happen back there anyway?

She hung up, cursing her worthless broken cell phone, thanked the manager, and headed outside into the warm, breezy Outer Banks afternoon.

♦♦♦

Amy Miller was just about at the end of her rope. A sleepless night spent recalling the day she found that poor girl's dead body rushed headlong into a day full of nervous anticipation of the arrival of the agents from Raleigh. Her first balloon popped when she discovered that it would be just one agent, not a slew of investigators, coming to Nags Head. Then, the arrival time of noon had turned into 12:30, one o'clock, and now two o'clock. Worst of all, Amy had discovered that the agent was a woman.

Amy didn't know why she felt so disappointed in finding out the agent would be a woman. In fact, she felt guilty for her disappointment and anxiety at the prospect of getting a female agent sent in for the case. Shouldn't she be cheering from the rooftops for the sisterhood?

Unfortunately, the reality that was Chief Anderson was

more than enough to suck the last bit of girlfriend pride out in Amy. He floated in and out of the world of good ol' boys and the new wave of yuppies with ease. Everyone respected him for one reason or another. His massive frame and strong personality turned most people into quivering jello, and no man or woman had ever stood their ground against him.

Just as her mind started to wander on about Anderson, Amy saw the outer door of the police station open and a fast-moving profile of an athletic-looking woman pass quickly through the inner door. With a purpose, the woman strode confidently up to the front window of the reception desk, straight auburn ponytail swaying with a purpose, flipping open her jet-black jacket as she produced something out of her inside pocket and held it up to the window. Sergeant Jones smiled and nodded for her to follow him over to the door leading to the back.

As the door buzzed and clicked open, Amy stood up and called over to the woman. "Excuse me!" she blurted out. "My name is Amy Miller, I called about the Kirkland girl. If you need anything, Sergeant Jones there has my number. You want me to wait here?" Her nervous blur of words didn't seem to faze the professional-looking investigator, turning to walk over, striking facial features warming into a reassuring smile as she extended an arm to shake Amy's hand.

"Thank you Miss Miller. My name's Michael Francis, State Bureau of Investigation. I'm sure Chief Anderson and Sergeant Jones have most of your report. You can't help right now, although I'll be looking forward to talking to you while I'm here. Why don't I call you tonight, if that's okay?"

Amy tried to hide her excitement at the prospect. "That'll be fine, thanks," she said. The agent nodded in confirmation, then passed by the Sergeant and into the back room. As she watched the door slowly shut, Amy slumped back into her chair, overwhelmed by adrenaline.

She leaned forward, putting her head in her hands. As she breathed out a heavy sigh, she noticed her hands were warm. Was it her hands, or her head? She moved the back of her hand to her forehead and realized she was sweating, then checked her cheeks and realized they were warm.

Standing up, Amy caught a glimpse of herself in the round mirror in the corner of the room at the top of the wall.

I don't believe it. I'm blushing.

◆ ◆ ◆

Bart Taylor sat in the outer office of State Senator Skip Pennington's Raleigh headquarters, reclining in a deep-back leather sitting chair. Its dark brown material was almost a perfect match for the room's rich chocolate paneling. Leafing through a Time magazine, Taylor didn't want to think any more about logistics or planning for potential events yet to unfold; he had spent 30 hours straight now putting pieces into place with the Raleigh SBI office and Chief Anderson in Dare County, playing both sides of every coin he could turn over, and he needed a clear head to talk to his boss.

The door to the inner office opened, and Skip Pennington's lean six-foot-two-inch frame pushed out slightly ahead of a much smaller man going over some paperwork thrust into the Senator's face. "Right, just get it to Paulsen's office by end-of-day, alright?" the Senator instructed the much younger aide.

Taking the smallish wire-frame glasses from his salt-and-pepper coiffed head in one stroke while moving past Taylor, Pennington regarded his Legislative Director over his shoulder with an amused smile. "Bartholemew, you still hanging around?"

Forcing a laugh, Taylor stood and replied, "Yes, Senator, I wanted to catch you before you left for the weekend."

Continuing toward a door leading out into the reception area, Pennington gestured for Taylor to come along. His mannerisms were not particularly forceful, but those around him seemed to sense his power and follow his commands. Walking just off Pennington's left side, Taylor leaned into his boss' range of hearing to talk in a low, hushed tone as they got to the door to the reception area.

"Senator, I'm wondering if this is such a good time for you to head back east," Taylor said bluntly. Having opened the door halfway, Pennington stopped, straightened-up, and regarded the smaller man. His face awash with curiosity, Pennington craned his neck out to the reception area and called to a girl behind the desk. "Molley, can you please call Johnny and ask him to get my car around front? I'll be down in five, thanks." With that, Pennington shut the door and leaned back against it crossing his arms.

"Why is this not a good time for me to head back east, Bartholemew? Could it be because one of our young staffers was murdered at the beach, right before I'm to announce a major development project that I've been busting ass on to get past the President pro-tem of the senate?"

"There have been some...developments back in Raleigh, nothing you need to be concerned about, I have good men on it. The Raleigh SBI office has opened an investigation into Kathy's murder," Taylor said, holding his hands crossed in front of his waist in a submissive gesture. "Although I doubt any media have caught wind of it yet, they might, and you've already sent out your itinerary for the week. They'll know you're at the beach, and they'll look for you for a sound bite. With the Tucker bill coming up for committee vote next week and with the Peterson –"

"Right, right, and with the Peterson thing going down this weekend we can't have any negative publicity attached to my ugly mug that might screw things up," Pennington interrupted. Looking skyward seemingly for guidance, the senator shook his head and jerked himself free of the support of the door he was leaning on, pacing across to an open window overlooking the legislative building across the street. "I just bent over for Paulsen, that whiny little Jew. Dammit, Bartholemew, I just sent him revisions on the friggin' bill takin' out everything he wanted to guarantee enough votes on the committee to pass the damn thing. I compromised, Bartholemew, and I don't like compromising!" Pennington paused for a second to let out a deep breath and calm himself, straightening his lapel and staring at the floor. "Now that little peckerwood's got me right where he wants me. I've already taken out 75 percent of what he wanted out, and now if anything breaks out east he'll use the publicity to stall the bill in committee." Looking up at Taylor, Pennington frowned. "Does he know anything – and I mean anything – about Peterson?"

Taylor thought hard for a moment. If he lied to please the senator, he'd be screwed later. If he told the truth now, he'd be screwed the same, just sooner. "He's no dummy, Senator."

Pennington bit his lip, then turned back to the window. A moment of silence passed. Without turning back to face Taylor, Pennington asked him, "So Kathy's murder. They have any clue?"

"Not yet, sir."

Pennington looked down at his feet. "Fit the profile of the others?"

"Looks like it, Senator. I'm on the case though, sir, and I think we've got a handle on the SBI."

Raising his gaze once again out the window, Pennington stared blankly in the direction of the legislative building, his mind wandering and his voice trailing off. "That's half the battle now, isn't it? It's the other half that's the tough part."

"Yes, sir."

"S'pose we'd better go out there anyways, then,"

Pennington said, turning and straightening his tie as he walked slowly toward the door.

"You sure you don't want me to go alone, sir?"

"Bartholemew, you're a good man. This is too big, son, too big. I've got to be there in case something develops. I'll need to act quickly," he said, placing his hand on his young aide's shoulder.

The two men shared an understanding glance, then Senator Pennington walked through the door to his outer office.

"Molley, send flowers to Kathy's family for me, would ya' sweetheart? Bartholemew and I are heading out east in a bit," Pennington tapped on his secretary's desk as he passed. "I already have, sir, two days ago," she called after him sweetly.

"Well, send some more then, dear. And make sure it's a rather large assortment. The biggest one they've got," Pennington said, slipping into a nearby private bathroom.

Once inside, the Senator locked the door and took out his cell phone to send a text. Back in his main office, his aide was doing the exact same thing.

Unbeknownst to one another, both men were texting the exact same person for different reasons.

◆◆◆

"Hi Momma, yeah I'm doing transport today. I'll be in Raleigh around 4 p.m., should be done by 5 at the latest, y'all good with an overnight guest?" Brad said into his phone. "Yes baby, yes of course! I'll call your cousin and we'll have a nice dinner together," came his mother's sing-song reply.

The orderly loved getting transport assignments every now and then, especially when they were going to his hometown of Raleigh. He'd left to play basketball at East Carolina University, where he'd gotten interested in medicine after suffering a major knee injury that had derailed his college sports career. After graduation, he was recruited to work at the lone hospital in the Outer Banks. The work was rewarding yet hectic in-season, and this summer had been no different. Lots of tourists getting weird injuries while letting loose at the beach. He appreciated this break in particular, even if it was transporting a body.

He'd come to develop a respect for the dead he carried in the ambulance from time to time. One thing he'd learned on the job was that death is a powerful antidote to careless, irresponsible behavior. Most of his friends in OBX had boring, everyday jobs they escaped by drinking at each other's apartments and trying to sleep with anything that moved.

"This sound alright, ma'am?" he said, looking into the rearview mirror into the back of the ambulance where Kathy Kirkland laid in a black body bag. Some smooth R&B filled the vehicle with solid, rhythmic beats reminiscent of Motown.

Brad was getting into the groove, his mind wandering as he pushed the ambulance through the traffic of Manteo and out onto the wide-open stretch of Route 12 that passed through the center of marches before opening into grassy fields at the end of the island. He much preferred this scenic route over the quicker bridge shuttling vacationers back and forth from the mainland across the Alligator River to Manteo and then over the Roanoke Sound to Nags Head and the Outer Banks.

The bridge to the mainland across the Alligator River loomed about a half-mile ahead. A white SUV passed Brad on the two-lane highway, then popped in front with a quick swerve. Had he been going faster, he might have had to slam on his brakes.

He noticed the SUV speed up, then start to slow down significantly without brake lights, as if the driver had taken his or her foot off the accelerator. Brad leaned forward and tried to see if the driver was having a heart attack or panicking or something, but he couldn't get a good look.

About 50 yards ahead of him now, the SUV started to swerve back and forth violently and list over to the shoulder, finally pulling off just before the entrance to the bridge across the Alligator River. It pulled into an unpaved fishing access area.

"Oh come on now, why you got to ruin my vibe? And why do I have to be such a damn fine human being?" Brad wondered aloud, slowing down and turning on his blinker before pulling into the access area behind the SUV.

The two vehicles were the only ones in the lot. Parking parallel to the highway near the entrance to the access area, Brad threw on his flashers and cut the engine. The SUV had pulled up pretty far away, under the bridge near the water's edge, practically out of sight. Brad shook his head.

If he's gonna need a tow, he isn't in a good spot.

"I'll be right back, ma'am," he explained to his passenger. He leapt out of the driver's side, shut the door and started half-jogging, half-limping up to the SUV. "Yo! You alright in there?" he shouted, just as he started to trip over some loose rocks and debris in the mud and gravel lot, looking down to watch where he was going.

He didn't see the SUV backing-up in front of him.

The sound of gravel flying and engine acceleration caught Brad's attention. The SUV was plowing back into him, and as he turned to leap out of the way his right leg was tagged by the truck's bumper, bending backwards unnaturally. The vehicle's left rear tire then ran over his leg, hip, and arm.

The left front tire did the same.

Brad tried to scream out in pain when his leg cracked back, but a searing sensation and bright light filled his head. He felt the back of his skull hit the ground, then all the sounds around him were sucked into a vacuum of silence. He blacked out.

The SUV cleared Brad's body, stopping some ten feet back, shifting forward and slowly, methodically drove up and over Brad's head, chest, and pelvis, crushing each part of the Good Samaritan's body with a dull popping smack. The vehicle stopped and the driver's window came down, the day silent except for the quiet hum of the SUV's engine. The driver surveyed the scene, seeing no witnesses.

The driver's window went back up and the SUV circled back around the body and to the side of the ambulance, away from the highway to an area where it was partially concealed from passing cars, behind the rising embankment of the bridge. Exiting the vehicle, the driver walked over to the rear of the ambulance, pulling on latex gloves along the way.

CHAPTER 8

Brian Francis sat in his car outside the Raleigh SBI office, trying to pull everything together. He was having trouble focusing, images of the recent shootout dominating all his thoughts.

Of his shooting a man dead.

He had killed men before, as an Army Ranger. Seven confirmed kills of Iraqis who were guarding what was then thought to be a biological weapons depot. The military had decided not to bomb it from the air lest they release toxins into the wind which blew toward Army and Marine encampments. Brian was part of a squad of Rangers assigned to parachute in and take over the depot. Hitting the ground 50 yards inside the perimeter defenses of the Iraqis, Brian's group had received fire right at the start, but by the direction of the bullets it was clear the Iraqis shooting didn't have night vision goggles, a real bummer for him as he sat in the most forward gun battery. A grenade lobbed by Brian found its mark, and two Iraqi soldiers lay dead.

Soon after, Brian's squad came under fire from a machine gun 35 yards away, and its aim was truer. Two of

Brian's troops caught hits, but both were wearing light Kevlar and only one got hurt, taking a grazing shot to the arm. Figuring the shooter had night vision, Brian and three other men ran round the right to draw fire, and a couple of guys left back at the drop point tossed exploding flares in the direction of the gunner. A cry of pain told them he had been temporarily blinded by the bright light, which counteracted the night vision goggles, and Brian and his cohorts swooped in with M-16's blazing. They shared the two hits on the machine gunner and the man feeding him ammo.

The other three were during a firefight at the depot itself, which was mercilessly undermanned. There should have been 50 Iraqi soldiers overall according to intelligence reports, but including the four they killed when landing Brian's squad could only find 16. The rest must have run, Brian had figured. With the adrenaline and the knowledge that this was probably the only fighting he'd be doing, seeing how the war was moving so quickly, Brian never had time to think about the four lives he had taken. Later, back in the states, he had seen a psychologist about it, but it was nothing really. Part of the job.

This was different.

This was personal.

Brian remembered he was consumed by hatred and anger chasing the intruder through his house, and in shooting the man down Brian was not so much trying to wound and incapacitate the felon as he was trying to punish him for threatening his family. For a moment, the thought crossed Brian's mind that maybe there was more to it. Perhaps he had gunned-down the man not so much in self-defense of his family, but out of sheer frustration over his marital predicament.

In the desert, Brian was like a machine going through the motions, matching his actions to his training. At his home in Apex, North Carolina, Brian was acting on pure emotions. He was sure that made him a murderer somehow, no matter what others were telling him.

His train of thought was interrupted by Sergeant Tomlinson sliding into the passenger side. "Here, listen, I got some calls back from some military contacts. They found records of a Marine disciplinary action, dismissing Cooper. Three months ago. He disappeared for a while, then got another job."

Tomlinson paused and stared at Brian.

"Where?" Brian asked.

"Security for the North Carolina State Legislature."

Brian blinked his eyes and stared out the windshield in confusion.

"Was he guarding anyone in particular?"

"Dunno," Tomlinson said, shaking his head. "Not sure how to go about finding that out."

"I do," Brian said, turning the key in the ignition.

◆ ◆ ◆

"How long have you been with the Department?" Michael asked her host. Hunched over a tall silver coffee urn at a sink in the break room of the Dare County Public Safety Building, Sergeant Toby Jones replied lazily over his shoulder, "Four years."

"Just four years, huh?"

"Yeah," the good-looking officer said, handing over a paper cup filled with black gold. "Long enough, 'spose. Know everybody up and down the beach, that's for sure."

"Where were you before here?"

"This part of the interview?" Toby asked half-jokingly in his smooth southern drawl. "Nah, kidding. Actually, I was fresh out of the Police Academy in Columbia, South Carolina. I'd worked security details for six or seven years in Myrtle Beach, wanted the pay guys on the force got. Two openings in Myrtle, one up here at higher pay, moved north."

"How'd the opening come up?"

"Old deputy quit the business, moved down to Florida. Even married the ex-president of Dare County Chamber of Commerce, she followed him down last year."

"You getting along well with Anderson?"

"I'd say we do just fine for ourselves," came a gruff voice from behind Michael. In the doorway to the office was a hulking, semi-balding man with some serious wear and tear on his face. Chief Curtis C. Anderson looked like an ass-kicking waiting to happen. "Chief of Police Curtis Anderson," he said with a forced good-ol'-boy smile, extending his hand and moving toward Michael. She stood up and introduced herself, accepting his handshake with the expectation that he would try to crush her hand to announce his dominance; instead, he was polite and gentle, as if greeting a neighbor in church.

"Nice to meet you, Chief Anderson. Your sergeant and I were just getting acquainted; sorry I was late. I ran into some trouble on the road."

"Back in Bulah, I heard," Anderson spat, walking over to the coffee machine and filling a cup. "I hear everything east of Raleigh, Agent Francis. I even heard why you're here, why you were in such a rush to leave the scene of a horrific accident."

"I sure would hope that you know why I'm here," Michael said, partly embarrassed.

"You're not here about the Kirkland girl, I'm not talkin' about her," Anderson said, turning to look at Michael while he stirred sweetener in his coffee. "I'm talking about why you were called here. I heard Amy Miller called around lookin' for someone outside our circle to come in and check up on us. And that's fine," Anderson said hurriedly, waving his hand in front of him to dispel any thought Michael might have that he was angry about having an S.B.I. agent to watch over his shoulder. "You're here 'cause if you don't come here you're gonna catch hell in Raleigh. That's fine, really it is. If we're missing anything, well, I sure would appreciate it if you'd enlighten us to our mistakes."

Anderson walked past Toby and Michael out of the break area. The two stood silently contemplating the situation; Michael looked over at the sergeant, and he just shrugged his shoulders and shook his head. "Agent Francis, if you'd be kind enough to come in my office we can get to know each other a bit," Anderson called.

Michael took a deep breath, closed her eyes and cleared her mind. Immediately, she disliked Anderson, having dealt with his type before, just like in the SBI break room. She didn't need to psyche herself up because this man was nothing but a blowhard scared that he might look bad doing his job. She grabbed her portfolio, slugged down the last of her coffee, crumpled the paper cup and threw it to her right across the room five feet or so toward a trash can. The cup bounced off the rim and onto the floor.

Anderson let out a snarky guffaw at her miss.

She could feel her eye twitch starting back up.

"So Mrs. Francis," Chief Anderson said with a gesture for Michael to have a seat while he himself slunk down in an oversized leather chair behind his desk. "This your first time in the Outer Banks?"

"Yes it is," she replied hurriedly and with force, reaching into her briefcase and retrieving three file folders worth of background on the Kirkland case.

Angered by her eye twitch, Michael took her frustration out on the prick in front of her, slamming the folders down with a loud smack on the Chief's desk. "First time," she said, looking up at him with a grin.

Anderson just leaned back in his chair, smiling.

"Well then, let's hope you see the sights while you're pokin' around so you come back with the man of the house and the kiddies sometime soon, hmm? Before it all blows away in the storm that's brewin' out there. Could get nasty for a pretty little thing like yourself." Leaning forward, Anderson reached to the side of the folders and retrieved a glass tray full of walnuts. He held it up to

Michael, but she shook her head at his gesture. Bringing the tray back to his side of the desk, Anderson took a walnut and methodically began cracking it open. "Those files there; those for me?" he said, finally acknowledging Michael's files on his time. "Looks like a helluva lot of information on one young girl."

"You're free to look at that file, but it's my only copy," Michael replied. "I gathered all of the information I could in a short amount of time. I did find a history of crimes in Dare County over the past ten years," she said politely yet forcefully. Instead of leaning back to wait for Anderson's reply, Michael started to direct the conversation, opening the top folder and turning it around so Anderson could see the top page, strategically placed there by Michael ahead of time.

"I was curious about the multiple missing persons' reports filed in Dare County in that timespan," she said.

Using his fingernails to pick the meat out of the walnut, Anderson seemed unmoved. He was intently separating the nut from the shell and sucking the meat off his fingertips. Without looking up from what he was doing, he said, "Which ones are those Agent Francis?"

Still smiling politely, Michael leaned forward and pointed to several highlighted names. "If you look at these, you'll see the missing individuals have something in common with each other and Kathy Kirkland," she said. "They were all young women, all visiting the area, and from their physical descriptions all very attractive with characteristics similar to the Kirkland girl."

Anderson cleared his throat and leaned back in his chair. With a condescending smile, he spat at Michael, "Yes ma'am, we've already noticed that ourselves. So what's the connection? That is, as you see it."

Smiling, Michael closed the folder, turned it back around and placed it neatly on top of the other two. She grabbed all three folders, stood up, and held them across the desk toward Chief Anderson. As he rose out of his chair in a knee-jerk southern boy reaction to a lady rising and grasped the folders in his massive hand, Michael held tight and said, "That's something I'd really like to find out."

She released the folders, reached down to grab her briefcase and turned to leave the office.

Anderson chided her, "You wanna dig around, Agent Francis, you gotta get permission and I ain't sure I wanna give it to you just yet."

"Why's that?" Michael said sharply.

"Nothin' personal. I just don't like where you're goin' with this. All you been tellin' me so far is pure conjecture, standard prime-time crime solver TV show bullshit. See, those other missing person's cases? They're missing because there wasn't any murder. You need a body, or some evidence at a crime scene for it to be a murder. You should know better, Agent Francis; you should know better than to draw a conclusion and try to find evidence supporting your conclusion. I am not going to allow my investigation on some poor girl's death to go chasing ghosts about what may or may not have happened to any missing persons. Those cases are still open; we solve this one, we'll move on to those. Right now, one ain't got nothin' to do with the other."

"Hey, Chief, maybe if we're lucky we'll solve all ten before anybody finds out that you've got mysterious disappearances up and down the Outer Banks on your watch," Michael said, turning and striding through the door out of Anderson's office

As Michael left, Anderson slapped the files down onto his desk. As he did, the wind from the folders swept the walnut shells onto the floor.

"Shit," Anderson muttered, walking slowly over to his phone, lifting the receiver, and placing a call.

CHAPTER 9

The beauty of the ocean stunned Michael as she drove down Beach Road, glancing between the houses up against the dunes. The water looked silvery, matching the overcast sky above. Whitecaps broke far out over sandbars, and flocks of pelicans sailed low over the water, dipping the tips of their wings on the crests of the waves. Soon she caught sight of her destination -- the Ocean Sands motel, a squat, one-story cement block, lathered in tacky teal green and plastered with dolphins and sand dollars.

She was surprised at how difficult it was to find a room at a motel at the beach. Pretty much the entire strip of the Outer Banks from Nags Head up north to Currituck was full of beach houses, some large enough for a small army, but no large-scale hotels. The few motels that dotted the scene were holdovers from the 1950s. Or so the woman from the Ocean Sands told Michael as she checked in, going on and on at length about the local rules against laying concrete to support high-capacity hotels that would crowd the beaches, only leaving options like the Ocean Sands.

The long diatribe by the desk clerk combined with the tacky teal walls of Michael's room to dampen her sense of wonder. The room's bright green ceramic push button phone caught her eye, at once making her cringe due to its clashing color and making her think about calling Robbie Cartwright.

I should call him, but if I tell him about my accident he'll want me to come back.

She wasn't about to do that now.

She glanced at the alarm clock next to the bed. It was a little after three o'clock. She had the afternoon to do a little research before heading out to check out her surroundings and prepare for a full day of interviewing on Saturday. She made a mental note to call the girls after they got home from school, probably around 5:30.

She broke out a pen, notepad, and her laptop, lay prostrate on her bed and logged into the Internet. Her uneventful first few months in the Raleigh SBI office had allowed her time to peruse the various online databases that North Carolina's law enforcement agencies shared. Once she got the case, she'd run some initial searches on Kathy Kirkland. Now she began to pull together a more complete profile of the young girl.

She learned that Kirkland grew up in Winston-Salem, about three hours west of Raleigh. She came from an educated family active in their community. As a girl, she continued that tradition: she was a Brownie, Girl Scout, cheerleader, point guard for her high school basketball team, and delegate to the model U.N.

Instead of attending local Wake Forest University, Kirkland followed a Carolina girl's dream by completing four years at the University of North Carolina at Chapel Hill. While getting her degree in public policy, Kirkland had interned twice, both in Raleigh: once at her late uncle's law firm and once at Senator Pennington's office.

Pennington was the most influential state legislator in North Carolina, the leader of the state senate for twelve years running. His family pretty much ruled the eastern section of North Carolina, including most of the Outer Banks. A stand-up guy, according to SBI notes, not into anything controversial. It just happened that his family had deep, deep roots in the state and their old money translated into a helluva lot of power and influence. Kirkland's uncle was Pennington's lead lawyer.

In the summer between her freshman and sophomore year at UNC, Kirkland was busted with three friends in a bar parking lot for marijuana possession. Although her three friends were charged, her charges were dropped, thanks to her influential lawyer uncle. About that time, Kirkland started to get involved with environmental advocacy groups, going door-to-door while working toward a degree in public policy at UNC.

After graduating UNC, she took a job as legislative aide in Pennington's office at the State Capitol in Raleigh. She was promoted last April to Assistant Legislative Advocate and worked with the Legislative Director, Bart Taylor. The professional trail ended there.

Michael dug deeper.

After the stints at her uncle's firm and Pennington's office, Kirkland began to turn politically to the right. Still keen on the environment, she kept her membership active in several national organizations. But the type of work she must have been doing for Pennington's office couldn't have been too environment-friendly.

That kind of conflict would have to weigh heavily on a young neophyte, Michael imagined. Breaking her train of thought, she glanced up at the clock at her bedside.

6:15. I'm behind schedule. Gotta call the girls and get moving.

Michael closed her laptop and put it on the bedside table. She took her pen and notepad and opened the top drawer of the table to stow them away. As she did, she noticed a couple packs of condoms in the drawer.

Her heart began to race. Her left eye started twitching.

Thoughts about June fifth invaded her mind. The pure fear of being discovered cheating on Brian in their own bed. The adrenaline rush that came with the fear, and the overwhelming sense of guilt and despair that followed.

"Stop!" Michael screamed aloud, standing bolt upright from the bed. She walked to the window, placing a hand on the wall to steady herself. She took some deep breaths and pulled back the curtain to focus on something else, anything to get her mind off June fifth. Out in the parking lot, some people were unpacking suitcases from an SUV, next to her beat-up Crown Victoria.

The Crown Vic. Michael thought about what was in the trunk.

The pump-action shotgun.

The thought of why she'd brought it along gave Michael chills. She shook them off, stood upright and closed the curtain.

"Call your girls," she told herself.

Call your girls.

♦ ♦ ♦

"Mom has to know about this," 14-year-old Megan Francis announced to her father, arms crossed in front of her as she paced across their neighbors' living room. All three Francis girls had been assembled, with their "Aunt Sue" watching pensively from the couch as the girls' father addressed them.

"Megan, I know; it's not every day that someone breaks into your house with a gun and takes a few shots at your father. I'm trying desperately to tell Mom, I just can't reach her," Brian said. "She's on the road and she isn't picking up her cell."

Twelve-year-old Mary Francis raised her fixed gaze from the floor and excitedly blurted out her idea. "Why don't they call the people she's going to meet?" Brian walked over to his daughter and dropped to his knees to regard her at eye level. "I've tried that, honey, when somebody sees her they'll get in touch with her."

"Bullshit, Dad, this whole thing is bullshit," Megan said, plopping down in the couch next to Sue McCairn and dropping her head into her hands, sobbing.

"Megan, watch your mouth," Brian snapped, then, talking more softly, added, "Baby, don't worry. I'm leaving in ten minutes to drive out there myself. In the meantime, stay here with Aunt Sue."

"You're WHAT?" Megan yelled. Her sister Anna's elfish voice piped up from the other side of the room, "What if, you know, someone else comes to the house?" Brian turned and smiled at his eight-year-old daughter. "Don't worry, baby, Uncle Harry should be home soon. He's coming with a driver to take me out to where Mommy is, and he's staying here with Aunt Sue tonight. You'll be safe. Look, there he is pulling into the driveway."

Reacting as if she'd heard Santa had arrived, Anna ran to the window and broke into a wide smile when she saw the hulking figure of the 6'4", 250-pound chiseled Marine in his fatigues walking at a quick step up the front walk. A freshly washed camouflage-painted SUV sat idling in the driveway, another Marine waiting patiently behind the wheel. As the front door opened, Anna ran into the foyer next to the living room where everyone waited and threw her arms around the legs and lower torso of Major Harry McCairn. Taking off his baseball-style camouflage hat and exposing his crew-cut red hair, Harry let a huge smile envelope his broad Irish face as he returned the young girl's hug and turned to address the family before him, laughing, "You know, I could get used to this!"

♦ ♦ ♦

The two friends sat across from each other in the McCairn kitchen, the burly Irishman with his hands folded before him, staring intently at Brian, who was hurriedly scribbling phone numbers and names on a sheet of paper. "My sergeant down at the Raleigh P.D., he's a friend, knows where I'm going and what I'm doing," Brian said, turning the paper around to show Harry and pointing to one of several names. "This is the guy you want first, the rest are regular emergency numbers."

"I'll keep calling Michael's cell on the half-hour," Harry said. "Don't worry. The girls, they'll be fine. We're all gonna camp in the media room. There are no windows and only one door, and I'll have my piece. I've got a buddy to come over on his day off to switch watch with me, nothin's gonna touch your family while I'm around. And Max; he won't let them out of his sight."

Brian could feel his stomach flip-flop. Half-nervous and half-relieved by what his friend had just said, he rose from the table and offered Harry a firm handshake, never raising his eyes from the table.

"I'll call you from the road," Brian said, turning and walking out of the kitchen into the family room.

In the center of the room, the McCairn's huge German shepherd, Max, lifted his head and cautiously regarded Brian's approach.

That reassured Brian slightly as he wiped away a tear, took a deep breath, and went to hug his girls goodbye.

◆◆◆

The phone kept ringing at the Francis home, which frustrated Michael to no end. If the girls weren't there, she at least wanted to check her messages quickly and then see if her girls were at the McCairns. Maybe she hadn't dialed the right number. Looking down at her watch, Michael realized she had less than five minutes before her 6:30 meeting with Amy Miller for drinks to talk about the murder. "Pick-up, dammit," Michael muttered into the phone as she waited for a connection.

Watching the phone ring before them, the two

uninvited guests at the otherwise empty Francis home exchanged glances, wondering what to do. They had unplugged the phone line from the answering machine so any incoming calls wouldn't connect as they were playing back messages, and here the phone was ringing at the most inopportune time. The shadowy figure on the right made a move to plug in the phone line to the answering machine, but his arm was intercepted by the figure on the left. Expressive eyes from behind a black ski-mask met those from his similarly attired partner. They both turned from the phone and continued rummaging through the Francis family office, carefully keeping their ears alert to any sounds of cars approaching the driveway from the silent street out in front or footsteps across the walkway.

In the heart of Nags Head, The Purple Turtle rose before Michael like an oasis in a sea of weathered cedar shingle beach houses, gift shops with extravagant facades, and an old-timey miniature golf course adorned with giant dinosaurs and a flying saucer. She found a parking spot, noticing a patchwork of out-of-state license plates as she walked through the gravel lot to the bar. Inside, a crowd of young people attired in tank tops and Hawaiian shirts milled about the place. She spotted Amy Miller sitting at a four-seat wooden table at the back wall away from the main bar. She had called her right after trying to reach her girls back home to set up a meeting at the nearby watering hole.

As she approached, Michael smiled sharply and stuck out her hand. "Sit down, please," Amy said somewhat hurriedly, trying to hide her anxiety with a nervous smile. "Pretty crowded!" Michael semi-shouted above the din of some old E.L.O. song over the speakers. "Sushi night," Amy replied.

"Sounds good to me, but man it stinks in here!"

Michael felt herself almost yelling. Indeed, the entire bar smelled like old beer, stale tobacco and beach sweat. Amy just rolled her eyes and smiled, somewhat embarrassed that she had to choose this particular dive to meet.

A waitress came over quickly and stared at the two women with her pen and pad. "Uh, Miller Light, please," Michael ordered.

"Bottle or draft?"

"She'll have a bottle, me too," Amy interjected, telling Michael, "It's on special."

"You two gonna eat?" the waitress asked.

"Yes, thanks darlin', we'll both have the sushi sampler."

Once the waitress left, Michael leaned across the table to be heard above the noise. "Thanks so much for meeting me tonight, I know it's been crazy for you lately and I figured instead of just rehashing what happened when you found Kathy Kirkland's body we could just chat a little about what's been going on around here, see if we might identify some possible clues local law enforcement may have missed."

Catching a whiff of her guest's subtle, feminine perfume when she got close, Amy smiled, and stared into Michael's piercing green eyes. Her blushing in the public safety building wasn't a fluke; Amy was smitten.

"You have great eyes," she blurted out without thinking.

"I'm sorry?" Michael replied, furrowing her brow.

A look of embarrassment shot across Amy's face.

Reaching her left hand across the table, she patted Michael's right arm. "I'm really sorry," she said apologetically. "I hope I didn't freak you out there. I'm pretty forward, and I'm pretty tired. I didn't see a wedding ring, and, well, you ... well, you're very attractive, darlin', let's leave it at that."

Michael sat back in her chair and just stared. She looked down at her left hand, rolling it over to see the back of her fingers. She wasn't wearing her wedding ring, hadn't been wearing it in weeks. She noticed there was still a white band burnt into her skin where the ring had rested all those years.

"So you were married, but not anymore?" Amy asked.

Michael lifted her gaze to the real estate agent and wasn't quite sure what to say.

"That's not important."

Amy cleared her throat and looked away as the waitress showed up with their beers. After she left, Amy crossed her arms, tilted her head, and shot Michael a curious look.

"So I'm gonna say still married then, but separated. Maybe trying to work things out? But maybe not interested in working them out. On your part, that is."

"Listen, Amy, this -- "

"Look, Agent Francis, I'm sorry. I've been going through hell lately, and I'm not seeing anybody and, well, let's just say it's been a while. I saw a super-hot lady and took a shot, let's move on."

Super-hot lady.

That made Michael smile.

"So about Kathy Kirkland. Did you know her at all?"

"Not really. I met her, seen her once or twice, at Chamber functions. She wasn't family, if you know what I mean? So my interest waned."

"Family?"

"Queer."

"How did you know she wasn't, uh, family? Do you have to register?"

Laughing, Amy answered, "Not really. Hit on her, kinda had the same result as just now, actually. Gotta work on my game."

"So you didn't get to know Kathy, but you had seen her at Chamber functions. Did you know who she worked for?"

"Yeah, she was here lobbying for Perry Peterson's construction gig up north of Kill Devil Hills. She worked for Skip Pennington's office back in Raleigh. Really wasn't much to do with the project, though. It was going through pretty smoothly. Pennington usually helps Peterson cross all his Ts and dots all his Is back in Raleigh before moving on anything, ya' know? A couple of environmentalist groups, the usual locals in opposition, but her work really was just schmoozing people already on board."

Amy's eyes dropped to the table.

"She seemed very young, very pretty. Probably had a lot going for her. She was the belle of the ball at a big party the Chamber threw for Perry at the local hospital just last Monday, lots of suits and ties, lots of money flowing. Perry had a damn wing named after him, greasing the palms so local folks don't mind that he's skirting the rules to get his development in, you know the drill. A couple of us were laughing at all the guys hitting on her, pretty funny actually. Well, then she's dead, just like that. Not so funny anymore I suppose."

Michael sat passively, taking in the conversation. She noticed the pain in Amy's voice, it was something you couldn't fake.

"Look, Amy, I don't want to drag you through anything here," she said. "To tell you the truth, I've been sent here to pretty much just make an appearance because of the pressure you put on my boss at the SBI in Raleigh."

Amy looked up and squinted at Michael, angry. "No. You're not going to blow this off. These assholes already tried to bury this. I find it hard to believe a woman of your obvious caliber and intellect is just an errand girl. I would think you're here to see if there's any shenanigans goin' on, right? I mean, you can find out where Kathy worked and who she was with, all that jazz from police files."

Michael didn't answer.

Amy leaned forward.

"Agent Francis," she spoke forcefully, under her breath. "I know everyone here. You probably know that, and aside from the fact that I discovered the body, and you feel the need to appease me with a visit because I called you here from Raleigh, you want to get the inside scoop on things. That's fine, just fine. Granted, I've only been in my job 18 months, but I damn well sure know everything that goes on around here. That redneck horse's ass Anderson doesn't want to do anything with this case because he doesn't want any pressure from anybody about upsetting things."

"Upsetting what things?"

"Anderson's a big fish in a little pond, and he doesn't want that to change. You know how they say all politics are local? Well, in OBX, all politics are family. And the biggest family is Pennington, kin to Perry Peterson, who is related to my boss and half the business community and government in Dare County like the local medical examiner Chris Lane, he's Skip Pennington's nephew. The local big shots like having Anderson around to keep things in line. If outsiders find out there's been a murder here, that's one thing to upset the tourism industry. But if they find out it's a staffer of Senator Pennington, and they start sniffing around, and some national network news crew gets down here and starts asking questions about why Perry Peterson gets to build his big ol' resort in an area zoned residential without environmental impact statements ever being filed, well then..."

Amy cut herself off when the waitress came over with their sushi. The two women were momentarily silent as they went about arranging their silverware and plates.

"Looks good," Michael said.

"Yeah, best place in OBX to get it, one of the bright spots to that motherfucker," Amy said, gesturing with her head over Michael's shoulder toward the bar. Turning around, Michael spotted a thin, late-twenties surfer dude with long dirty blond hair and a scruffy chin behind the bar mixing drinks. "The bartender?" she asked, turning back to Amy, who nodded.

"Yeah, that's Bruce Pennington, he owns the place. Daddy bought it for him to keep him busy so he don't ruin the Pennington name by doing anything stupid."

"The senator's son?" Michael asked.

"Yeah, that's Skip Pennington's boy, son of the next great United States Senator from the Tar Heel State. Real champ; was all over me like a cheap suit when I first got here. Found out I pitched for the other team, started dissing me whenever he got the chance. His cousin Chris, he helped set him straight one night when Brucie was all over me. He's a good guy, Chris, helped Bruce get this place up and running. Handy with the DIY projects around the house and what not. Hangs out here from time to time, keeping an eye on Bruce, helps fix shit from time to time. Hell, I'd take any excuse to get away from the morgue."

"Pennington's son didn't know Kathy, did he?"

"He's probably who killed her," Amy said with a laugh and wave of her hand.

Michael just stared.

Amy didn't flinch. "That's the reason I thought I'd bring you here. I figure, you know, you need suspects, right? I mean, the Chief, he hasn't done shit on this case, I just figured...well, ol' Brucie there, he's usually all over the fresh meat that flows in here. Him and that switch-hitting ex-girlfriend of his."

Michael stopped chewing and held her hands out openly, gesturing for Amy to conclude her thought. Amy noticed and laughed. "I'm sorry, I'm dishin'. That's the southern belle in me rearing her ugly head," she said in increasingly southern tones. "Bruce and his ex have a pretty good deal going, if you're into it. Open relationship, occasional threesomes with some of the prettier new girls in town is what I hear."

Amy took another swig of beer and dabbed at her mouth, leaning in to talk more softly to Michael. In a serious tone, she said, "Agent Francis, I didn't see them together at any Chamber functions. If you're asking me if lil' Brucie could've done those awful things to that poor girl, well..." Amy trailed off then coughed, trying to keep her composure. "I'm sorry, but you should've seen her poor body like I did. No, Brucie boy fancies himself a Valentino, not a Hannibal Lecter or anything. He's a pretty big wuss. But hell, I figure you gotta start somewhere, right?"

Michael sat still for a moment, gathering her thoughts. "Alright, I'll take that under advisement. I'm not looking to gossip about who may have done what to Kathy Kirkland, I'm trying to find people who may have been in contact with Kathy Kirkland. Did you see the police report?"

"No, why?"

"The last place Kathy Kirkland was seen that night was in here, Monday night, the night of the hospital Chamber reception you mentioned."

Amy sat back in her chair, astounded by the revelation. Before she could say anything, Michael piped in, "Now I'm not saying Bruce Pennington or his girlfriend had anything to do with it. It could have been someone she met in here, a vacationing surfer or a drifter or somebody or it certainly could have been someone with no association with this place. Maybe it was someone from the reception she brought with her, who knows. But I'm eventually going to have to interview the younger Pennington to see what he knows, so the more I know about him before I talk with him, the better I can approach things. In fact, I think I want to talk to that girlfriend of his before I talk with him so he doesn't shut her up before I get to her. You know where I can find her?"

"Well, I don't know where she lives, don't have her phone. I used to see her at The Wagoneer, a dance club up in Duck, when I first rolled in here. She stopped going about a year ago. She has her own boat, the Shoal Surfer, does charter fishing tours, runs out of the marina down at Oregon Inlet. Tomorrow's Saturday; you might be able to catch her if you're up early enough."

"What's early enough?" Michael said with a smile, sipping from her second beer.

"I'd guess she'd leave around 6:00 without a tour scheduled to do some fishin' for profit, or 8:00 or 9:00 with a tour. With this weather rolling in, I'm thinking we might be in for quite a blow. You best get over there first thing."

First thing. Michael was exhausted, physically and emotionally. A look of gloom passed over her face; she tried to hide it, but Amy noticed and gave a big smile from behind her fourth pint of beer.

Michael turned around in her seat and tried to spot Bruce Pennington.

He was standing behind the bar, washing out a mug, staring straight at her.

For a moment, they locked eyes. Then Pennington turned, hung the mug on an overhead rack, tossed his dishtowel over his shoulder and walked out from behind the bar and down a short hallway to a back room.

Turning back to Amy, Michael heard her say, "Well I guess he's figured out you're bad news."

◆◆◆

"Can I help you gentlemen?" Robbie Cartwright asked through the open door of Agent Francis' office at the SBI building. The two men standing to the left of her desk, dressed in matching baby blue oxford shirts and dark slacks, turned their attention to the fat man with his tie and topmost button undone. The taller of the two, the one with close-cropped blonde hair, smiled sheepishly and moved slowly toward the door.

"Sorry, we were looking for an Agent Michael Francis," he spat, stopping just inside the doorway. Robbie regarded the man, sizing him up. White, well over six feet, athletic, steely gaze, late twenties; probably military. Looking past him at the companion intruder, Robbie figured him to be the lower in rank, along with being of slightly lesser build, plain features, and longer brown hair.

Damn. Two military in one of his agent's offices, unannounced. Robbie looked down at his cold cup of coffee and wished it was something more menacing.

"Who y'all? Got any identification?"

"Who might you be, sir?" offered the leader, moving outside the office and extending a hand.

"Robbie Cartwright, special agent in charge, who are you and why you here without an appointment?" he asked, forcefully moving in to grasp the man's hand and then brushing by him into the office. The lead intruder seemed to fumble a bit as Robbie moved past him, perhaps not expecting him to be so aggressive. The smile left his face and he mumbled something as Robbie moved into the personal space of the second intruder, grasping an I.D. badge on the left side of his shirt.

"Peterson, Todd Peterson, U.S.M.C. Military Police," Robbie read the badge, turning to the leader. "You his commanding officer?"

The lead man broke again into his smile as the other man laughed briefly behind Robbie. "No sir, hardly. Brian Laviolette, special investigator. We're both MP's outta Lejeune, sir. You weren't at your desk when we tried to buzz in at the front desk, and your man down there sent us up here to wait."

"Y'all follow me to my office, we can chat a bit," Robbie said, clearly irritated. Peterson started to respond from aside the desk, but a quick glare from Laviolette shut him up. Both men followed Robbie out of Michael's office and down inside his own.

Plopping down in his chair, Robbie leaned back and regarded the men.

"Y'all came without having your C.O. give a call. Why's that?" Robbie asked.

There was a brief silence, then Laviolette started to turn

his head toward Peterson when the smaller man spoke up. "We were called in last minute by our C.O., sir. He had to leave ahead of us by five minutes to attend to some business." Robbie nodded his head, and began rocking slowly back and forth in his big leather chair. The smooshing of the leather accentuated the growing stickiness in the room; Robbie could see Laviolette starting to turn red in the cheeks and on his brow. He wondered if it was the stifling heat, his approach to the two men, or how the younger MP had acted so far.

"Got it. Figure it's about that fella shot down at the Francis house?" Robbie asked. He had gotten the info from Brian Francis' sergeant, Bart Tomlinson, who had called earlier to get in touch with Michael to let her know about the whole awful event. "Yessir," the younger man continued, who was then interrupted by Laviolette. "We wanted to interview Agent Francis if we could, sir."

"Sorry, Agent Francis is unavailable. On assignment."

"Where might that be, sir?" the younger man asked, almost too anxiously. His question was greeted with an icy stare from Laviolette.

"Sorry, boys, but I don't give out details on a case unless elements of the agent's case are directly involved," Robbie said, standing from his chair. "Now, if that's all, y'all can just get outta here and give a call if you need any info."

The change in tone surprised the two Marines. "Oh, uh, fine, no problem sir," Laviolette said, offering his hand. He squeezed Robbie's strongly as he said, "We'll be checking in. The victim at the Francis home was from Lejeune. Our C.O. wants it all squared away ASAP. You understand."

Robbie scowled. "Ain't no victim, friend. He tried to blow away one of the good guys. Check in when you need to."

Laviolette quickly made his way out of Robbie's door while Peterson moved over to shake his hand without eye contact and rush to follow his partner.

Robbie plunked back down into his chair, nerves beginning to jump, his stomach starting to feel queasy. They said they were looking for the agent involved in the shooting of their buddy, yet they came looking for Michael, not Brian. Why were they coming to the SBI looking for Michael and not down at the Raleigh P.D. looking for Brian?

Robbie had sent Michael out to Nags Head by herself. A newbie sent into a difficult situation; the political bosses had asked for someone to tread water, find nothing, and keep quiet. That's how Robbie had pitched them on Michael, but the joke was on them. Robbie, trying to play both sides, wanted to get someone in there who would do a good job, do what was right. The pride Robbie had felt after he decided to send Michael, an agent he actually expected to make a true blue effort on the case, a new friend he cared about, had faith in, and who needed a break was now being replaced by second-guessing and guilt over sending a quality agent into a situation that was unfolding into something that very well could be much more than just over her head.

It's okay. She's good for this case; she needs this case. She'll use it to get herself on track, there's more to it for her than just the motions.

He had a good feeling about Michael Francis.

But, Jesus, Robbie thought. Her husband shot a Marine in her house, in front of her kid. She's been out of contact all afternoon and can't be reached. That cop Anderson in Nags Head said they haven't seen her. Now some shady fellas from Lejeune came looking for her without explanation.

His ringing cell phone interrupted his musings. He checked out the number: 828 area code, out east, Outer Banks.

"Robbie Cartwright," the SBI veteran muttered.

"Hey Boss," came the faint voice of Agent Michael

Francis on the other end.

"Francis?! That you, girl?"

"Yeah, Boss. Can you hear me?" came the choppy reply, her voice muffled from background noise.

"Yes indeed, missy. Where you at?"

"I'm at a bar interviewing a witness, getting some details on this murder. It's pretty loud, but I'm outside on a deck in the back on someone else's cell phone. The wind's picking up a bit, but I can hear you."

"Listen, Agent Francis, you doin' okay? We're seeing news reports of a nasty squall, weather guys say it might turn soon. You need to get it all done and quick, girl. You hear me?"

"Yeah, Boss, fine. Listen, I can't seem to get a hold of the girls. Nobody's answering at my home number and the neighbors' phone is busy."

"Yeah, there's been an incident but your girls are safe," Robbie said. His exclamation of assuredness was met by silence on the other end of the line.

Over some difficult minutes, Robbie Cartwright laid-out the major details of the shooting, leaving out the aspect of Michael's eight-year-old daughter being in the line of fire and the visit from the military police. He answered as many of Michael's harried questions as he could, but would not lead her into speculation about the shooter, deciding instead to leave it as a possible robbery gone bad.

"Agent Francis, you come home now, hear? You come home ta' your girls," Robbie said in the sweetest down-home voice he could muster.

Holding the phone to her ear, Michael looked out from the deck of the Purple Turtle into a crowd of rowdy young 20-somethings playing volleyball in a tiki torch-lit backyard pit. The bobbing heads, flying hair, bare midriffs and wide smiles seemed to be moving in slow motion. One girl, a young blonde with cut-off jean shorts, dove for a ball and went face-first into the sand. A tall boy with dirty-blonde hair fell over her, and they both rolled around a bit, laughing. Kathy Kirkland could have been playing here just a few nights ago.

"Sorry Boss, I'm not through here."

"What? I couldn't hear that."

"You heard me. You sent me here to do a job, and I'm gonna do it. You said the girls are safe, right?"

"Look, Agent Francis, I sent you out there – "

"Boss, they're at the McCairn house, right?" Michael cut him off.

Robbie shut his eyes in defeat. "Yes, that's where Brian's Sergeant said they are. Just listen, I want daily reports, morning noon and night, on my cell, you got that?"

"I'm on a borrowed cell phone. Mine got damaged..." Michael caught herself before going into details of her car wreck. She didn't want that information getting back to the girls. "Look, I'll call you tomorrow. Got to go, Boss."

"Agent Francis, listen, you – " Robbie heard the other phone click off. He turned off his cell phone and tossed it angrily across his office.

He shook his head.

Francis hadn't even asked about her husband.

Robbie got up from his seat, put one hand on his hip and pinched his temples with the forefinger and thumb of the other as he looked out his window. He reached down, and pulled up the window, then moved over to the other and did the same.

Robbie started to feel as if he had left something burning on a stove somewhere.

Robbie Cartwright began to sweat.

◆ ◆ ◆

Outside the Purple Turtle, Amy and Michael talked for a good fifteen minutes. Amy told Michael she should look for a girl who goes by the name of Jules, who pilots The

Shoal Surfer at Oregon Inlet. She was Bruce Pennington's part-time girlfriend, and Michael wanted to get her take on things before she hit-up her boyfriend for info, playing one against the other.

She began to feel overwhelmed. Her eye began to twitch.

"Agent Francis? You alright?" Amy asked, noticing the twitching.

"Here's your phone. Thanks for letting me use it."

"You keep it for the weekend, Agent Francis. It's my work phone, I don't need it, I'm not working. I've got another one at home. You keep it to stay in touch with your family," Amy said with a sympathetic smile.

All Michael could do was smile and try to keep her eye from twitching wildly.

"Thanks," she muttered, and slipped it into her purse.

The two women eventually parted ways and Amy watched Michael disappear behind a group of parked cars. Walking in the opposite direction across the Purple Turtle's lot to her blue Jetta in the darkened lot next door, Amy fished her keys out of her pocket and fumbled around until she could feel the automatic unlock button with her thumb. She depressed it once, then twice as she moved within ten feet of the vehicle. She should've been greeted by a beep acknowledging the alarm system deactivating and the doors unlocking, but heard nothing.

Concerned, Amy walked faster, stretching her arm out toward the car and pointing the keychain as she rapidly depressed the button over and over.

She walked around a white SUV to her driver's side door, and tried the latch several times, to no avail. She was locked out of her car. "Shit," Amy cursed under her breath. She was in a dark gravel lot off Beach Drive. There was a good deal of Friday night traffic, so walking home was not out-of-the-question; if she had any trouble, she could flag somebody down. Still, it was a good eight blocks to home and she was wearing heels.

She turned to head back into the bar. To her right, she heard rustling in the gravel parking lot. It was jammed-full of cars, but nobody was around besides her. There was a banging against one of the cars, across from her, which made her jump a bit. Figuring it was a bottle or beer can blown by the wind, Amy turned her attention back to The Purple Turtle. She could see its neon lights across the lot.

Amy heard some moaning.

It sounded like somebody was hurt toward the backside of the parking lot, right next to the small strip of grass dividing it from the gravel lot next door. "Hey, anybody there?" Amy yelled. "Uhhh," came the reply, a man's voice. "My head," he mumbled.

Amy made her way into the lot, and about six spaces in began to look between cars. Turning, she saw a man in a tee-shirt and jeans, down on one knee, both hands over the back of his head, between two cars, near the rear of a white SUV.

"You alright?" Amy called, walking over to the man.

"My head," he mumbled again.

"Let's go over to the bar across the way and get you some ice," she said, reaching for the man. When her arm was about a foot from his shoulder he sprang up, head down, and ram-tackled her in the stomach, knocking her to the ground.

All Amy could utter was "oof," as the wind was knocked out of her and she tumbled backwards. The back of her head hit the ground, and she saw stars. She started to open her eyes, but they were blurry because of the pain and alcohol. The man rammed his left knee into her crotch, sending searing pain up her stomach.

She shuddered in agony.

The man did it again.

And again.

Amy blacked-out.

♦♦♦

Michael Francis drove south on Beach Road from the bar to her hotel. After parking in front of her room, Michael fished around in her pocket for the room key. She located the impossibly large diamond-shaped green plastic key tag with the bright silver 9 on it, and was almost at her door when she heard something behind her.

Stopping, Michael strained to listen to what had caught her attention.

Wind and waves.

Michael turned and looked across the street from the parking lot in front of the motel. Grassy dunes stood between two houses about 50 yards apart, long stalks making shadows in the moonlight as they danced in the wind. A large wooden support beam stuck out of the ground; must've been a beach house there at one time, probably washed away by a hurricane. Michael stood there and listened to the waves. She shook her hair out of her face, thinking that she couldn't believe it took several drinks and exhaustion to get her to slow down enough to actually hear the ocean. Here she'd been in Nags Head for, what, eleven hours and she hadn't even been down to the water yet.

Exhaustion creeping in, Michael closed her eyes and breathed deep, taking in the soft, warm salt air. A stiff breeze was blowing it across the street, right into her face. Her whole body felt enveloped by the smells and sounds. Opening her eyes, Michael made her way across the parking lot, stuffing the key back into her pants pocket as she headed toward the beach.

Crossing Beach Road was easy, as there were few cars in this part of Nags Head at eleven o'clock at night; most everyone else was heading north toward the strips with the bars and restaurants. She felt her shoes hit the sand after crossing the street and started up over the dunes toward the beach. As she did, she remembered Amy Miller's cell phone in her jacket pocket, and took it out and held the face of the phone up to the moonlight to help her see the semi-lit dials. Michael tried her children once again at the McCairn house. She wanted to hear their voices, but she didn't want to tell them about her car accident; they had enough to worry about with a man getting shot at their house. Michael figured everyone needed a little reassurance right about now.

This time, her neighbors were off the phone. Sue McCairn explained that Harry had been trying ceaselessly to contact Michael on her cell. As her friend went to get her eldest daughter from the family room, Michael made it down the other side of a dune, and walked to where the dry sand met the high water mark. She sat down and brought her knees up to her chest, watching the moon highlight the white caps blown by the stiff wind. She could see thousands of stars in a clear night sky. Without clouds, Michael was amazed the ocean was bringing in such a wind, and was humbled by the force of nature before her. Safe in her happy place, loaded semi-automatic gun at her side, Michael felt completely independent.

When she heard her daughter's voice, she felt suddenly vulnerable, and a little scared, and was surprised as she was overcome with so much emotion. Michael looked over her shoulder and for a split-second thought she saw her father standing behind her. She turned back to face the ocean and stared out at the moonlit tips of the waves crashing onto the shore, talking calmly to her daughter, trying to explain what she was doing so far away from home.

To herself, as much as to Megan.

CHAPTER 10

Six o'clock in the morning brought rapping on Michael's hotel room door. Years of training forced her eyes open and she half-rolled over to her nightstand, instinctively reaching for her holster. Unfortunately, her weapon was M.I.A. after the accident, leaving Michael tossing the empty leather carrying case onto the floor.

Fuck.

Michael sat up in bed, shaking away her frustration and realizing the front desk had given her their version of a wake-up call. "Got it!" she yelled to whomever was on the other side of the door.

Stretching her lithe body as she stepped out of bed, Michael could feel just a tinge of her long night out that had capped an extraordinarily challenging day. It took a while longer for her body to recover than when she was in her twenties, bringing with it a longer wake up routine. Michael sat on the floor, spread her legs straight in front of her and did several toe touches, holding for a ten count with each stretch. She then spread her legs apart at a 45-degree angle and brought her head to her knees, one at a time, holding for a ten count. She continued the stretching until she felt less like a 39-year-old mother of three and more like the 25-year-old police recruit who had learned to turn her love of sports into a way to build and maintain an efficient tool and fighting machine called the human body.

Usually, Michael would get dressed in sweats and run for a few miles. This morning, however, she needed to run into Bruce Pennington's girlfriend down at the Oregon Inlet marina between 7 and 8. A quick shower, followed by a half-ass makeup job, wet hair tied back into a respectable ponytail along with a pair of shorts and tank top got her out the door by 6:45. She got directions from the clerk at the desk and drove up Beach Road for two blocks to Whalebone Junction.

Whalebone Junction was an intersection which gave travelers a choice of going right toward the mainland or heading straight into the sparsely populated Pea Island Nature Preserve heading down the southern end of the Outer Banks. Michael drove her car straight into the preserve, and what little development there was disappeared as wide marshes popped up to her right and dunes reared their heads to her left.

Michael must've seen two dozen rabbits alongside the road in the short 15-minute drive to Oregon Inlet. She figured she must've seen as many, if not more, pickup trucks with plastic tubing on their front racks transporting impossibly long fishing rods. She passed a lighthouse with horizontal white and black stripes on her way to the marina with the sign Bodie Island Light. Just before a bridge climbing up into the sky then back down again somewhere over the horizon, the marina appeared on her right. Michael parked in one of the few spaces left as truck after truck pulled in line at the boating access ramp to drop their vessels into the water. She got out and reached back into the car, taking her handgun out of a small backpack, checking it for ammo, then placing it back inside the backpack, which she zipped closed and slung over her shoulder.

Walking over to a long pier, Michael took in the sights of the morning fishing rush. A stiff, warm breeze blowing out of an overcast sky brought incredible smells of salt air, coffee and fish. Sounds of lightly idling outboard motors and larger inboard models dared not disturb the 5 mph speed limit of the marina's waters. As she made her way along the beginning of the pier, Michael could see fishermen near the marsh actually in the water, with hip boots, up to their waists casting and recasting where the tides gave them something to stand on. It seemed like another world.

Michael made a point to look over the Coast Guard station at the other side of the marina. Several guardsmen were out hosing down one of their boats, and there seemed to be a good dozen cars and trucks in their parking lot. On the roof of the station sat two rotating radar antennas, as well as a large radio or microwave station.

Amy Miller had mentioned that Pennington's girlfriend's boat was a fairly good size ship named The Shoal Surfer, and Michael began peering at the backside of the boats moored to the pier. There must have been about 20 or so similar fishing and touring boats moored, with several tour groups fitting themselves with life jackets and clumsily boarding with picnic coolers. About three-quarters of the way up the pier, Michael caught sight of The Shoal Surfer.

She was a 30-footer, Michael figured. Five fishing rods sat in tubes on the back railing, with a cabin taking up the front two-thirds of the ship. Atop the cabin was the deck with a wheel and some navigational instruments. There was nobody on deck.

Michael walked up on the pier until she was about halfway up the side of the boat. She leaned forward, cupping her hands around her eyes and pressing them against the tinted window to see if there was anybody inside the cabin.

There certainly was.

Michael's hands and face were about three feet from a woman, naked from the waist up, with her back to the window. She reached down and grabbed a shirt, then pulled it over her head. As she did so she turned, and Michael was taken aback by the sight of the young woman's firm round breasts. "Jeesh," Michael laughed nervously, recoiling in embarrassment.

Hoping the woman had not seen her, Michael moved quickly to the back of the boat and waited for someone to come out the cabin door and onto the deck.

A few uncomfortable seconds later, a mop of wavy brown shoulder-length hair poked out of the cabin, followed by the bright face of a fair-skinned girl in her early 30's with dark eyebrows. She turned and saw Michael, and smiled hello.

"Hey there," the woman said in a friendly, semi-surprised voice. "How're you this morning?" she asked sweetly with the tinge of a southern accent.

"Just fine, thank you," Michael replied with a smile, trying hard to hide her embarrassment while matching the woman's friendly demeanor. "Are you Jules?"

"Juliana," the woman said, putting her hands on her hips and cocking her head slightly to the side. "Juliana Gray. Who might you be?" she asked.

For just a moment, Michael hesitated. This woman seemed more like a celebrity actress or supermodel than a fishing boat captain. Michael shook her head slightly and stammered, "Michael Francis. Agent Francis. I'm with the North Carolina State Bureau of Investigation."

The woman's smile seemed to darken a bit, but she held out her hand in greeting nonetheless. "Nice to meet you. Come aboard?" she asked, still holding out her hand. As Michael nodded yes and took a step onto the boat, Juliana grabbed her hand and pulled her the rest of the way on board with strong athletic prowess. Michael shifted her weight and landed gracefully, matching the woman's athletics.

"What can I do for you, Michael Francis? Agent Francis," Juliana asked.

"I was hoping to ask you some questions. I was having dinner with Amy Miller last night, and she said I should look you up." Juliana's face brightened, and she leaned her head back a bit, looking Michael up and down, head to foot and back again.

"She did, did she?" Juliana said playfully. "Well, you found me. You want to head out with me for a bit this mornin'? I just dropped a new engine in this puppy and need to give it a run through the chop before my tours start around 10:30."

Slightly confused, Michael looked at her watch. "I'm really just interested in a few questions."

Juliana smiled and crossed her arms over her chest. "Unless I'm under arrest, I'm heading out on this boat. You're welcome to tag along and ask your questions, or disembark. Your choice."

She needed this interview, Michael thought. "Fine."

"Great. Get those two ropes aft, and the one fore. I'll get the engine started," Juliana said. Looking from side to side, Michael located the ropes in the rear of the boat tied to two pilings on the pier. She jumped off the boat, untied both and threw then onto the boat, then ran up to the one toward the front of the boat, untied that one and walked quickly to the back of the boat and jumped on as it started to ever so slowly pull away from the pier. Juliana revved the engines from above the cabin.

"You can come up here, we can get to know each other on the way out," she yelled down.

Michael scrambled up the ladder at the rear of the cabin, and stood behind and to the left of the supermodel fishing captain as they slowly pulled away from the marina.

♦♦♦

"Sheriff, we got a call this mornin' from Jenny

Cooper," Deputy Alan Marshall said in an anxious southern drawl. He pushed past the swinging waist-high wooden door separating the outer reception area of the Bulah County fire department and Sheriff's office from the inner administration area. A small setup in the rear of Town Hall in the town of Bulah, the office housed three desks: one for Sheriff Sinclair, and two more for his deputies/firefighters.

Normally, nobody would be in on Saturday morning and everyone would be on call via 9-1-1 dispatch. But Friday was no ordinary day, what with a horrific and highly suspicious accident on the main thoroughfare of 64 East, and an almost totally incinerated pickup truck and a badly burned, unidentifiable body in the car of a known drug dealer.

Sheriff Boyle Sinclair figured he'd probably be in Sunday after church as well.

"What's Jenny got to say? She want us to come about the trailer park next door again? Geez, how'd she find out we were here today," Boyle said shaking his head and slapping down his spiral notebook, tossing his pen on his desk and leaning back in his chair.

"No sir, she said she hasn't been able to get in touch with her son Mike."

Boyle's eyes opened wide. "Mike, huh? Now whaddaya know 'bout that? Art Swanson's comrade in arms, his little transporter of illicit goods."

"She said she drove over to his place, but he wasn't around and his dogs were hungry, like they hadn't been fed in a spell."

Boyle leaned forward in his chair and clasped his hand in his lap. He looked down at the floor, lowering his head as he mumbled, "Well that's unusual even for a shit heel like that. Alan, you ask Jenny what kind of vehicle Mike drives?"

"Yessir, she said it's a 2000 Toyota Camry. Black, moon roof, four doors," Deputy Marshall replied.

Boyle looked up from the floor at his deputy and forced a smile. "Alright," he said. "You call Pete, tell him to pick you up and go get the truck and bring it over to the Smith Brothers garage. Then you and Pete, you go get that burned-up wreckage, all you can find, and bring it over here. We need to pick through it one more time. I'm gonna go talk to Jenny, tell her we're lookin' for her boy, then I'm comin' back here and pulling files on Mike Cooper and Art Swanson. Then we're putting out an A.P.B. on that Camry."

"We lookin' for Jenny's boy now too then," the deputy said.

Boyle looked down at the floor again. "Well," he said slowly. "We find that Camry, Alan, we gonna find us either Mike or Art drivin' it. And whichever one we don't find, well, let's hope for Jenny's sake we find her boy drivin' it."

Looking up, Boyle took a deep breath and stretched his back. "And then," he continued, more forcefully, "Then I'm gonna go get that hard-ass Agent Francis, sit her down and find out why some she was in such a rush to get outta here yesterday."

Deputy Marshall stood hands on hips, trying to make sense of everything. "You think she's involved in somethin' more than an accident?"

Boyle regarded his deputy seriously. "Somehow. Whether she knows it or not, that's the question that I want answers to."

Deputy Marshall shook his head, a vacant stare of incomprehension crossing his face. Boyle considered it for a moment. "Why don't you come with me out to the beach? You got anything planned this weekend?"

The deputy's face lit up. "No, sir! I'll get Pete on the line right now."

Boyle put on his hat, adjusted the brim, and walked out of his office before he decided to change his mind.

The waters of Pamlico Sound were choppy and a bit rough as The Shoal Surfer made its way slowly out into the midst of the Oregon Inlet. Tall saw grass and reeds seemed to fold in sections as the wind whipped across their tops. Gulls flew everywhere, and Michael saw several pelicans fighting the stiff breeze, flying low to the water's edge, along with many funky-looking ducks.

The boat headed toward the bridge that shuttled vehicles across from the northern beaches of Nags Head and beyond to Pea Island, which was a long stretch of nature preserve. Michael passed several fishermen in their waders along the sides of the inlet, and many more in small boats casting their lines among the weeds. As they reached the bridge, Juliana opened-up the engine a bit and The Shoal Surfer headed straight for the edge of the inlet, where it opened its shores like two outstretched arms to the vast Atlantic.

"This is incredible," Michael shouted over the engines. Juliana turned around and smiled behind Bono-style bug shades. Michael kept her hand above her eyes, shielding them from the sun in front of her to the East. "Is this the mouth of a river or something?"

"No, this is just a piece of the sound where it meets the ocean. It didn't always used to be this way. Back in the 1800's a hurricane tore a hole in the island and created the inlet, connecting the ocean to the sound. The first ship to pass through was a paddlewheel steamer named The Oregon, so this became the Oregon Inlet. You don't have any control over things out here on the water, really. Whatever she says, goes," Juliana replied.

"She?"

Juliana nodded. "The sea. She rules all out here, no matter what you might think of yourself. Fish, birds, people, beaches, shoals, it doesn't matter. You just gotta go with the flow; you can't fight it. Sometimes she gives you something good, sometimes she gives you something bad. In the end, she gives you what you need, really. This case, she gave us a great fishing spot, great access from the Coast Guard Station."

Juliana opened the throttle more as they hit the somewhat choppy ocean proper, and the rear of the boat sank lower, the front rose up a bit, and Michael had to grab on a railing to her right to keep from falling, while grabbing onto her backpack strap to keep it from slipping off her shoulder. "Hang on," Juliana yelled.

The Shoal Surfer smashed through several breakers and eventually hit smooth ocean water about 100 yards from shore. Juliana turned the boat south toward starboard and held her ground about 200 yards from shore. Michael looked right at the wildlife refuge beaches, and spotted only a few people who had parked alongside Route 12 and made their way through the dunes to the unspoiled beaches beyond. Some were fishing with their elongated eight-foot fishing poles, some seemed to be searching for shells.

"Where we headed?" Michael asked.

"Down the beach here a bit, not far, that's my turnaround spot," Juliana said, smiling.

"Sounds great. Listen, I've got some questions and Amy said – "

Juliana interrupted her, turning with her smile gone. "Amy says a lot. Not much of it's true." The two women stared at each other for a minute, Michael making sure to keep her painted-on slight smile, which she was trained to do when conducting informal interviews so as to keep her subject at ease. Juliana turned back to the ocean in front of her.

About 20 minutes later, the boat was coming up on a stretch of beach with the world-famous black and white stripes of the Cape Hatteras lighthouse looming off in the distance.

Waves crashed on the shore to their right, and several surfers, some in wetsuits, were challenging the larger waves not too far from The Shoal Surfer. A couple were on wave runners. One in particular was driven by a tall, muscular young man who stood out with a blonde ponytail wearing a bright yellow and black stripe wetsuit. He was charging waves and doing amazing leaps and semi-flips and turns over the crashing surf.

For a moment, Michael forgot why she was on the boat and was simply in awe. "Wow! That's just amazing!" she heard herself shout.

Juliana turned and smiled. "Recognize him?"

Michael stared blankly. Juliana turned back to the ocean and said, "Thought you may have already met Toby Jones, he's law enforcement. Also the best friggin' surf rat on the island."

"That's Sergeant Jones? Huh," Michael said in disbelief.

"Aw, come on now, don't tell me you didn't notice Toby now!"

Michael just smiled. "Not my type."

The Shoal Surfer turned slightly to port and made its way along a sand bar with gulls, pipers and other waterfowl standing about, the wind ruffling their feathers, about 100 yards from shore. Michael could see exquisite beach houses peeking out from among the dunes across on the beach. Juliana let up on the throttle and pulled to an isolated spot toward the edge of the sandbar that made Michael feel like she was in the middle of the ocean. Juliana shut down the engine, and brushed past Michael, slid down the ladder, and made her way toward the rear of the boat.

As Michael looked on, Juliana, with her back to Michael, reached down and pulled her tank top up and over her head. She was not wearing anything underneath.

Michael raised her eyebrows in surprise as Juliana turned around to face her from the deck below.

"Come on down and join me."

As the woman looked up at Michael with a smile widening across her face, Michael averted her eyes.

"You wanna put that on first please?" Michael yelled down.

Juliana shook her head and put her tank top back on.

Michael made her way down the ladder and faced the captain.

"So we're clear," Michael said sternly, "I didn't come here looking for a date, I'm investigating a case. That's why Amy sent me here."

Juliana shrugged her shoulders and walked away from Michael to start moving equipment around the deck. Turning and smiling, she said, "I'm just tryin' to get an all-around tan, sister. Don't flatter yourself. And you can ask me all the questions you want, it's gonna be a colossal waste of your time."

When Amy Miller awoke, she could see only blackness. She felt cold, smelled mud and dirt, lying flat on her back somewhere. As her eyes began to focus on some light above her, she felt pain in her head. Reaching up with her right arm to feel her head, bending her left leg at the knee to bring her foot up to steady herself, a searing pain shot through her lower body. Amy bent her leg back down quickly and instinctively shoved both her hands in between her legs where the pain was. She had shoved them there too hard, accidentally pushing several broken bones in her pelvis in a manner which caused the pain to intensify. Amy felt bile rush up in her throat, saw stars, and blacked-out.

CHAPTER 11

R obbie Cartwright woke at 6:15 a.m. Saturday morning when he heard his wife grinding coffee beans downstairs. He'd gotten home late the night before after a crazy, extra-long day at the Raleigh SBI office to his loving wife of 24 years who'd welcomed her husband with a hug and kiss, no questions asked. She'd helped him get changed and he fell asleep as soon as his head hit the pillow.

Clearing the morning fuzz from his eyes, Robbie got up, washed his face and brushed his teeth, threw on some sweatpants and a t-shirt and stomped down the stairs toward the smell of fresh brewed coffee.

Halfway down he heard voices. One belonged to his wife.

Another belonged to a man.

Turning the corner at the bottom of the stairs, Robbie Cartwright walked cautiously into the eat-in section of his kitchen.

"Oh, Robbie, this officer came to see you. I was making you both some coffee," Maggie said.

At the table before him, Robbie saw Brian Laviolette,

close-cropped hair and all, his oxford shirt and slacks replaced with a golf polo and jeans.

"Sorry about the surprise, Agent Cartwright. I have a sensitive matter to discuss, ASAP," Laviolette said.

Robbie could feel blood rushing to his face. He breathed deeply, trying to relax himself.

"Let's talk in the den. Maggie, would you mind getting' me a glass of cold milk?" Robbie asked.

The two men moved through the kitchen, across the dining room, and into a den with leather chairs, a loveseat, nice wooden desk and French doors. Maggie brought in some coffee and milk, and both men politely thanked her as she left, closing the doors behind her and giving a reassuring wink to Robbie that made him smile.

Thank God for her, he happily thought.

Turning to Laviolette, Robbie's disposition was more sour. "Just what in the hell do you think you are doin' bringin' your sorry jar head ass into my G-D house unannounced?"

"Totally understandable, my apologies sir. I had to see you alone, without Corporal Peterson because I'm not really sure I can trust him."

Robbie ran his hand through his unwashed hair and sat on an ottoman across from Laviolette. "What do you mean by that? What is this James Bond roleplay, Mister Laviolette?"

"I'm doing a very high-level internal investigation on orders from up in D.C., United States Marine Corps Central Command. Corporal Peterson is from Camp Lejeune. He is a local operative attached to my investigation," Laviolette said.

"What investigation?" Robbie demanded.

"The Marine shot in Agent Francis' home, Michael Cooper, we were investigating him for dealing drugs in and out of Camp Lejeune. After 9/11 drug deals showed up a lot clearer on everyone's radar, especially drug rings on military bases. Washington takes these things a lot more seriously now. Cooper was being protected by his C.O., a Colonel Jenkins. When we got close, and Jenkins got wind that we found out he had a daughter engaged to Cooper, he discharged Cooper."

Robbie just stared silently at the Marine investigator.

"Look, the only way Jenkins could know we were that close is if somebody told him. Corporal Peterson is not beyond suspicion; his father is a very influential developer in eastern North Carolina and is well-connected to local and state government, so even though I'm not 100 percent sure he let the Colonel in on things, I can't be sure. That's why he's not here."

"Yeah, yeah, little boy blue ain't here, who gives a rat's ass?" Robbie said loudly. Calming himself, a little more softly he asked, "But why are you here? I mean, you already know most of what you need and your suspect's dead."

Laviolette sipped more of his coffee, then leaned forward in his chair. "We searched the Francis home after we got word Cooper'd been shot," he said, at which point Robbie started to glare and raise a hand to make a point. Laviolette cut him off. "Look, look, look, I know, I know. Listen. I'm here now, just listen. Agent Francis; she's in the Outer Banks, right?"

Robbie leaned back a little and straightened-upright in the ottoman. "Right," he acquiesced.

The Marine nodded at Robbie's cooperation. "Thank you. I wish you could've told me that in your office; actually, no, I'm not. Corporal Peterson would've heard, and I'm glad he didn't. Look, Agent Cartwright,"

"Robbie," his host interrupted.

The Marine nodded with appreciation.

"Robbie, look. Cooper was assigned to Senator Skip Pennington's private security detail. He has special privileges as speaker of the North Carolina Senate, he gets to pick his own men. He picked, or rather, someone in his office picked Cooper personally."

"So what?" Robbie asked.

"So they had to know of him, and if they knew of him, they must've known about his drug history," the Marine said, leaning in closer. "I'm still trying to make connections here, but I do know that the drug ring Cooper was involved with did a lot of business up and down the beaches of the Outer Banks. We think we isolated the shipping routes from central North Carolina through Raleigh out east to the beaches. We think he had a connection in his hometown, some podunk place called Bulah, on the way to the Outer Banks down Route 64. Cooper had to have some influence over local law enforcement or judges or something for his low-level pushers to work undeterred over the past couple of years; this was big stuff they were pushing, okay? Not just pot. Everything else, all the hard stuff. So I've got Cooper running this thing, working in the office of the most influential public officials in the state, who, by the way, is building a war chest to run for U.S. Senate, with roots so deep out east they stick out in China. I've got a major developer named Peterson out east with ties to people like Pennington, and when I start getting' close to Cooper Lejeune assigns Peterson's nephew to the case."

"That'd be your partner, who ain't here. I see where you're comin' from, and I appreciate it," Robbie said.

Laviolette took a breath before continuing. "Now, as far as why I'm here, well, Pennington's office says that he is on an extended weekend trip to the Outer Banks. Your girl is headed out there. The same girl whose house Cooper was shooting-up just yesterday."

"So this is some big drug ring conspiracy handled out of the speaker's office in Raleigh? If it's that big a deal, why don't you call in for more help?"

"I know, I know. If I call in more help that's gonna alert the wrong people with connections. What I'm trying to do now is –"

"Don't worry about all that B.S.," Robbie said

forcefully. "My girl is out there in no-man's-land, and she could be heading for a bunch of trouble neither of us saw comin', that's all I care about. Now, Mister Laviolette, I need you to wait here while I shower, then we need to get back to my office to check some things."

"I have to meet Corporal Peterson at ten o'clock," Laviolette said.

"I'll get you where you need to go soon enough," Robbie shot back.

Opening the French doors, Robbie turned to Laviolette and held out his hand. The Marine took it and the two men engaged in a firm, healthy handshake.

"I'm glad you came, Mister Laviolette. You did the right thing. Not too many people care to do that nowadays."

"I just wish I could've nailed Cooper before he messed with the Francis family," Laviolette said.

As the two men walked out of the office, Laviolette asked Robbie, "Just what do you think we'll be able to find out this morning?"

Robbie snickered. "I do not know. But hell, even a blind hog sometimes finds an acorn."

◆ ◆ ◆

The two women had drawn-up white plastic lawn chairs across from one another on the deck of The Shoal Surfer, Juliana sitting facing the wind, and Michael with her back to it.

Juliana crossed her legs tightly in front of her and crossed her arms across her chest. She just stared at Michael with a slight smile, her eyes hidden behind her sunglasses.

"Okay, then, I guess we didn't get off on the best of footing here," Michael said somewhat lightly as she reached into her canvas backpack at her feet, withdrawing her notepad, pen, and identification wallet. She flipped it open and showed it to Juliana. "Like I said, my name is Michael Francis, and I am an agent with the North Carolina State Bureau of Investigation. I am here investigating the recent death of a girl named Kathy Kirkland."

"Pretty formal. So you're not just some hot piece of ass new to the island that Amy sent my way?" Juliana replied cattily, her smile widening with exaggerated head movements as she delivered her remarks.

Michael just stared at her from behind her mirrored aviators.

"Sorry. Amy and I go way back," Juliana blurted out laughing, uncoiling her legs and standing. She moved behind her chair and fiddled with the fishing poles, her back to Michael.

"I wouldn't worry too much about that," Michael replied. "I guess I should be flattered. Let's move on."

Juliana turned her head, raising an eyebrow above her sunglasses. "Flattered?" she said coyishly.

"Let's move on," Michael repeated.

"Pity. You seem like you'd be right up my alley."

Michael looked down, unsmiling, and leafed for an open page in her notebook. "You said you and Amy Miller go way back. How far back?"

"I grew up out here. My family were long-time islanders, from Kinnakeet, now they call it Avon. Real Bankers, that's what they called the old Outer Banks families. My father was a fisherman, my grandfather was a fisherman. When my dad died 12 years ago, I took over his boat and changed it into a sport-fishing rental and sightseeing operation. Amy was a marketing rep on Manteo then, working for The Lost Colony historical play they do every summer, doing some freelance work. I got her name from a friend, and hooked-up with her."

"Hooked-up with her?" Michael asked.

Juliana just smiled. "Amy's really smart. She helped me get this thing up and running, took me on as a freelance marketing client. Went even so far as to coming out on tours with me, schmoozing with my passengers. She met a lot more people that way, people who were here visiting their friends and relatives in the business community. Soon word of mouth spread and Amy had me booked solid nine months out of the year."

"This was 12 years ago?"

"Nah," Julia laughed, standing again and walking with her arms crossed slowly around the deck, regarding the light reflecting off the glassy calm waters. "It took time to even think this was gonna work. I was still bartending at The Purple Turtle."

"That's where Amy and I ate dinner last night," Michael interrupted.

"Oh yeah, sushi night. Nice! So you know that place is the bomb, right? Always busy, made some good cash. It really held me together during tough times."

"So, you had tough times financially, then? Did Amy help you out with money as well?"

"Yeah, we moved in together," Juliana recalled, staring wistfully out across the water. "We knew right off that we were both gonna get together. Err, well, she moreso than me. Does that bother you, my talking about this?" she asked, looking down at Michael with a flirtatious smile.

"Don't worry about me."

"Oh yeah?" Juliana teased.

"I need information from you now, not head games. Kathy Kirkland is dead. I intend to find out what happened."

Juliana nodded.

"So you and Amy were an item. What happened to the relationship?"

"Well, you know how it is with lesbians. On the first date, we show up with a moving van. After that, it's only a matter of time before the whole thing fell apart. Well, Amy and I didn't really fall apart, it's just that she didn't like the fact that I was bi, got a little jealous, actually a lot jealous.

We'd go up to Anton's in Currituck, it's a dance club. From time to time I'd spot a straight guy there with some lesbian friends, and, well..."

"Okay, that's fine," Michael said. "Let's fast-forward a bit. I'm assuming Amy got her job at the Chamber through contacts?"

Juliana nodded. "Yeah, she's pretty well-connected all across the eastern part of North Carolina. Not in any powerful way, mind you. She still has to pay speeding tickets, but she can get a free meal anywhere."

"So in her capacity as Chamber Director and general schmooze-hound-in-residence, Amy would have had ample opportunity to meet Kathy professionally, as the girl was a lobbyist," Michael stated as fact rather than question.

"Met her at Anton's actually. The only spot really for any fun around here if you like dancing. She was here the summer before, and I ran into her at Anton's but she was super-straight, colder than even you about it, minus the bullying," Juliana said with a slight smile.

"So she was straight and hung out at the club. Now, what bachelors on the make do you have in Nags Head?"

"Can't say. They come and go with the summer crowd. The locals are pretty slim pickings, you know?"

Michael wanted badly to hit Juliana with the Bruce Pennington information Amy had given her. She tried to bait Juliana into offering it up, but clearly there was something holding her back. She obviously had opportunity to get to know this man who ran the bar she worked in, she had intimate knowledge of the social scene in and around Nags Head, and she even knew the murder victim.

Although Michael felt uncomfortable with it for some reason, she had to consider Juliana a suspect, if not in the murder of Kathy Kirkland than complicit in the act of covering it up.

"Thanks for the info," Michael said, breaking into a wide smile. Juliana, relieved, returned an equally large smile.

"I don't suppose you'd head back early just for me?" Michael asked playfully.

Juliana studied her passenger. "Guess I could." She looked at her watch, then out to the overcast sky. "I can have you back at Oregon Inlet by 9:30. Maybe my next group'll come early, if they don't cancel with this weather. Something's coming, that's for sure."

◆ ◆ ◆

"Margie! You are looking fine, young lady, just fine!" Skip Pennington greeted his long-time friend and employee rather loudly in front of an early-bird dinner crowd at Pennington's, his family's namesake restaurant. Showmanship was one of the Senator's trademarks, and his constituents were standing and applauding his antics like they were welcoming home a conquering hero.

"Senator, it sure does my eyes good seein' you again," one elderly gentleman said, grasping the Senator's outstretched hand with both of his in an eager embrace.

"Well now, that's just a fine, fine greeting sir. You get back to your banana puddin' there before I get to it first!" the Senator joked, receiving an overwhelming wave of laughter from his captive audience.

Taylor was standing in the doorway to the dining area with Elizabeth, the day manager and second cousin of Skip Pennington. "He's occupied for a good half-hour, 45 minutes, I'm gonna step out to run some errands before I get him over to the Chief. I'll be back to get him. If he asks where I am, just tell him I ran out."

"I'll slide a plate of blueberry cobbler in front of his nose and keep fillin' his coffee cup. He'll be fine," Elizabeth reassured him with a smile. Taylor smiled back and gently patted her on her back and slipped out the front door.

Walking over to his Lincoln Town Car, Taylor looked

back to check if anyone was looking out the front of the restaurant then slipped in behind the wheel. He took his cell phone out of his jacket pocket and hit his speed dial. When the voicemail on the other end of the line picked-up, Taylor said, "I don't have a lot of time. You need to get with our friend and take care of the house. Burn it. Buy something, spread it around, and burn it, as soon as you can. Be discreet, but get it done in the next 48 hours."

CHAPTER 12

Chief Anderson craned his next and yelled from his office, "Jones! Did you get Agent Francis on the phone yet?" Sergeant Jones came bounding in, wearing his uniform shorts and buttoning his shirt. "Jesus Mary and Blessed Joseph. Can't you dress BEFORE you leave the house?" Anderson snapped.

"Sorry, sir, I was catchin' some waves this morning, big swell coming up you know. Uh, I called the hotel she's at, they said she left at the butt-crack of dawn, no idea where she went. I left word that when she checks back in, she's to call here immediately."

"That's not good enough. She needs to be back here precisely at noon. We've got company coming, and she needs to be here to explain herself."

"Sir?"

"Never mind. Listen, get your ass in your Jeep and go to the crime scene. She's bound to show up there sometime today. Wait there for her, and then bring her here."

"Crime scene?" Toby replied. He knew damn well which crime scene Anderson was referring to, but just wanted to push some more buttons. Anderson just looked up from his papers, glared, and motioned his head toward the door. The Sergeant smiled and left.

"Prick," Anderson muttered.

At 9:25, The Shoal Surfer cruised back into the marina at Oregon Inlet and steered toward the dock, gliding in effortlessly next to some pilings. Michael looked up top of the wheelhouse and saw Juliana shut off the engine and pause to check her messages on her cell. She decided to jump off the deck and grab a rope from the aft deck and tie the top to one of the pilings on the pier. After a few minutes she walked to the front of the boat, grabbed another rope, and slipped it over another piling while Juliana finally made it down the ladder.

"Hey, you're good! I should bring you along more often." she said, tossing Michael's backpack to her.

Catching it one-handed, Michael said, "Maybe. Listen, I may have to contact you more about this. Got a business card?"

Juliana went into the cabin for a moment, then returned with a business card with her work number on the front and a hastily scribbled home number on the back. She handed it to Michael, but did not immediately let go of it once Michael grabbed it.

"I'm sorry about that Kirkland girl. I wanna do what I can to help," Juliana said.

Michael smiled as the athletic tour boat captain released her grip, then said, "Thanks. I'm sure I'll need all the help I can get."

"You know, if you need to just talk, look me up."

Michael's smile dissipated. "Thanks. I'll get back to you."

♦♦♦

Michael drove back across the northern end of Pea Island, passing a long line of traffic headed the other way. Tourists were all over the beaches this weekend, and why not, Michael thought. Despite the lack of beaming blue skies, there was pleasantly warm but not overwhelming weather, thanks to a constant breeze that was whipping up some serious waves for boogie boarding.

Without trying, she started to have flashes of the past day and a half burst before her eyes. Saying goodbye to her daughters in the morning Friday. The fatal accident on the way to the Outer Banks.

Tears started to form in the corner of her eyes. Her heart began to pound. Her eye began to twitch.

The accident. Someone was trying to run her off the road. Was he looking for her in particular? Was he just an aggressive driver? Whatever the case, a man was dead.

She felt her eye twitch stop. She shook her head and composed herself, stopping along the highway at a pull-off. Michael got out of the car and walked back to the trunk, opened it, and took the shotgun out of its rack. Checking to make sure no traffic was coming and nobody was watching, she climbed over the nearby dunes to a deserted beach.

Kicking off her shoes, Michael walked into the water, gun hanging down at her side. She stood there, breathing deep, watching the breakers about 20 yards out.

She looked down at the gun. It was like she wasn't holding it. Somebody else was. Michael told herself to lift it up, move it in front of her, but her arm hung limp, motionless.

She knew what she wanted to do. Why she had grabbed the shotgun at the SBI in the first place.

To end the fear, get rid of the pain.

Stop thinking about all the tragedy. About her life.

About her father.

About June fifth.

About Kathy Kirkland.

Looking back out at the sea, Michael began to cry.

Kathy Kirkland. She said the name again in her head.

Kathy Kirkland. Jesus, Michael thought, what that girl must have gone through.

Michael wondered if it was anything like her own experience.

Poor girl. She didn't even get a chance for a husband and family like I did. Or love, for that matter. She was just caught up in someone else's nightmare. She could've used some help.

She looked down at the shotgun again.

At her hand near the stock, finger outside of the trigger guide.

She turned the shotgun over, staring at her finger.

The sounds around her seemed to fade away.

So close to the trigger.

A glint of sunshine hit her watch, forcing her to squint.

Sound rushed back in. Michael looked at the time.

Jesus, I've been here 45 minutes.

As if waking from a dream, Michael hustled back to her car, stored the shotgun back in the trunk and sped past mile after mile of sawgrass down Route 12 to Beach Road, eventually stopping-in at her motel. She used the bathroom, wrote down some thoughts into her notebook, transcribed some other notes onto her computer, and did a little research for about an hour and a half. She left her room, and drove down past the street with the Public Safety Building, down to 3042 Beach Road, a two-story gray beach house on the right with vertical siding. There wasn't any police tape, nothing to indicate it was a crime scene.

As she pulled into the sand and gravel driveway out front, Michael double-checked the address. It was the right house.

I hope they secured the scene, she said to herself.

She stepped out of the car and stood, door ajar, looking

at the house, and to the side out toward the sea. She could smell the salt air coming in on a steady wind. She could hear the waves crashing from somewhere out back.

Just like earlier in the morning when she had considered doing the unthinkable.

Michael closed her eyes and took a deep breath.

"She deserved better. We both did," she mumbled out loud, opening her eyes and reaching into her shorts pockets for some white rubber gloves before heading into 3042 Beach Road.

♦ ♦ ♦

Robbie Cartwright sat at his desk leaning in toward his computer screen, peering at the date contained in the files he was opening one after another. He enjoyed unfettered access to data on nearly anyone and everyone in North Carolina and beyond. The trick was finding exactly what he was looking for.

This Saturday morning Robbie was running dual searches for Michael Cooper and Kathy Kirkland. As Robbie searched through network drives, Brian Laviolette looked through personnel files on Agent Michael Francis, the same files Robbie had refused to share upon the Marine's initial visit just a day earlier.

"Her husband was in Iraq?" Laviolette asked from his reclined position on Robbie's short-back leather guest chair. Robbie just nodded his head and kept moving his mouse, opening and closing files. "She wasn't military, though. Where'd they meet?" Laviolette asked.

Robbie muttered, "If I recall correctly, they both met upstate New York, when she was in college, well before the war."

"Interesting," Laviolette said "She got kick-ass scores at the Police Academy. I'm guessing she can take care of herself, then."

"Yup, probably learned it from her daddy, he was a

cop," Robbie said.

Laviolette looked up from his paperwork at Robbie and furrowed his brow. "Isn't it practice to send agents in sets of two? You didn't have anyone else available?"

Robbie turned in his chair and faced the Marine. His vision jumped to the man's left hand holding open Michael's file. He had a wedding ring on.

"How long you married?"

"Two years now."

"You love your wife?"

The Marine sat upright in his chair and answered sharply, "Of course."

"You'd do anything to protect her, wouldn't you? I feel the same way about my wife. I feel the same way about my kids. You got any kids yet?"

Laviolette shook his head no.

"I've got two, both grown-up now. Two girls. Michael Francis there. She reminds me of my youngest. I'd do anything to protect her."

Robbie got up and walked around his desk, sitting on the edge across from Laviolette. "This is strictly on the QT. I got a request from a judge who's got a niece named Amy Miller out in Nags Head to send agents to investigate a murder. The Judge got my name from another SBI office that was scared shitless to take this case. Claimed they was too busy."

"That's a load of bull," Laviolette chimed in with a slight smile. Robbie reciprocated with one of his own.

"Yeah, I checked up on it. Fella who runs the office out east gave me that same line when I called him, his agents and all that. I called the local police out there in Nags Head, a Chief Anderson. Got the cold shoulder. I start puttin' everything together, figuring folks likely don't want to make a big deal out of this murder case at the tail end of a weak tourist season. I figure if the folks out there see an army of agents descending like flies on the Outer Banks and scarin' off what visitors are left, everybody'd catch hell, especially my office."

Laviolette shook his head in disgust.

Robbie looked down at the floor. "Yeah, I hear ya', I made the wrong call," he said, then, looking back up at Laviolette he continued "But in a way I made the right call. I sent someone fresh, unattached to the old boy network here in Carolina who I can trust to give me the real skinny. Francis is the only one I got on staff not from here, believe it or not. So I send her along, figuring she'd actually do an investigation, the best she could on her own, and come back here to me with all the real facts, not some cover-up malarkey, so we could actually fix this in the off-season."

"I think you sent a pit bull into a locker full of poison meat," Laviolette responded, shaking Michael's personnel file in the air.

"Yeah, she's not gonna pussy foot around, that's for sure. With all the nasty types involved, you think I compromised my agent?"

Laviolette exhaled in exasperation. "You got an agent out there on her own, under somewhat false pretenses, knowing one tenth of the story."

Robbie stood up again. "When I talked with her on the phone yesterday, I told her about the shooting. She still wouldn't come home, and I don't know what the connection is with your case."

"Well, one way to get her home is to help her figure things out. We're looking for a connection; well, one connection is the Statehouse. That's where Cooper was working on security detail and that's where Taylor is at," Laviolette said, pausing. "And that's what scares me."

Michael had trouble handling the small key for the front door through her disposable rubber gloves. The gloves were made of a material good for running fingers over railings in search of blood and so forth, but with the key the glove was more cumbersome; every time Michael tried to move a finger to adjust her grip, it stuck on the side of the key and she found herself fumbling around with it, finally dropping it onto the woven welcome mat at her feet.

As she bent down to pick it up, a strong gust of wind came across from her right, blowing some sand into her face. Still hunched over, Michael started laughing, eyes closed, spitting sand out of her mouth.

She had the distinct impression that the Outer Banks were out to foil her day.

Michael shook off the feeling and stood up with the key in an exaggerated fashion in front of the lock. Slowly, she moved the key forward and into the lock.

After wiggling it around for a while, Michael turned the knob and opened the door of the beach house. Stepping inside and shutting the door behind her, Michael was taken by the stale smell of the house. It was dank and stagnant, as if no air conditioning had been circulating for quite some time nor had a window been opened to let in fresh air. She walked over to the wall across from her and checked the thermostat; it was set at 74, and it read exactly that. A newer home, it must have been built pretty much air tight to avoid leaks.

Michael flicked on the lights and walked up the stairs onto the main floor with the extended living space. Some police tape was laid on the furniture, an amateurish attempt at keeping people off of it. Michael reached into her pocket, retrieving a small notepad and checked where she had read in the police report the body had been found. She read her notes that the girl's body had been propped-up in a seated position by the fireplace.

Walking around to the left, Michael saw dried blood stains on the floor. A large puddle was evident, and some stains on the front of the fireplace. Michael rubbed her gloved index finger around the edges of the dried blood circle on the floor.

Michael stood up and walked around the living room, looking on the floor, furniture, and walls before heading downstairs, stopping at the landing to stuff the notepad back into her pocket.

That's when she heard a creak.

Michael cocked her head to the left, listening intently for more noise. There were two stories of living space in the house – the first floor where she now stood by the front door, which had several bedrooms and a bath, and the upstairs with the living room, kitchen, some bedrooms and an outer deck. The squeaking was too close to have been the deck; it must have come from inside.

Although it seemed like several minutes were passing as she analyzed the noise she had heard, Michael had only spent about ten seconds running through her options. If someone was in the house, chances are they weren't supposed to be.

Michael thought about running out to the car for the shotgun.

Another creak.

Too late.

Michael crouched slightly and moved quietly across the landing toward the two bedrooms at the back of the first floor. Slowly, she moved to the right door, which was open all the way. She poked her head in quickly and scanned the small room: a bed, a dresser, a nightstand and no closet. Unless someone was hiding under the bed or on the other side of the bed on the floor, it was clean. Michael walked in slightly, jerking her head behind her to keep an eye and ear on the landing. She scooted quickly to the other side and saw nothing, then moved back to the door, peeking outside. Hearing nothing, Michael knelt down and with her left hand quickly drew-up the dust ruffle of the bed to look underneath, seeing nothing.

As she stood back up, Michael heard quick footsteps above her head, and a sliding sound. She bolted into the hallway and raced up the stairs.

When she got to the second-floor landing, Michael burst out into the main living area, making a beeline for an open sliding glass door across from her. Wind was blowing the white curtain into the house as she stepped quickly through it. As she did, she heard someone running down stairs to her right.

She raced across the deck wrapping around the right side of the house, running over to outdoor stairs at the far end and swinging her head over the side to look down. The stairs zig-zagged back and forth across landings halfway down the second floor and first floor to the ground. She thought she could make-out a figure underneath the boards down almost to the ground level.

"Freeze!" Michael shouted as she took the steps two at a time. At the first landing, out of the corner of her eye she saw a blur racing underneath the other way, back under the deck away from the beach house, toward the dunes.

Michael turned and raced down a flight of stairs to the next landing, at a gallop. She misjudged her final set of steps and went sprawling down the last few feet, landing hard on her left side with a sickening thud. Rolling as she had been trained to do, Michael popped up onto her feet and began running back under the deck toward the dunes, bolts of pain shooting up her side. Looking up ahead of her, Michael saw sand flying as a blur of a figure went down across the other side of the dunes.

"Freeze!" Michael yelled again in vain, lurching through sawgrass and out onto sand, up an incline about ten feet to a dune which shot up another ten feet. Really slogging through the sand, she breathed heavily as her legs, unaccustomed to running in the sand, shot out from side to side as she stumbled up the small hill. Falling once, twice, Michael began swinging her arms to forge ahead, flailing as she made the last couple of feet to the top of the dune.

At the top, Michael dropped to her knees. She scanned the beach in front of her, left to right, searching frantically for anybody who was running. All she saw was assorted groups of families and groups of friends, with some couples strolling quietly along the water's edge.

Nobody running by themselves. Nobody suspicious.

Michael kept looking for some time, chest heaving to catch her breath. Michael turned and looked back toward the beach house, scanning the empty grass fields behind her.

"Damn," she muttered as her attention turned back to the beach, hearing laughter and chatter from happy vacationers above the steady wind. Michael leaned back on her haunches and rested, feeling angry and frustrated despite the tranquil scene before her.

Her hip began to throb and burn.

"Damn," she repeated.

CHAPTER 13

Pain shot up Amy Miller's hips as she opened her eyes to the damp darkness surrounding her. A brief moment of lucidity told her that she needed to keep completely still unless she wanted the pain to get worse. As she figured it, she probably had moved her hips in her sleep which had awakened her.

Her mind began to recant what had happened; last she knew, she had opened her eyes in the same location moments earlier, but searing pain down below had made her black out.

Think. You need to stay still if you want to stay awake.

She moved her right hand down and tried to feel around her shorts pocket, then remembered she'd given her cell phone to Agent Francis. Her heart pounded and she began to cry.

The pain was still throbbing, and she was aching to move a little to try and adjust her body to lessen the hurt. She rationalized with herself that it would do more bad than good, so Amy tried to think about something other than the pain between her legs and see if any other parts of her body were hurt.

Keeping her eyes closed, Amy wiggled her toes, which made her thighs hurt somewhat, but not too bad. She moved her feet from side to side, turning her ankles; that felt okay, too. Amy took a moment to lay still and breathe deeply, gradually waking herself up and clearing her head while she imagined herself reclining at the beach.

After a few minutes, Amy wiggled her fingers. She moved her wrists. She bent her elbows up so her forearms were at 90-degree angles to the ground; this hurt a little, as her back muscles pulled a bit and she felt it in her lower body. Amy waited a moment, then, keeping her upper arms on the ground, brought her hands up to her cheeks and felt her face.

She felt something sticky on her fingers.

Dried blood?

Amy smeared her right index finger into whatever it was on her cheek, then brought it up to her nose; yep, smelled like blood. Her head began to swim for a minute, and then Amy noticed that her head was starting to throb.

All right girl, she told herself. *Get a grip. Calm down.* She breathed slowly, smoothly, bringing her arms back down to her sides.

Then Amy opened her eyes.

It took a few seconds to adjust to the darkened room. Darting her eyes from side to side without moving her head, Amy tried to locate some light, some slivers of anything but darkness. Just black, everything a thick, cool, damp black.

Cool. Damp. *I must be below ground*, she thought.

Amy squinted her eyes and tried hard to see above her, to try and make out some type of ceiling, to get a frame of reference. She couldn't make out anything, and brought her right arm up off the ground to reach out and see if she could touch anything. She took it slow, first bringing the forearm off the ground. Then, she tried lifting her upper arm off the ground.

Pain shot up her side. Her arm fell flat onto the floor

and she cried out a little in pain.

After her arm had hit, Amy realized it felt like cold concrete. Basement, she thought.

But whose basement?

Amy stopped thinking and just listened. Empty silence. As her eyes focused on nothing above her but the darkness and her senses stretched out into her surroundings, Amy suddenly began to feel uneasy.

Calm down, she told herself.

But the fear kept coming. Something was wrong; something was coming, something was after her, Amy could feel it. But what? She listened more intently, but there were no sounds. She felt someone watching her. But where? Who was out there? The dark in the room felt as if it were closing in around her, pressing in on her from all sides. She felt as if she would suffocate and started to hyperventilate.

Instinctively, Amy tried to squirm away and scream. As she did, searing pain shot up from between her legs to her head, and the blackness began to swirl.

She tasted bile, then passed out.

The stiff breeze kept blowing directly into Michael's face as she knelt at the top of the dune looking out at the ocean not 50 yards away. A group of people were pointing out at some waves breaking far from shore, and some others ran over with surfboards and began to make their way out under a now overcast sky. Her mouth felt dry. Her throat felt tight.

"Dammit, don't you cry," she said out loud to herself.

Michael cleared her throat, blinked her eyes in rapid succession, and stood up. She regarded the beach one more time in each direction, then turned and headed back toward the house.

As she walked, Michael felt a pull in her side by her hip,

and her shoulder on that side hurt a little as well. She took a look at her sand-caked shorts and shirt, dusting them off as she walked.

"Agent Francis!" Sergeant Jones called to her from the deck of the beach house some 20 feet in front of her. "What the hell you doing?" Toby asked excitedly.

"You're a little late, thanks for nothing," Michael yelled up.

"Late for what?"

"There was someone here in the house, they ran off. I yelled for them to stop, but they scampered over the dunes."

"Who was it? Did you get a good look?"

"No, they were just out of sight. Look, don't worry about it; probably a teenager or something. But you gotta do a better job of securing this place, dude. I didn't see any forced entry anywhere, but the door was open."

"No kidding?! Man, what the hell?!"

"Sergeant, why are you here?"

Toby stared blankly at Michael. "Uh, well, I've come to collect you, actually. Chief's got some people coming in from Raleigh thought you wanted to talk to."

Michael stopped at the bottom of the stairs and put her hands on her hips. "Right now?" she yelled up.

The Sergeant made his way down to where she was, giving her a once-over. "You don't wanna clean up or anything first, do ya?"

Michael turned away and stared back toward the dunes again.

"So who are these people your boss wants me to meet? And how did he know I'd be here investigating a crime scene?"

No reply.

Michael turned back to see the deputy peering at the sky overhead.

"Weather's turning. You know there's a tropical storm brewing, right? News reports say it might become a Cat 1 hurricane by the time it gets here, won't be long now."

"You're kidding, right? A hurricane?" Michael asked incredulously.

Jones nodded. "Probably some tasty waves, too."

All Michael could do was shake her head. "Well, alrighty then. Murder investigation, suspect runs away from a crime scene, a hurricane coming and you're thinking about tasty waves. You know, I actually saw you out just past the inlet this morning on your wave runner," Michael pointed out.

"Been surfing out here since I was, oh, ten I guess. Got my own wave runner now, take it everywhere with me, hook it up to the Jeep on a trailer. It's sitting in the back lot at the office right now. Really good waves down toward Hatteras, but these usually aren't that good. Looks like six, seven-foot waves at this time of day. Stuff pops up here all the time. Better call my buds when I get off work, catch a ride or two before it gets bad. Wait – you said you saw me out this morning, didn't you? What, you go fishing or something?"

"I was in a boat down at Oregon Inlet, took a quick trip."

"Who took you out there? You don't have a boat of your own, do you?" Toby asked, smiling as he cozied-up to a bar stool at the eat-in kitchen not six feet from the dried blood spots on the living room floor.

"Nah, I took a charter, The Shoal Surfer."

Toby's wide smile sharpened into a sly grin. "Ooooh, Jules' boat, huh?" he said with some sarcasm. "You, uh, chose her yourself, or was she the only one out there?"

Michael furrowed her brow. "Actually, Sergeant, I wanted to talk to her about the case. She was someone Amy Miller had mentioned."

Toby shook his head, laughing silently. "Oh yeah, Amy and Jules, they go way back. Waaaaay back."

"Jules? You know her pretty well, then?"

"Yeah, everybody here knows everybody," Toby said.

"And everybody knows everybody's business, if you know what I mean."

"She one of the good guys?"

"She runs with a wild crowd, has a bit of a racy history, nobody really knows her too well. She's harmless, though. You should pump her for info; she has her pulse on everything going on around here. Listen, I better get you to the office. I'll bring you back here later to check things out. And don't worry, I'll have this place tight as a drum," Toby said.

"That'd be an improvement," Michael chided.

Senator Pennington led his small entourage down the back hallway of the Dare County Public Safety Building to the inner office, a suite centering three glass-walled offices. Chief Anderson stood in the doorway of his office, hands folded across his chest, watching a television set across the room. An anxious looking meteorologist was in front of a blue screen with superimposed satellite images of the Carolina coast reloading over and over, showing white patches of heavy weather approaching from out to sea.

Nodding toward his visitors, Chief Anderson said disapprovingly, "Can you believe this? Out of nowhere. Mmmm-hmmm."

"What is this?" Pennington asked incredulously. "Bartholemew, what is this?" he repeated to his legislative aide, who shook his head and held out both hands palm-up.

"You didn't hear?" Anderson asked.

"Hear what?"

"Tropical storm, they thought it was headed out to sea in the Caribbean, wasn't too strong. Decided to turn on a dime northwest, headed our way. Freak thing, really. They say if it mixes with a front from the west it's gonna be fierce. Looks like we've got a hurricane evacuation on our hands."

Both of Anderson's visitors stared in disbelief. "Chief," Pennington said with a smile. "You must be mistaken. I don't have time for any storms this weekend. I'm a very busy man."

"I've already begun my calls," Anderson deadpanned, pointing at the television. "It'll be announced soon. Soon as Pete's done with his weather update there, he's coming over here for a statement. I've called in everybody on the force; it'll hit the airways at the top of the hour at six."

"What's at six?" Sergeant Jones asked from the hallway. He entered just ahead of Michael Francis. "Hello Senator. Toby Jones, we've met before," he said, shaking the senator's hand. "This is Agent Michael Francis, from the State Bureau of Investigation, Raleigh office."

"SBI?" Pennington replied, impressed, as he shook Michael's hand. "You here on any important business the state senate should be aware of, Agent?"

"Not at this time," Michael replied straight-faced. Pennington's smile dropped a notch.

"Bart Taylor, legislative aide to the senator," the smarmy staffer introduced himself, shaking Michael's hand.

"Wow," Toby said from in front of the TV. He had just gotten the gist of the news. Turning to Michael, he said, "Agent, you better – "

"Jones," Anderson interrupted, "why don't you go get the front room set-up for a quickie press conference? TV station's on its way in short time. Agent Francis, Senator, Mr. Taylor, why don't we go sit in my office and talk about all this."

Toby glared at the Chief, then looked at Michael. She half-nodded; Toby reciprocated and went out to the front.

When everyone was seated in Chief Anderson's office he began with, "Now, this isn't a hurricane, not yet, anyways. But I am still moving forward with a voluntary evacuation."

"Is that wise?" Taylor interrupted.

The senator laughed and held up the back of his hand to his aide, who sat perched on the arm of a leather chair behind his boss. "Bartholemew, please, the Chief is running on protocol here. He has a job to do. Now, Chief, I am certainly not gonna sit here and tell you what to do. In fact, I wanna get the hell out of here, secure my relatives and get my ass inland. But I have some things to do, some meetings to get through with tomorrow, and an event I think you're aware of."

The Chief nodded. "Yessir, we'll get to that. I'm just tellin' you what I'm gonna say on the TV," he said, slightly irritated, with half a glare.

The senator's smile widened. He looked over toward Michael. "Agent Francis, right?"

She nodded.

"The Chief here is afraid I am going to tell him to hold-off on announcing a disaster preparedness plan. He's afraid I want him to tell everyone to remain calm, at least until after 11 tomorrow morning." The Senator paused and looked at Anderson. "But I'm not going to do that. Chief, you know I'm not going to do that."

"Well then, my curiosity is piqued. What are you going to ask me to do?" Anderson snapped back, leaning back in his chair.

Taylor interjected, "The Senator has been working over a year and a half on a proposal to bring millions into the local economy here long-term. I don't expect anybody here to understand the true weight of this matter, but we are depending very heavily on news coverage of a groundbreaking up on the beach in Duck tomorrow. Call it ammunition for future legislation."

The Chief sat bolt upright. "Look, boy, come Tuesday there might not be anything left of the beach up in Duck."

"Well I really don't give a damn if there's beach left or not," the Senator howled, standing and turning away from everyone. After a tense pause, he ran a hand through his hair and began pacing around the office. "After tomorrow morning, the beach could slide back into the ocean for all I care. It's the image that counts. The powerful image of progress."

The Senator stopped talking when he saw Michael sitting demurely in her leather chair, legs crossed casually, hands on her lap, leaning back and smiling innocently. "What's your take on all this, Agent?"

Michael's expression turned serious as she looked around the room. "I'm afraid I have to side with those looking for a delay. For those not in the know, I'm investigating a murder of a young woman who was on the good senator's staff. My investigation is about to be made all the more complicated with this oncoming hurricane."

Chief Anderson started to interrupt her with, "It's not a hurricane yet."

"I don't care what you call it, to tell you the truth. All I know is that if you call for an evacuation of Dare County and the surrounding areas before I have the chance to interview my subjects, I'm screwed."

The three men regarded her with raised eyebrows.

"I need two days," she stumbled defensively.

"Two days for what? To get clobbered by Mother Nature? Forget it! I'm supposed to wait until the National Guard is here and the freaking storm is in my streets before I call for people to get to safety? That's nuts!" Chief Anderson yelled at Michael.

She raised her hands for the Chief to calm down. "Look, look, that's not what I'm saying. I'm just asking you to tell people to get ready to evacuate, but don't give the green light to go until Sunday afternoon. I can interview my people tonight and tomorrow morning, then work on the physical evidence Monday."

Before the Chief could issue an objection, Pennington chimed in. "Chief, listen, you've got some competing interests here. This storm is coming, there's no doubt. Now, you can tell everyone to get out tomorrow, clog the roads, send everyone into a frenzy, or you can tell people to remain calm and tune in tomorrow afternoon for an update. That'll help us all out and nobody gets hurt."

The Chief started to say something, but the senator interrupted. "Nobody. Gets. Hurt. That girl was on my staff."

He stared wide-eyed at Anderson. The Chief laughed, "You're all nuts."

"Chief," Michael said, getting up from her chair and walking over to his desk. "We can help each other here. I'm still investigating this case, just hold on. I'm heading up to Duck to chase a lead."

"You're not even supposed to be here!" Anderson blurted, walking out from behind his desk.

"Chief! Chief, let me talk to you a second," Taylor called nervously after Anderson as the Chief stormed out of his office, walking forcefully toward the hallway as he rubbed the back of his neck. The aide caught up with him and placed a reassuring hand on his left shoulder. The two men started to talk in hushed tones.

Michael cocked her head.

Not supposed to be here? What did he mean by that?

Senator Pennington leaned in close, whispering in Michael's ear, "You're witnessing something you probably don't want to. The good ol' boy network. This is how it's done down here. Watch."

Michael got a sick feeling in her stomach. Soon, the two men turned and walked back into the office. Chief Anderson looked up, and with some resignation in his voice, said to Pennington and Michael, "I'm going with the 'be-prepared-don't-panic' speech tonight at six. I'll tell everyone to stand by, don't pack just yet, tune in Sunday afternoon. I'm still moving forward with mobilization, though, but I'm not calling a full evacuation."

Pennington smiled and extended his hand. The three men started talking amongst themselves, but Michael felt miles away as the reality of what she had just put together hit her: she had two days to solve a murder before all the suspects could scatter to the ends of the earth. They'd know someone was poking around soon enough; she'd lose her element of surprise. She had to hit them up soon.

Before the storm hit.

◆◆◆

"Yeah Harry, this is Robbie," the rotund and sweaty leader of the Raleigh SBI office said from a bench out in front of the North Carolina statehouse in downtown Raleigh. He wiped his brow with a handkerchief. Sweat stains showed on his white button-down short-sleeved shirt. Since it was a Saturday, the eternal professional was going tie-less.

"Listen, I got past security and into the public safety office. That's where they keep the lists and bios of all the security folks. Lots of locked file cabinets, I can tell you that," Robbie said.

"Did you find anything?" Harry McCairn asked on the other end of the line.

"Not much. There was a board in the main area with initials of people assigned to various legislators. Our guy's initials weren't there."

"Who'd they have listed for Pennington?" Harry asked excitedly.

"Didn't have anyone listed. Pennington's name wasn't on the board."

"If his name's not on the board, then the head of the Capitol Police doesn't assign security to the man, does he?"

Back on the park bench, Robbie smiled and sat upright. "No, he does not."

"Then who would?" Harry asked.

"I believe that'd have to be the Senator himself. I have to head back to the office, can you pick me up in about an hour? I could use your help."

♦ ♦ ♦

Heading out of the Dare County Public Safety Building, Michael caught sight of Senator Pennington getting into his Lincoln Town Car with his legislative aide. "Senator!" she called after him, half-running down the steps to catch him before he left.

"What can I do for you, Agent Francis?" Skip Pennington shouted out over the top of the car, flashing his deadly politician's smile.

"Thanks. I just wanted to know if you could please let me know where you'll be over the next couple of days."

The senator stood silently smiling at her, whispy hair blown by a strong wind.

"In case I need to reach you for background information on some of the goings-on out here in the Outer Banks."

"Now Agent Francis, there's plenty of fine folks 'round here who can help you with that. You sure that's why you want to talk to me?" the senator said, slipping into the passenger seat of the car and closing the door. Michael moved over to his door and watched as the power window opened.

"Actually, sir you could help me out with one thing. Do you own any rental property around here?"

Pennington's smile faded just a touch. "Me, no, Agent, I do not. My son, well, he owns a few places aside from his eating establishment up and down the beach. I'm going to assume you have some place in mind? Somewhere specific, perhaps where my poor young staffer was found?"

Michael just stared back at the senator, matching his gaze.

"I'm going to assume then, Agent, that you most likely could surmise that, yes, my son does in fact own that property, he's part owner with a very reputable individual living right here in OBX, I won't mention who because it is not relevant to your line of questioning. As for my son, he has nothing to hide, I have nothing to hide. Now, I'm going up to visit my family in Duck, Agent Francis. Funny name, 'Duck' don't you think? Sounds funny every time I say it. More like something you do when something dangerous is heading your way, not the name of a town."

"You're from Duck?" Michael asked. "I hear there's a popular dance club up there. You ever been?"

Pennington didn't miss a beat, laughing. "No, young lady, I don't dance."

Michael just smiled back. "I'm heading up there in a bit, actually, Senator, you know, for the investigation and all. Funny thing, that."

"Funny thing, that, yes, that's good Agent Francis, very good," the senator chuckled, shaking his head and looking away. He motioned with his hand for his driver to pull out of the driveway. "Give a holler to Anderson if you need me. I'm not going back to Raleigh before Monday, or unless this damn weather gets too bad."

Michael gave a half wave as the car backed out into the road and then sped away. Pennington's family is from Duck. Duck is home of the dance club Kathy Kirkland used to frequent.

And her body was found in Bruce Pennington's rental property.

Five minutes later Michael was pulling into The Purple Turtle. There was just one other car in the parking lot, a black pickup truck. Michael parked and walked up the ramp to the front door. Finding it unlocked, she opened it and stepped inside the darkened bar.

"Hello? Anybody here?" she called out. From behind the bar, the Bruce Pennington popped his head up. He smiled weakly behind his goateed face and looked at Michael with confusion. "Yeah, can I help you? We're not open yet."

Michael moved forward and flashed her ID at Pennington as she approached. "Hi, I was in here the other night with Amy Miller. My name's Michael Francis, and I'm an agent with the North Carolina State Bureau of Investigation." She paused and watched for a reaction. Pennington leaned over the bar and looked at her ID. "Name's Bruce Pennington. I run this place," he said, and extended his hand. Michael shook it and noticed it was cold and wet.

Pennington noticed Michael wiping her hand on her shorts and clamored, "Oh, sorry, I was washing the bar glasses. Messy work."

"Can we talk for a minute?" Michael asked. Pennington shook his head yes and gestured to a bar stool. "I'm here investigating a murder of a young lady."

"Murder?" Pennington exclaimed, standing upright away from the bar with shock. "Been a while since someone's been murdered around here."

"A while since when?" Michael asked, digging out her notepad from her pocketbook. An uncomfortable silence followed, and Pennington turned and walked a few feet to a small refrigerator, returning with a couple of bottles of Diet Coke. He slid one across the bar to Michael. "Where was she murdered?" he asked.

"Can't say for sure," Michael lied. "Listen, Amy Miller mentioned something to me the other night over dinner. I was asking her about the social scene around here, and Amy said you were pretty popular with the ladies."

Pennington laughed and sipped his drink. "That right? Well, I do alright, I guess."

"Okay. Well, this young lady who got killed, she was single, and pretty good looking. I was wondering if you maybe knew her or had met her?"

Pennington stared straight at Michael, unblinking, with a pasted-on smile. "What's her name again now?"

"Kathy Kirkland."

Pennington squinted and gazed upward in thought. "Name don't ring a bell. I tell you what, I see so many of them summer hotties comin' through here, I lose track, aside from the ones I hook up with."

"Did you hook-up with Kathy Kirkland?" Michael asked bluntly. Pennington half-smiled, half-sneered, shaking his head no.

Michael jotted down something on her notepad, then flipped it shut and put it back into her pocketbook as she stood up. "Thanks for your time. I'm going to need to talk with you again tonight, if that's okay."

The smile on Pennington's face quickly faded. "Workin' tonight. Gonna be a good crowd in here, lookin' to have fun before the storm."

"I'd like to come check out the scene, look over some of your patrons. I was busy talking with Amy Miller the other night and didn't get to look around much."

"Listen, Agent Francis, this is a place of business. I can't have you snoopin' around, hassling my customers, asking a lot of questions. That ain't right."

"Oh no, I won't be obtrusive," Michael said with a reassuring laugh. "I'm just gonna order some beers, hang out. I won't hassle anybody."

Pennington regarded her for a minute with a look of confusion, stood up, and spoke in a conciliatory tone. "Alright, look, I don't wanna do nothin' to get in anybody's way here. You wanna come poke around, fine, I'm not getting in your way. I would just ask that you respect my rights as a businessman just as I'll respect yours as law enforcement."

Michael smiled, realizing her suspect was the first person she'd encountered in the Outer Banks who'd offered to let her do her job. "You know Mr. Pennington, you've got yourself a deal. One last thing," she added, "It's my understanding you are co-owner of this place. Who might the other owner be?"

Pennington grinned slyly, then leaned forward with both hands on the bar. "That's a matter of public record, ma'am. I would direct you to the Town Clerk's office for more information, or I suppose you could bring me in for, uh, shall we say more 'direct' questioning?"

Michael smiled again, this time in disgust, and turned to leave.

"Just stick around, I'll be in touch," she yelled over her shoulder.

◆ ◆ ◆

Amy Miller was dreaming of a little girl with braids, licking an oversized lollipop, sitting on the beach all alone. The tide was coming in, reaching her feet, then her bottom. But the little girl didn't move, just kept sitting there licking her lollipop. Suddenly, the water was up around her arm pits, dragging her down toward the deeper water.

Amy's eyes flashed open, her mind snapped back into reality by the smell of the dank dark cellar.

Laying still, she decided not to try moving again. She didn't know how long she had been passed out since the last time she was awake, but she was sure it wasn't long enough to allow healing of her serious wounds. Since she couldn't move her body, Amy tried honing some of her other senses.

She closed her eyes and listened. Her mind felt as if it had hands, reaching out farther and farther to her right and left and above her head, up into the dark. She could hear her own heartbeat.

And a shuffle-thump.

Amy's heart beat faster. She listened again.

Shuffle-thump.

It was coming from above her, in front of her face, how far up she wasn't sure. Thinking quickly, Amy settled on footsteps as the cause of the sound. Shuffle-thump. Somebody was definitely above her somewhere, moving around.

The need to shout out, to cry for help or summon her abductor loomed strong in the forefront of her mind.

However, she held still, listening.

The noises above her stopped. Perhaps the person had left, or gone into another room.

Instead of feeling safe from her abductor, she felt a rush of anxiety. The noise, friend or foe, was her first link to sanity that she had felt recently. The sudden realization that the source of the noise had left and she was again on her own filled her stomach with butterflies. Amy felt bile start to form in the base of her throat.

She was about to swallow it down when, for some reason, Amy's mind leapt into survival mode. She couldn't move, had no weapons or tools, no communication, and was unsure of her surroundings. The only thing she had was her badly beaten body. Amy had an idea.

She swirled her tongue around and moved her mouth back and forth, building up as much spit as she could muster. Carefully, she opened her mouth and formed a tube-shape with her lips. Taking in a deep breath through her nose and curling her tongue, Amy spat straight up into the air as hard as she could.

As the liquid left her mouth, Amy concentrated hard on listening for a splatter. In short order, the spit fell back to earth, some on her forehead and the rest on the floor. She swirled her tongue again, worked up more juice, then took another, deeper, breath and spat, straining to hear if it hit anything. In a second or two, it fell back down onto her. She spat again a third time, with similar effect, and then swirled around the last of her spit in her mouth with her tongue, opened her mouth, took in a huge breath and strained to launch a loogie as hard as she could lifting her head ever so slightly off the floor with a jerk.

Ker-splat.

She hit something.

She started to cry and laugh at the same time, quickly silencing herself because of the pain the laughter was causing. She quickly rehashed the spitting scene in her head, and guessed that she had hit a ceiling of some kind, maybe three feet above her head. She figured she couldn't have spit any farther.

Some of the spit dripped off the ceiling onto her neck. Instead of grossing her out, it filled her with a sense of pride and gave her some hope.

Amy didn't even want to think about what that meant. She just hung onto that feeling for as long as she could.

CHAPTER 14

Michael drove the 17 miles from Nags Head to Duck in about 45 minutes. The heavier-than-usual Saturday afternoon traffic was full of families who should be heading from the beach to the tourist traps with pirate themes and seafood restaurants, but were instead packing up and heading home.

Word of the storm, not to mention the overcast sky and stiffening wind, had people spooked.

How sad, Michael found herself thinking. She continued to marvel at the sheer magnificence of it all: mile upon mile of shoreline, jutting out far into the Atlantic, almost daring the ocean to overtake it. These people weren't going to get to enjoy it.

Michael's thoughts drifted back to a summer several years ago, on Lake Ontario in upstate New York. Her young family had rented a lakefront house for a week. Brian had rented a catamaran; the winds off the great lake were so hard, he had Michael and the girls in stitches as the family man fell ass over teakettle time and again trying to sail the damn thing not ten yards from shore. He never did get it going, try as he might day after day. Michael had

161

liked that tenacity; found it charming, Brian's hard work at pleasing the family.

That seemed so long ago.

Michael shook her head, clearing the thoughts from her mind.

Stay sharp, girl.

She continued along the coast, seemingly far removed from the tourist areas of Nags Head and Kitty Hawk. Short, wind-swept pines formed a constant fence line to Michael's right and left, with intermittent driveways leading to multi-million dollar estates and exclusive condo developments. The highway turned from ashen asphalt to near-new blacktop. Finely coifed bike paths followed the highway. Saabs and BMWs and Lincoln Navigators ruled the road.

About ten minutes into the upscale area, Michael passed a wood-carved Welcome to Duck sign at a point where the highway entered a narrow branch of the northern Outer Banks. The road twisted and turned sharply, and Michael entered a commercial area with what looked like English renaissance architecture marking the sub shops and pizza joints to her left and right; fifty or so yards beyond each of the establishments was the ocean and, to the left, the sound.

Soon enough, she came upon The Wagoneer, Anton's place Juliana had mentioned. Michael pulled off the road, walked up the steps to a porch, then through a large door into a completely different world.

Kitschy deep red vinyl covered the walls of the windowless, darkened establishment. Garish mosaic flooring stretched out for a good thirty feet to a mahogany-top bar dressed in black leather that seemed to go back for miles, at least to the back of the long barn. To the right was a dance floor, and to the left and back around the other side of the bar and then back the other side were cheap metal tables and chairs, with flaming red tablecloths. Darkened disco lights of all kinds hung from up above, and a thumping techno beat was playing at what Michael guessed was a much, much lower decibel than would be heard later that night. A few people mingled at the bar, and a bartender was washing glasses. The entire place stank like old beer and cigarettes.

Michael walked up to the bar. "Hi there!" she called cheerfully to the bartender, flashing an eager smile. The bartender, a thirty-something white male who looked like he had given up covering for his growing widow's peak, resigned himself to walking over with a why-are-you-bothering me smile.

"Hi yourself," he deadpanned.

"Yeah, hi. I'm looking for Anton," Michael asked, reaching into her pocketbook, fumbling around as if looking for her wallet.

"Oh? Who's looking for Anton?" the bartender hissed back, stretching his arms out in front of him to prop himself up on the bar. Michael dug out her identification and flashed her SBI badge in the man's face. "North Carolina State Bureau of Investigation," she said loudly, so the few other patrons could hear. She didn't stop smiling.

As a small group of people mingling at the bar looked on, the bartender sheepishly gestured Michael to the opposite side of the rectangular bar as he hopped up and over the side, then led Michael to a nearby table.

"I'm Anton," he said, sitting down, looking concerned. He leaned in close as Michael sat down across from him. "Look, I don't deal anymore. If someone sent you here about that..."

"No, no, don't worry about any of that. I'm not here for you," Michael said with a take-charge voice. She flipped open her notepad and began talking fast and pointedly, looking Anton straight in the eye. "I'm conducting an investigation and need to know if you know a girl named Kathy Kirkland."

"Kath? Of course, she's great. She's just a kid, she can't be in trouble or anything?"

"I just have some questions about her, that's all," Michael shot back.

"She won't be getting into any trouble? You promise?"

Michael felt a catch in her throat. "I can promise you that. So she never hooked-up with anyone?"

"No. No, definitely not. Liked dancing, never hit on anyone, never went home with anyone other than friends she seemed to know."

"Did she ever hang out with any regulars?" Michael asked. Again, Anton shook his head.

"No ma'am. The regular fellas would try to hit on her, but she snubbed them all."

"The regular fellas?"

"Oh, Paul Masterson, Rick Pruitt, Bruce Pennington –"

"Pennington?" Michael interrupted. "You said Pennington? He was a regular fella? Did he try to hook-up with Kathy recently?"

Anton curled his lips as he thought hard for a moment. "Hmmm....You know, I don't remember exactly. I mean, he hit on everything with a hole. Come to think of it, though, I don't really think I saw him hitting on her recently."

Michael leaned in close. "Did he or didn't he? It's very simple, and it's very important."

"I can't say for sure. I'm sorry, I really am."

◆ ◆ ◆

The nondescript Ford Taurus pulled up next to Robbie Cartwright outside the SBI office in Raleigh, and the oversized man yanked open the door and slid into the passenger's seat. Harry McCairn pulled away from the curb and made his way out toward the 440 Beltline.

"What were you able to get?" he asked.

Robbie raised his eyebrows and exhaled dramatically. "Well, I called in a lot of favors from people who owed other people favors, really burned up a lot of cell phone lines, bothered people at home. Law enforcement, staffers in the legislature, whole nine yards. Here's the skinny: people remember Cooper as an annoying pit bull, totally loyal to Pennington and his boy Taylor. Came into the Capitol straight outta Lejeune."

"That normal?" McCairn asked.

"It is when your C.O. is your father-in-law. Word is his fiancé's daddy didn't want him in no two-bit crap job. But it gets better. Taylor was pushin' hard to get Cooper on staff, he lobbied for him, actually had Pennington call Lejeune personally, see about grabbing him up as soon as his tour was up."

McCairn shot a look of disbelief at his best friend's boss. "Did he know Cooper?"

Robbie stared out the window and answered slowly, as if in defeat. "Yeah, you could say that. They grew up together out in Bulah," he said, then turning to Harry, "Rumor has it they were using contacts back home to funnel drug money into a slush fund that Taylor was looking to tap for Pennington's U.S. Senate run. Taylor's the brains. Cooper's the muscle."

Harry felt his face getting flush with anger. "Jesus, Mary, and Joseph, we gotta get Michael and Brian."

◆◆◆

Skip Pennington stood in front of a huge wall of windows on the third floor of a soon-to-be-completed upscale beach house in Duck. He sipped a glass of Patron Silver on the rocks as he watched white caps rolling across the ocean before him like ants popping up out of some dark blue sand. On the horizon, the cloud-covered gray sky melted into something darker. Tall reeds beneath the beach house, on top of the dunes, blew wildly in the ever-increasing gusts of wind.

"You're late," he called over his shoulder to the visitor

coming up the stairs.

Julianna Gray tossed her keys onto a coffee table, kicking her sandals off halfway across the room.

Pennington smiled at the sight of sand flying everywhere and sipped more of his drink.

"I can see you're very busy. Too busy to come down to see me? Maybe I should leave," Julianna said flirtatiously, approaching Pennington from behind and placing her arms around his waist. She pressed her body up against his back and closed her eyes as she held him tight.

She felt a rush of warmth pulse through her body.

"Maybe I can work something out," the senator said, turning around to put his drink on a corner table and take his lover into his arms. The two kissed deeply, passionately, hardly coming up for air.

Julianna smelled the tequila on Pennington's breath mingle with his too-strong aftershave. To some girls, the scents would seem repulsive. To Julianna, the smells were reassuring.

"Mmmmm," she said, curling her head underneath his chin into the crook of his neck. "I've missed you."

"Bull," Pennington said pleasantly, smiling down at his mistress, holding her close. "I know you get around. Frankly, I don't care."

Julianna playfully pushed away. She walked over to a wet bar and poured herself some cognac. "What are you going to do when this place gets sold?"

"Maybe I'll just have to buy it," Pennington replied, picking up his drink.

"Or we could go back to the old place," Julianna said quietly, almost under her breath.

Pennington stared at her coldly. "That's not the least bit funny."

"Sorry," Julianna answered, taking a swig of her drink. "Aren't you worried about somebody connecting your name as owner of the beach house? I mean, it's gonna come out sooner or later. Especially with the police sniffing around."

"The police are busy. Don't worry about it. Bartholemew's going to talk to Amy Miller about buying it and bulldozing the lot. He got the keys from Anderson today, nobody's going in there again."

"You can do that? Right now? I mean, you know some state investigator is poking around, don't you?" Julianna wondered, walking over to join her lover by the wall of windows.

Pennington grinned playfully. "So you've met our little miss from Raleigh now, have you?" he said.

Julianna frowned and looked at the floor. "She came by."

"Came by where?" Pennington demanded, albeit in reserved tones.

"The boat."

"The boat," Pennington repeated. He turned and faced the windows, walking toward them with arms outstretched wide to his sides. "The boat! That's great. The boat. How did she find you on the boat?"

"Amy sent her my way."

"Wonderful. Any reason in particular why she'd send her your way?"

"She was asking about Kathy Kirkland. I guess Amy said I knew her."

Pennington turned, glaring. Sarcastically, he asked, "And did you?"

"A little."

Pennington stood upright and looked askance at her. "How much is a little? Like your other little friends?"

Julianna crossed her arms in front of her chest and walked to the opposite end of the windows. "Why do you have to be so hateful? No, I didn't know her like that."

"Well, what a relief. Someone on this island you didn't sleep with."

"I didn't know you were so jealous of your son," she spat. "You've gotta get over that. Hell, you're the one who introduced us. I don't know why you've got such a problem with that."

"Who said anything about my son?" Pennington yelled. "My son spends his time picking up beer sluts at his bar. Hasn't ever had a steady relationship since he flunked out of med school. He is the bane of my existence; the bad seed we don't talk about during my campaign. Do you know I once had a reporter beaten-up who interviewed my son? I'm just dumbfounded one of his slut bags doesn't run to the News and Observer with a story about dear old dad."

Pennington looked down at the floor, pausing to collect himself.

"I don't give a rat's ass what piece of trash he lays. When I referred to people you haven't slept with, I was talking about those bush bumpers you pal around with when I'm not around."

Julianna laughed at Pennington and downed the last of her drink. "I'm outta here," she said, slamming her glass down hard on the wet bar as she stormed across the room to the stairs.

"Wait. Wait. Wait!" Pennington shouted. Julianna shut the hall door behind her and bolted down the stairs outside. Turning back to the windows, Pennington scowled at the slowly boiling sea stretched out before him.

◆◆◆

In her Jeep on Beach Road, Julianna dialed Amy Miller's cell number. She got voicemail.

"Hi Amy, this is Julianna. Listen, I wanted to talk to you real quick. Can you meet me for drinks tonight? Call me," she said, then hung up. Just about ten seconds later, her phone rang. "Hello?"

"Sorry," Skip Pennington blurted.

Julianna waited for a moment, trying to decide what to say. "Yeah, sorry. Whatever. Look, when do you want to meet?"

"Seven will work. Your place."

"Make it eight. I'll be there," Julianna said angrily, hanging up her phone. At a red light, she thought for a minute that she was going to cry. She was letting her guard down and it made her mad. She leaned her head forward until it touched the top of the wheel, then raised it, took a breath, and accelerated when the light turned green.

♦♦♦

In her dark tomb, Amy Miller focused all her energy and concentration on her left arm. She was going to move it under her back, using her fingers to walk her hand where it needed to go in order to cut down on the stress to her body.

One. Two Three.

Amy took a breath and grimaced as she worked her hand and then forearm under the small of her back. She exhaled; she had done it! The pain was bad, but not too intense. She tried rotating her shoulder; ouch, that hurt.

Waiting for the pain to subside, she counted to three again, took a breath, and muscled her upper body over onto her left side with one great heave, using her left hand and arm as a pivot. She almost overcompensated and threw herself onto her stomach; instinctively, Amy moved her right leg, trying to swing it over to catch her body.

The pain made her scream. In a split second, Amy decided to avoid the pain and not pay attention to whether her attacker heard her, and continued to try and swing her leg over. She used her right hand, positioned on her right lower thigh, and arm to help her leg over, swiveling her hips. The pain was excruciating, and Amy let out several of the loudest primal screams she thought she'd ever heard.

She was on her left side. She was in great pain and started to cry, tears of joy mingling with the tears of pain. She would wait a while, then try for her next goal: to sit upright.

♦ ♦ ♦

It was about quarter of six when Michael Francis walked out of the bar and back to her car. When she passed the back of the large blue minivan parked next to her, she stopped in her tracks.

Her two driver side tires were flat. She rushed around to the other side of her car; those tires were flat, too.

She heard squealing tires and out of the corner of her eye saw a white SUV peel out of the parking lot down Route 12.

Michael dug through her pocket for Amy Miller's cell phone. She laughed at herself; was she really going to call local law enforcement? Hell, Anderson would probably leave her out there, she thought.

As the screen on the phone came to life, Michael noticed a missed call notification. She pressed the button to clear it and another window launched with the number of the caller who had been listed in Amy's contact list.

"Jules," Michael read out loud.

She clicked the return call button and the phone began to dial.

CHAPTER 15

Sergeant Jones was standing at the front desk of the Public Safety Building, speaking sternly but clearly into the phone to the television reporter on the other end of the line. "Dammit Pete, how should I know? You realize, we could have a hurricane roaring into town oh, let's see, about 72 hours from now, and I honest to God have no idea where the Chief of Police is, I'm a little stressed myself. I have no clue what he is doing. I can tell you, off the record, he is going through regular channels to prep everyone on the storm that's coming, by the book. He wants to talk to you; he just had to run out. Promise me you won't say anything without talking to him first?"

The outer door to the building swung open, shooting blustery wind into the lobby. A stranger in a police uniform entered, followed by another similarly dressed stranger.

"Can I help you?" Sergeant Jones shouted, somewhat irritated, covering the mouthpiece of the phone.

"Sheriff Sinclair from over in Bulah," he said, then pointing to his companion, "This here's Alan Marshall, one of my deputies. We're looking for someone sent your way earlier today." Deputy Marshall moved forward with a smile and grasped Toby's outstretched hand. "Stubborn lady from Raleigh SBI office name of Michael Francis, you seen her?"

Before Toby could answer, Deputy Marshall said, "Oh Sergeant, do you know you have an abandoned ambulance out on Route 12 West? We stopped by to check it out on the way in here, tried to call in but guess your receptionist wasn't here. No driver, nobody in the back, nothing. Might wanna get that towed and out of the way for your evacuation here."

♦♦♦

Michael watched a cappuccino-colored Jeep Wrangler with the top town wait for traffic to clear then turn into the lot. Julianna Gray smiled behind her sunglasses as she pulled up to Michael's car.

"Jesus, what'd you do?" she hollered.

Michael just smiled as she climbed aboard. "Long story."

Julianna turned the Jeep around and headed back down the road to Nags Head. "You know, I was really glad you called, even if it was from someone else's cell phone."

Michael smiled as she slipped-on her sunglasses. "Listen, I appreciate you coming. I really didn't want the local authorities to have to rescue a damsel in distress. Wouldn't help my investigation."

Julianna looked over and smiled. "You must trust me then, huh? Well, that's refreshing."

"I was thinking since we have some time together I could ask you a few more questions?"

"Ah-ah-ah!" Julianna replied, waving her index finger back and forth in front of Michael's face. "You don't get to make the rules; I'm the one helping you out, remember?"

"I have to talk to you again eventually," Michael said.

"It's your call when we do it."

"Well, if that's the case, I'll talk to you tonight, at my place, over a few drinks."

Michael regarded her cautiously. "I'll try and make this perfectly clear. I'm interested in talking to you about a murder, that's it."

"You happily married?" Julianna blurted.

"What?"

"Are you happily married? Simple question."

Michael was taken off guard, and let her mind drift from her questioning and control of the situation. "That's, well, it's really none of your business."

Julianna snorted.

"Hey, look, I'm happy. Let me at least ask you some questions now, then some more at your place." Michael could feel the blood rushing to her face, and her heart was racing. She was a bundle of nerves, exhausted. She felt like she just drank three cups of coffee, but her body ached with exhaustion. She needed a nap.

"Fair enough," Julianna said, a look of satisfaction spreading across her flawless face. "We may not have enough time for questions tonight."

"Why not?"

"Haven't you noticed the wind? It's been getting stronger all day, and now it's gusting irregularly. When fronts come in, they blow strong and the temperature changes. The wind today and now tonight has been cold, but the overall temp is still hot and humid."

"And?" Michael prompted.

"And that usually means nasty weather is on its way, that's all," Julianna said, glancing repeatedly to her left over the dunes and beach houses to the ocean. "You can't see it real well right now that it's getting dark, but there is some serious cloud cover coming in. The radio was reporting nasty fronts converging, hurricane weather."

Michael looked toward the water. The horizon seemed darker than the early evening sky overhead, like something ominous was out there, waiting to pounce. "Yeah, I know what you mean. The Chief actually filled me in on it today. A tropical storm is brewing, maybe something bigger, might hit Monday, just like the TV is saying. He's calling for an evacuation."

"Sonofabitch!" Julianna yelled, slamming on her brakes a bit too hard as they came to a red light. "I knew it! Why hasn't that twit called for it sooner?"

"Actually, I think it might be partly my fault," Michael said. "I asked him to postpone the announcement until I could talk to a few more people."

Julianna looked at her angrily, hair whipping violently in front of her face. "Why the hell did you do that?"

"People know I'm here. They know an investigation's going on. Like you said, everybody knows everybody. If there's an evacuation, then all bets are off. Suspects can leave and tell me they'll be back, but they don't necessarily need to tell me where they'll be if they don't know. Could be a week after the storm is over, could be a month, could be never before they come back. At that point, the trail would be pretty damn cold. Not to mention the crime scene may very well be halfway to Africa."

"Yeah, freakin' beach house. That could go in a hard storm, couldn't it? Huh," Julianna said softly.

Michael regarded her driver. "What beach house?"

Julianna glanced over, confused. "The beach house. The crime scene," she said matter-of-fact.

Michael kept staring.

"What?" Julianna asked.

"I don't believe I told you anything about a beach house."

Julianna stared straight at the road ahead, smiling. "Like you said, everybody knows everybody."

The two women didn't speak much again for the remaining ten minute drive to Julianna's home.

Turning off of Route 12 in the northernmost section of Nags Head, the Jeep headed onto a long dirt road bordered by spruce trees. The vehicle playfully bounced on rocks and sticks as it barreled forward for a good 500 yards. The road curved to the left, and the spruces opened on either side to reveal the waters of Roanoke Sound. An old two-story converted fishing shanty was the only structure. Julianna pulled into the driveway and cut the engine.

"You can't see too much right now, but you can see the lights across the sound in Manteo when it gets a little darker. Really cool," Julianna said, hopping out of the Jeep. Michael climbed out and noticed the still fishy smell that hung in the air. The trees were guarding them from the encroaching winds from the ocean side of the peninsula; one could hardly tell a storm was coming.

"Come on in," Julianna said, leading Michael up the front dirt walkway to the door. Once inside, the two women moved through the short foyer into an eat-in kitchen area. Michael walked to some sliders that opened onto a deck overlooking the sound, which lie about 20 yards across some grass and sand. Julianna hit a button on her CD player on her way into the kitchen; some old 80's song by Split Enz kicked in on surround sound.

"That's too funny," Michael shouted in Julianna's general direction. "This is the kind of music I was listening to in college."

"What'll you have?" Julianna yelled back over her shoulder, head buried in her refrigerator.

"Anything cold," Michael replied. Julianna popped out with two bottles of white wine, one in each hand.

"I'm sorry, don't have anything cold. This is slightly chilled; I'm hoping it'll do."

Moving into an adjoining living room, adorned with painting upon painting of fishing boats and the ocean, Michael sat on one end of a very long couch, while Julianna poured her a glass of wine and then sat across the coffee table, cross-legged, on an overstuffed chair. The cozy room, music, and wine was a welcoming departure from her crazy day, Michael thought. Once she sat down, a wave of exhaustion overtook her. Michael felt that if she closed her eyes, she would surely pass out.

"You ready?" she asked with a tired smile, pulling out her notepad.

"Shoot," Julianna said, toasting her guest and then taking a swig of the wine.

"This morning, you said you knew who Kathy Kirkland was, that you'd met her at The Wagoneer. Correct?"

Julianna nodded, looking up at the ceiling and pursing her lips as if considering the question.

"I was talking to Anton today. He said he remembers you clubbing it up with Kathy on several occasions, but he never saw the two of you, uh,.."

"Together?" Julianna finished the sentence, sipping more wine.

"Right," Michael said. "He also said he can't recall Bruce Pennington hitting on Kathy Kirkland. Now, you said you know Bruce; did he ever mention Kathy to you?"

"Bruce and I used to date, but he and I are old news. We're just friends now. We weren't seeing each other when Kathy came onto the scene." She stood up and moved to the coffee table separating the two women, poured herself another drink, and then sat back down. "As far as I know, he never got together with her."

"I don't mind telling you, I've interviewed Bruce once already, and I'm going to see him again. It'd be nice if you could think real hard and tell me anything you remember about him and Kathy," Michael prodded, sipping some wine.

Julianna drank another gulp, then another, quickly. "So he's a suspect then?"

Michael just stared back, emotionless.

"The last time you saw Kathy Kirkland was last Saturday night, at the Wagoneer?"

Julianna didn't answer.

Michael had to look up. She put on an irritated look as

if to say, I'm waiting.

Julianna was staring, smiling. She looked across the room, stretching her legs out up the other side of the overstuffed chair, and began rubbing her left calf with her right foot.

"Yeah, well, I think that's about right," she replied. "I was there just looking to have a good time. I ran into an old friend, Margaret Chang."

"She a local?"

Julianna paused before answering, scratching her right thigh with her hand, her fingers reaching slightly up her shorts to get at the skin underneath, almost playfully.

"I spent the whole night with Margaret."

"That's fine. Now where – "

"We've been lovers on and off again for about three years," Julianna interrupted. "She's a lawyer, you know. She may know some people around here you should talk to. Real nice girl. Beautiful. Asian, long straight black hair, nice body, full lips."

Michael sat still and waited for Julianna to answer. When she didn't, and simply looked away and drank more wine, Michael leaned forward and took another small sip of hers.

Julianna looked over. "You want a nipple with that?"

"I'm just not in the mood for alcohol, thanks."

"I'll grab you a Coke, then, but it won't be cold," Julianna said, walking over to the kitchen and returning with a can of soda. Just as she was about to say something, the cell phone on a table next to the overstuffed chair began to ring.

"Excuse me," Juliana said, answering the phone. "Hello?"

"I'm coming over," Skip Pennington said matter-of-fact.

"I've got company. Just give me twenty. I've gotta run someone home real quick."

"Real quick."

Sighing, Julianna turned to her guest. "Need to answer the rest of your questions on the road, I'm afraid."

Both women spent the first part of the ride back to Michael's motel in uncomfortable silence, watching the darkening sky and strengthening wind gust through palm trees lining the road.

"This could be quite the storm," Julianna mused. "So you're married. Any kids?"

Michael held up three fingers.

"Wow. Mother of three, and an agent with the SBI. Damn. Lookin' at you, you can see it wearing on you."

Michael kept looking out the window to avoid her gaze. The wind kept blowing in waves against the Jeep, and Julianna struggled to steer straight through some of the stronger gusts. She watched the road ahead closely as she spoke. "I can see you struggling. I've been around a lot of people in my life, and you just seem like somethin's not right."

"Give it a rest," Michael said sharply, shooting daggers at her driver. "I've got a job to do, and I'm gonna do it and I'm gonna go home to my kids."

"And?"

"And what?"

"And your husband?"

Michael looked away again.

"Ahh, the husband. Not goin' so well, aye?"

"You wouldn't understand if I told you," Michael mumbled. "You wouldn't understand. It's hard with kids. You should try having kids."

Julianna was momentarily quiet. "I did," she said.

Michael turned and stared.

"Well, kinda. I got pregnant. I thought I was in love with a man, somebody who swept me off my feet when I was just starting out adulthood, after my father died. He helped me decide the baby wasn't the best choice, for either of us. He was there through the abortion, helped me get back on my feet..." her voice trailed off.

Exhausted, Michael thought about just letting the conversation end. Oddly, though, she felt somehow drawn to the conversation.

"Where is he now?"

"He's around," Julianna said, pulling to a stop in the hotel parking lot. "Shows up in my life every now and then. My life's kind of a mess, so no big deal. Going to see him now, actually."

Both women just stared at each other.

"Don't judge," Julianna said defiantly.

Michael let herself out of the Jeep and turned back to Julianna, leaning in, holding the door open.

"Wouldn't think of it," she said. "My life's pretty messed up too."

◆◆◆

Brian Francis had flipped through a dozen stations, trying to find some news. He came across a faint signal and caught the last half of a news report.

"...shooting by a Raleigh Police Officer, identified as Brian Francis. Nobody can yet confirm if the officer is being charged in connection with the shooting at his home, or as to the location of his current whereabouts. Police are tight-lipped on the situation, and we'll bring you more information as it becomes available."

Brian slowed down. He checked his watch; it was creeping up on 8:20, but it looked more like 9:20 with the darkening clouds overhead. He looked at his speed – he was going 85.

A speeding cop who was just involved in a shooting, and who should not be anywhere but his home, would be a prize for any state trooper or local law enforcement.

He slowed to what felt like a crawl, afraid to go too much over the speed limit since he seemed to be the only vehicle heading East on Highway 64. In the Westbound lane, a constant stream of cars was headed away from the coast. He turned back on the radio.

"...a full evacuation has now been called for the entire Outer Banks, with State Police mobilizing roadblocks to keep vacationers from heading to the beach."

Roadblocks, Brian thought. If he tried to talk his way through to the beach, they'd ask for I.D. With his name plastered all over the airwaves, it was going to be tough to get to Michael without being detained for fleeing Raleigh while a live investigation was underway.

Brian had some thinking to do. Quickly.

◆◆◆

Skip Pennington adjusted his bow tie in the bathroom mirror, wet his hand and slicked back what remained of his receding salt and pepper hair. Putting on his gold, round wire-rim glasses, he felt as if his look immediately went from tired old man to intellectual power broker. Satisfied, he left the bathroom and walked over to the edge of the bed.

Julianna lay there, nude, the top sheet pulled up to her waist. Her breasts laid listlessly inches from the pages of a book she was reading on investing. She looked up expectantly.

"That'll be it for the weekend. I'm heading back tomorrow before this storm gets any worse, right after that damn press conference at the Chamber of Commerce. It'll be just a five minute thing on the way outta town so we can take a picture and say we did it," Pennington said matter-of-factly, smiling, as he lifted a white sports coat off a chair and put it on.

Julianna slammed the book shut and tossed it on the bed, rolling her eyes. "That's great. Thanks for stopping by. Phht."

"Look, you should think about getting gone, too," Pennington said, gesturing to Julianna's bedroom window overlooking the sound. Dark silver clouds gave the normal evening sky a wicked feel. Rain was beginning to come down, and the wind was picking up.

"Just check your homeowners insurance before you leave," he said, making his way downstairs and out the front door.

Julianna started to think about what she needed to do before she left the Outer Banks for the mainland. She should tie-down her boat, collect her instruments from the cabin, pack lightly and grab some bottled water for the trip in case traffic got tight. She slipped out of bed and walked, still nude, downstairs to her kitchen.

Julianna laughed when she saw the plain white envelope on the counter. Her lover never did seem to figure-out how demeaning that was. She would almost rather have him hand her the $500 dollars after one of their regular nights together. She walked past the envelope to the refrigerator and grabbed some juice, looking to the right of the counter and seeing the half empty bottle of wine from earlier.

Agent Francis.

Julianna's pulse jumped just a little, and she grinned.

CHAPTER 16

Tired as she was from her day before, Michael couldn't resist standing in the motel's side yard, looking out toward the water at the approaching storm. Despite a slight sense of trepidation, she felt calm overall, which surprised her. The chaos coming in over the water seemed to supplant the chaos in her own life.

"Good morning!" Toby shouted from his Jeep as he swung into the motel parking lot. The stiff wind whipped his bleached hair as he bounced over to Michael. "Definitely coming, picking up steam really fast. You ready?"

Michael shot him a curious look.

"When you called the hotel this morning they only told me you were coming to meet, nothing was said about us going anywhere. So where you taking me?"

"Trust me," Toby smiled.

Three blocks up from the motel on Beach Road, Toby turned off into the parking lot of the beach house at 3042. "What're we doing here?" Michael asked.

Toby winked. "Follow me."

The two walked up to the front door. "Try it," Toby

said, pointing at the doorknob. Michael tried to open it, but couldn't. She looked at Toby, confused.

"Locked it, just like I did when I tied-up the crime scene. I went over it a couple times, just can't figure out how you got into a locked house without a key."

Michael cocked her head. "Why, Sergeant Jones, have you been doing some honest-to-God police work?"

Smiling, Toby said, "Two people have keys to this house. Me and Chief Anderson. And I sure as hell didn't come by and open it for anybody, no way, no how."

"Where is he now?" she asked.

"He's supposed to be at a press conference at the Chamber of Commerce, we can be there in five minutes."

They both turned to walk over to the Jeep. "So an unlocked door means your boss might be dirty?" Michael asked quizzically as she climbed in.

"Not exactly," Toby said, sliding behind the wheel and shutting his door. "But it makes me think something isn't quite right when he told me to detain you."

Michael stared blankly. "Excuse me?"

"The call came in late yesterday afternoon; at least that's what the Chief said when he called me. Your boss, Agent Cartwright. He called you in, right?"

Michael stared for a moment, then nodded. "Not exactly," she answered, resignation in her voice. "We spoke two nights ago and he said I should come home, but he didn't argue when I told him I was staying put to continue the investigation."

"Well, Chief said he called, said you declined his invitation, I think that's how he framed it. The Chief said your boss told him you were AWOL and we needed to detain you until someone from the Raleigh SBI office could get out here."

Michael reached for the door handle.

"Hey hey, don't do that, just listen," Toby said, leaning in closer and speaking in a hushed tone. "I highly doubt your boss told my boss to hold you, that don't feel right.

This Kirkland case, the intruder you ran into...well, it's just not sitting very well with me. I want to help you get as far as you can with this, and then help finish it for you when you leave. But you gotta be straight-up with me; I know about your car accident in Bulah, I talked to Sheriff Sinclair. Something funky is going on with you, and you gotta tell me what you found out so far, so I can help you finish this."

"This probably isn't the time or place, you know?" Michael said. "But then again, I don't have anyone here I really trust, and you're the only one I think who's been up-front with me, so here it is: someone murdered that girl and I've got a feeling it's being covered-up. I think you do, too. It's got something to do with Pennington, and your boss is in on it somehow. At first, I thought it was because Kirkland was on Pennington's staff, but now I think there's something more. I've been through too much," Michael stopped short of telling the sergeant about her tires being slashed. "Anyways, I think Pennington's son knows something about it, and Julianna Gray knows something about it."

"Are they suspects?"

Michael's smile waned. She had begun to think of Bruce Pennington as a suspect, but why not Julianna?

"Agent? Are they suspects?"

"Yes," Michael heard herself say. The reality of her answer smacked her in the face. She stared blankly over the sergeant's shoulder at the beach house.

"Jules. You think Jules is involved," Toby mumbled in disbelief.

Michael didn't reply. She stared firmly, almost defiantly at Toby and nodded her head. "Yeah, they're both suspects, long-shots right about now. Truth is, Sergeant Jones, I have no strong leads, no evidence, and I'm days behind where I need to be."

"This press conference, Pennington will be there, you can talk to him one more time before he bolts, we'll just have to avoid the Chief if he's in earshot. After that, you can leave before the storm and come back to finish this up with me."

Michael smiled. "Thank you," she said. "But I don't intend on leaving before I'm through. I'm staying."

Toby stared in disbelief. "Why? What for?"

Michael looked away, toward the ocean, wiping her hair away from her face. As she started to think about the question her stomach began to ache. "You wouldn't understand if I told you. Hell, I don't think I understand." She looked back at Toby. "The point is, we don't have a lot of time. There's been a murder. I'm an agent with the SBI, and I'm here to do my job. I'm staying until it's done."

"I'm impressed, but I'm not sure if you realize there isn't going to be anywhere for you to stay in another day or so, SBI or not. You may think you're staying, but ol' Mother Nature, she's got other plans."

"Well," Michael said defiantly, "I'm a mother too, so we'll just see who comes out on top."

◆◆◆

Sue and Harry McCairn sat at their kitchen table, silently drinking coffee. A nervous energy filled the air.

"What're you going to do?" Sue asked in a hushed voice. Harry sat in silent contemplation for a moment, tapping his phone against his chin. He looked out the bay window into the backyard and saw a group of birds flying to and from a bird feeder. One of them was the male cardinal. He turned back to his wife.

"I know a guy who'll fly me out there," he said.

Sue felt her stomach sink, and she was suddenly overwrought with concern. "Oh, Harry, what're you doing? You sure?"

"You want me to do something, right? Well, this is it. Listen, I need you to take the girls to your sister's house, okay? We've kept the news media away from them so far; it's only going to get tougher if someone gets wind of them here and I'm not around to keep them at bay. Stay there and I'll call you."

"Where are you going?" Sue asked.

"I have to get to RDU. The guy I know has a refurbished Guard chopper, does aerial work for developers, he spends his whole day out there at the airport and is chomping at the bit to do some flying, legit or not. If I drive out east, I'm sunk. I'll hit a roadblock somewhere, they're not going to let anyone onto the Banks with the storm coming. They won't be able to stop a chopper in the air, we'll just land and B.S. the authorities until I find both of 'em."

"Babe, you're talking about going up in a helicopter in a hurricane."

"It's a tropical storm, they aren't sure if it'll get to hurricane strength. Most helos can handle 50 knot winds. My buddy's not going to risk losing his bread and butter, okay? If it's too much, it's too much."

"What if someone busts the two of you, then what? You're up shit creek," Sue hissed.

Harry became agitated, whispering loudly, "I thought we were trying to keep them together, like we talked about. That's the talk we've been talking, right? Well, now it's time to walk the walk." He rose quickly from his seat and left the room.

Sue turned her attention back to the television, with some talking heads discussing the coming storm. She closed her eyes, crossed herself, and prayed.

◆ ◆ ◆

"Alright, I'm glad y'all could come this morning. Seeing how the weather's gettin' rough behind me here, I figure we better get going," Perry Peterson addressed the assembled dignitaries braving the wind gusts and darkening skies above the choppy surf. About two dozen local town planners, managers, council people from Nags Head, Duck, and Corolla stood in the empty parking lot nervously waiting for the symbolic ribbon cutting to be over so they could get home to their families and get out of the way of whatever was coming.

Peterson was an institution in the Outer Banks. His father Red had built the first grocery store in Kill Devil Hills, and Perry had fought the environmentalists' efforts to throw the vacationers off the beaches. Instead, he rebuilt not only the vacation homes storm after storm, but he had used his own money more often than not to clean-up shopping centers ravaged by the flood waters and winds, and every now and then build new ones when the lines at the existing stores got too long for the locals to handle.

His latest development, his biggest in years, was why they were all there now. Surfside, the amenity-laden resort, sprawling over some ten-plus acres, was a Godsend to the local small businesses trying to compete with the larger private all-inclusive resorts up in Virginia. At Surfside, visitors would be able to do whatever they wanted, except eat; for that, they had to frequent the nearby tourist-trap restaurants and raw bars. That was part of the deal Peterson had brokered with the local folks; you want to build a 210-room monstrosity on the shore, that's fine. You just can't throw up a privacy wall and keep all your families secluded from the necessities of life. They'd have to spend their tourist dollars on the local businesses, so no restaurants or grocery stores in the resort, and local catering only.

It was a win-win in a big way, hence the crowd.

"I'd like to first, thank all of you, for coming here today," Peterson stumbled through his opening remarks, clumsily leafing through a couple of stained index cards. "I'd also like to welcome the local media," he said, gesturing toward a newspaper reporter and a TV news videographer.

"Most of all," Peterson continued, "I'd like to thank our good friend, Senator Skip Pennington for helping us get the land, the permits, and the local support to make this great project possible." The crowd burst with applause. Pennington ate it up, striding to the microphone, hair blowing in the wind, grasping Peterson's hand in a hearty shake.

"Perry, thank you. Thanks to y'all, not only for your support here today but for your constant, unwavering support all these years. This great project, Surfside, will be an economic and spirit boon for the whole Outer Banks. Its success will send a ripple down to Nags Head, and across the sound to Manteo, and even up into, dare I say, Virginia," Pennington said mockingly, eliciting laughter and cheers from the partisan crowd.

The Senator's smile faded as his gaze fell upon two late arrivals to the press conference: Sergeant Toby Jones and Agent Michael Francis. "All of you here today," he continued, looking in Michael's direction, "will bear witness to honest, hard work and the fruits of the labor of an entire region's belief in itself, North Carolina, and the United States. We have patiently played by the rules, we have filled-out the required forms, we have abided by state and federal regulations, we have ensured the environment is properly protected, we have graciously reimbursed our neighbors for their land, we have done everything asked. And now, we have the opportunity to show the world what good, decent folk can accomplish."

With that, Pennington and Peterson turned and yanked two ropes that pulled-off a large white sheet off a giant sign showcasing an artist's rendering of the resort, the sheet billowing crazily in the wind. Its gleaming white flat-roof structures, swimming pools, tennis courts, and greenery brought forth waves of oohs and ahhs as the crowd pressed forward for a better look. Applause soon followed.

"Thank you, Senator, thank you all of you for all your hard work. Let's get rolling," Peterson said to scattered applause, then he and Pennington left the makeshift stage and began glad-handing the crowd.

"They've been working on this for years," Toby said to Michael.

"Years seems long. Any particular reason for delays?" Michael asked.

Toby shook his head. "As far as I know, the enviro-wackos left this one alone. The state sent some engineers and such over two years ago and they bitched a little, but they went away."

Michael regarded Pennington moving through the crowd. "Does he have any stake in this monetarily? I mean, it's great for a lynch-pin for his running for higher office, I guess, but it seems risky to back something so strongly without a payoff, directly or indirectly."

"If he does, it's none of your business," came a reply from behind her. Michael and Toby turned to see Bart Taylor. "The Senator has always played on the up-and-up; any financial dealings he has with developers is public knowledge, Agent Francis, but it shouldn't be a concern to you."

"Actually, it is a concern to me," she shot back. "You're the senator's chief staffer, you were at the Public Safety building, so you know that there's a murder investigation underway out here, and that I would at some point like to interview your boss, like I tried yesterday. When he gets a minute, that is."

"Is the senator a suspect, Agent?" Taylor asked coyly. "Because if he's not..."

"The senator's son, Bruce Pennington, who runs The Purple Turtle. Why doesn't he have a high-paying consulting job in Raleigh? Why is he stuck schlepping drinks to tourists out here?" Michael asked, irritated.

"Bruce Pennington is from the Outer Banks. This is his home. The senator is proud of his son's business acumen."

"Did the senator buy his son that business?"

"The senator supplied some up-front – "

"So you do realize that if the Senator is tied to The Purple Turtle in any way, shape, or form, that he's implicated somehow in the death of a young lady named Kathy Kirkland? Before you ask how, I'll tell you; The Purple Turtle was the last place anybody remembers seeing Kathy Kirkland before she died. You know, she was one of your staffers? Chances are her murderer was in the bar with her, meaning the entire establishment is complicit in aiding a criminal if in fact the murderer was an employee or regular tied to the ownership at some level. Oh, and by the way, the place where the body was found? Yeah, your boss' son owns that property. But I'm sure you're eager to contribute to the investigation, as Kathy Kirkland was one of your staffers."

Taylor stood poker faced. "So what exactly are you looking for from the Senator?"

Michael stepped in close to Taylor's face. "I want a sit-down today. I want unfettered access, one-on-one. You can be there, but don't 'no-comment' me. If there's nothing to hide, then the Senator…"

Michael's voice trailed off as she caught sight of Julianna, over Taylor's shoulder, making her way toward Pennington. When they were finally face to face, the Senator extended his hand; Julianna shook it, smiling wryly, then the Senator stepped by her and continued glad-handing.

Michael saw him turn and look back at Julianna with a conceited smile.

"Agent, are you through?" Taylor asked.

"Yeah," she fumbled, regaining her focus. "Just get me some time with the senator."

"I'll see what I can do," Taylor said, melting away into the crowd.

Toby patted Michael on the shoulder. "You okay?"

"Didn't sleep much," she replied. A gust of wind

kicked-up and blew one side of the giant sheet that had covered the Surfside artwork loose, whipping the crowd. People shrieked, laughed, then made their way back to their cars. Michael tried to wade through the crowd, looking for Julianna. She lost track of her in a sea of smiling faces. Suddenly, out of the corner of her eye, Michael caught her heading over to her Jeep. Michael tried to push through the mass of people to get over to her, but by the time she did Julianna was driving out of the parking lot.

Michael spun around. "Toby, can you take me to the Oregon Inlet marina?"

Toby looked at his watch. "Well, we can try, but we have to get over to the Public Safety Building in 45 minutes for the Chief's evacuation briefing."

Michael nodded, and they both rushed over to Toby's Jeep.

CHAPTER 17

The wind from the darkening sky was whipping across the 200 or so yards of saw grass, bushes and short dunes on the left side of Route 12 as Toby and Michael drove down through the north end of the Pea Island Wildlife Refuge, past the Bodie Island lighthouse, heading south toward Oregon Inlet. Toby was struggling with the wheel to keep the vehicle on a straight line as he hauled ass down the deserted highway under dark gray skies.

"Don't see any tourists right about now," Michael yelled over the wind and engine.

Toby shouted back, "I can't say that I blame them, Agent Francis. I'm not so sure I think this side trip is a good idea right about now. You sure you need to see her boat?"

Michael looked away from her driver and out at the blowing sawgrass as she answered in a curt, professional tone. "Julianna Gray is, at the moment, a suspect in a murder and her place of business may very well be blown away by this storm."

Toby stared at her for a moment, then moved his

concentration back on the road. "This getting personal for you?"

Michael just kept looking at the sawgrass.

The Jeep struggled against the wind for another ten minutes until it reached the Oregon Inlet Marina. The large wooden gate leading into the parking lot was locked. "I guess park it here, and hang on. I'll be right back," Michael yelled, snapping off her seatbelt and jumping out. She jogged past the gate and began traversing the 50 yards of empty parking lot toward the first pier on the left, across an empty stretch of blacktop from a U.S. Coast Guard station.

The wind was loudly snapping the giant American flag and the assorted state and Coast Guard flags on the roof of the nearby station with such ferocity they sounded like watchdogs barking at an intruder. Michael felt like she was trespassing and got a little nervous. She looked around; she was the only one outside. If there was anyone next door in the Coast Guard station, they weren't coming out in this weather. As she reached the first pier, Michael stopped running where the asphalt met the wooden dock. It was moored, but it was a floating dock so it was pitching violently in the wind and waves, which were no doubt less foreboding thanks to the barrier of the inlet and peninsula keeping the largest waves out. Michael found the Shoal Surfer third boat in. It was bouncing against the dock, and Michael waited to time her jump on board. She half missed, and slammed her left knee into the metal railing aft. Tumbling onto the deck, Michael grabbed her knee in pain, but forced herself to get up and limp toward the door to the cabin. She tried the handle but it was locked.

Wind whipped her hair in her face, and Michael struggled to keep it out of her eyes. She slammed her elbow into the cabin door window, reaching through the broken glass and unlatching the door.

Once inside, Michael began scanning for cabinets and drawers. Each time she saw one, she flung it open and hurriedly rummaged through Julianna's belongings. Tools, fishing gear, lots of maps and navigational aids, but nothing incriminating. She moved forward cautiously to the pitching lower deck, which was more of a crawl-space, some five feet high. It contained a cushioned seat which ran all around the room, and more cabinets overhead. Michael started pulling open the doors and yanking-out blankets, life jackets, food stuffs.

Suddenly a photo album fell onto the floor. Michael stopped what she was doing and stood steadying herself in the swaying boat. She picked up the album and sat on the cushioned bench. Flipping through the pages, she saw pictures of the captain and her passengers, showing off their catches on deck. As she flipped toward the front, she came across pictures of a younger Julianna on her boat, probably when she was first starting out. There was one of her cutting a ribbon, one of her posing with local business leaders, and one of her with Skip Pennington. The two were standing, arms around each other's shoulders, smiling. Julianna had a drink in her hand.

Michael stared at the image for a moment, then opened the plastic sheet covering the page and took out the photo. She slipped it into her jacket pocket and clambered out of the lower deck. Michael stumbled out of the swaying cabin, moved back out on deck, walked to the side and threw herself onto the pier, steadying herself on a piling. She walked quickly back down the moving pier to the parking lot and onto the asphalt. The snapping flags on the Coast Guard station sounded like gun shots as she ran to her waiting ride.

"Get what you need?" Toby yelled over the wind as Michael opened the canvas and plastic door and jumped in. Almost on cue, the Sergeant's cell rang. He steadied the wind-shaken Jeep with one hand and glanced down at the number in the display.

"The Chief?" Michael asked.

"No. Local number, don't recognize it."

♦♦♦

If Amy Miller had her full senses about her, it would have seemed like hours since she had first painstakingly moved herself underneath the dripping water source now nourishing her beaten and dehydrated body. All she could feel, however, was the healing power of the water as the drops intermittently fell upon her lips and tongue. It was almost nirvana, a timeless dreamlike state Amy felt herself in. She had no worries, no anxieties. All she cared about was catching the next drop of water. That was all that mattered.

In time, her eyes started to dart to her right and left in the cool, dark compartment where she lay. There was no light, but Amy could feel her senses reaching out if she stared long enough in one direction or the other. While she was initially nervous, especially when she had rubbed up against what felt like another human body, Amy was now content, almost enjoying the simplistic task of catching the water.

As her mind began to focus more and more clearly while her eyes tried to make inroads into her surroundings, she started to realize that her mouth and tongue were numb because of all the water she had taken in. Thinking inward, Amy's stomach felt bloated, and she realized she had drunk enough water, possibly too much. She concentrated on her lower body and tried to pee, but she couldn't contract the muscles without pain and could not force herself to go. The damage must be severe, she thought.

The water kept dripping, about 20 seconds between drops, and was hitting Amy in the cheek as she turned her head from side to side, looking about. She moved her neck so that the water would fall just to the left of her head. Thinking clearly, Amy wondered about the source of the water. Could she be outside in a sewer or something, under a puddle? The water was not salty, so it wasn't seawater, and she didn't hear raindrops on a roof or anything. Could it be from a leaky faucet? The water she had collected in her mouth was extremely cold, numbing her mouth and tongue. Faucet water wasn't that cold.

Air conditioning condensation? It would have to be a lot of it to seep through a floor. A refrigerator? Well, there could be a leak, but it would have to be a rather large refrigerator to pump out so much water. What had large refrigerators? Or refrigeration units?

Restaurants.

Maybe she was in the basement of a restaurant, Amy thought. Closing her eyes, she tried to remember the night she was attacked. She had been at The Purple Turtle, in the parking lot next door.

The Purple Turtle. Amy figured she could be in the basement of the Purple Turtle. Did the restaurant have a basement, though? She had never seen one. And if it was a restaurant, why didn't she hear any footsteps from above?

Was Bruce up there? Amy thought briefly about calling his name, then hesitated. A chill ran up her neck.

Did he put me here?

For her own sanity as much as anything else, Amy Miller told herself she was in the basement of The Purple Turtle, and she was on her own. Now that she knew where she was, Amy thought, she had to figure a way out.

♦♦♦

Michael had trouble keeping her eyes open on the short 15-minute drive from Pea Island to the Dare County Public Safety Building, the sound of the wind and rocking of the Jeep lulling her aching body to sleep.

"Agent? You with me?" Toby nudged Michael with his elbow. She jolted awake, and scrambled to gain some semblance of order. "I just called that number back; that was Chris Lane from the coroner's office."

Michael just stared, confused.

"He called looking for you. Said he needs to talk to you in person, was very nervous. He doesn't want anyone to pick him up. He said he'd meet you at noon at the Bodie Island Lighthouse, then he hung up."

"Back where we just came from? Why the cloak and dagger act?"

"No clue. Said something about Anderson wanting some papers he's got or something."

In minutes they were in front of the Public Safety Building, which was surrounded by curious onlookers, some television cameras and a gaggle of public officials and law enforcement.

"Agent Francis," Toby said in a straightforward, serious tone as he leaned in close to her. "You wanna take care of yourself, you hear? He's gonna want you arrested as soon as he sees you."

"Listen, I can take care of myself, believe me," Michael replied. "Sergeant, do you have the keys to the beach house?"

"Why?" he said, digging the keys out of his pocket.

"Just give me the keys," Michael said, grabbing them before jumping out of the Jeep.

"Ladies and gentlemen, thank you for coming. I'm Chief Anderson, we have weather reports indicating a tropical storm is bearing down on us, picking up a little more steam and moving quicker than we had expected and bringing with it expectations of very high storm surge and flooding. I am hereby calling for the immediate evacuation of the Outer Banks from Duck down to Hatteras," Anderson said to the gathered throng filling the lobby.

The two reporters on hand peppered the chief for a good ten minutes, then he waved his hand and announced the press conference over. Officials began arguing in small groups, and the news media raced to get back to their newsrooms. Michael watched from behind a crowd in the corner as Anderson called Toby over and began an animated discussion with him. Toby looked dejected. Michael walked defiantly through the dispersing crowd toward the two men.

Anderson turned his gaze toward Michael. "Agent Francis, I guess my man here hasn't informed you. There's a detention order for you. I have it on good authority that you have refused a call-back from your commanding officer back in Raleigh. By all accounts you are an unauthorized presence eating-up my time in an emergency situation. I'm afraid you'll have to come with me," he said, gesturing for her to follow him.

Michael took a step toward him, getting up in his face. "You don't have the authority."

"I believe I do," Anderson shot back, loudly. "Your badge means nothin' around here if I don't want it to," he yelled, moving his hand behind his back to grab a set of handcuffs.

Michael's heart started beating like a jackhammer. Adrenaline coursed through her body as she jerked her head back and slammed it forward quickly, her forehead hitting Anderson on his upper lip and chin. Anderson stumbled backwards and fell flat on his ass, grasping his face with both hands. Michael bounced backwards slightly, and Toby instinctively lunged at her to try and grab her around the arms from behind, instantaneously going from comrade in arms to public safety officer, corralling a suspect. Michael took Toby's left arm and slid it off of her, grabbing and holding his wrist as she spun around and away from him. She jerked his wrist down, pulling his body down with it, and ramming her left knee into his stomach. A loud groan escaped the Sergeant's mouth as he buckled slightly, then threw himself at Michael.

Without balancing himself in his charge, Toby left himself open to be pulled along by his own force as Michael just took his arm and threw him past her. Toby stumbled and fell on top of Anderson in comical fashion. Onlookers gasped at the fight.

"Hey there!" came a friendly yell from the open front door of the building. It was Julianna. "Need a ride?"

Michael hurried out the door. The last ten feet to the Jeep she broke into a frightened run, not sure of the crowd. She jumped in and the two women sped off, the shouts of the crowd fading behind them.

♦♦♦

Julianna kept the Jeep in the flow of traffic on Route 12 heading south, out of Nags Head. The four-lane highway was empty going the other way, but a parking lot heading out, full of nervous-looking tourists and their families trying to find their way back to the mainland. About a mile from the bridge linking Nags Head with Roanoke Island, Julianna noticed the traffic signal at the large shopping center about 200 yards ahead was swaying pretty hard in the ever-increasing wind and blinking red. She saw flashing lights, and noticed two squad cars and two officers directing traffic, helping crowds of people leave the shopping center with their emergency necessities.

"Where to?" Julianna asked.

"Bodie Island lighthouse," Michael answered.

"So may I ask why you want to go to a lighthouse in the middle of an oncoming storm?"

"I may be all sorts of screwed-up right now, I don't mind telling you. But I'm still running an investigation into that girl's murder, and this is part of it. I'm meeting someone at the lighthouse who has information for me."

"You got any suspects?"

Michael felt her left eye starting to twitch.

"Couldn't tell you if I did," she replied.

"Shit, that's too bad. I know pretty much everybody here. If you had some idea, you could run it past me and I could help you."

"Look, I can't say, alright?"

As the Jeep inched to another short stop, about 50 feet

from some police directing traffic, Julianna shot her passenger a glare. "Why can't you tell me? Am I a suspect?"

Michael just looked straight ahead. The traffic cop motioned them forward, and they passed by the officer without a second glance.

"Shit, I'm a suspect, aren't I?" Julianna scoffed.

Michael wouldn't look at her.

Minutes passed before either woman spoke again.

Julianna asked, "Why are you doing this?"

"Look, I don't have one suspect, so everybody's a suspect, alright? Don't take it personally. I appreciate your kindness, and the ride."

"No, no, not why am I a suspect. I really don't give a damn. Why are you doing this?" Julianna asked with a sweeping gesture of her hand. "Why are you pushing this? Why can't you just let this go? Take the loss on this one?"

"I don't take the loss on anything," Michael interrupted.

The Jeep was at the intersection with its blinker on to veer left, continuing South on Route 12. Up ahead where the women wanted to go, two large wooden gates were padlocked over the road where it entered the Pea Island Wildlife Refuge. Julianna turned and looked at Michael.

"Go around," Michael said. Julianna smiled, then gunned it across the Northbound lane and up over some grassy dunes about five feet high to the right of the gate. The Jeep didn't miss a beat, tumbling down the other side and back onto the road.

"You do realize if the person who was gonna meet you at the lighthouse didn't get through here before the gates went up, this is all a waste of time," Julianna teased.

Michael shot back, "You got somewhere else to be?"

Julianna swung the Jeep around a curve and slowed at a sign to the Bodie Island Lighthouse. She turned right and slowly drove down the driveway. Pine trees and cypress on either side of the driveway blew wildly in the wind. Pockets of sawgrass shook like green pom-poms. Where the driveway opened up into a parking area in front of the lighthouse welcome center, Julianna pointed to a white SUV.

"Guess your buddy made it here after all," she said.

◆◆◆

"Curtis, Curtis, Curtis, how you doin' this fine day?" Sheriff Boyle Sinclair said walking straight over to the Chief's desk and plopping down in his sitting chair.

"Not now, Boyle, I'm a little busy if you haven't noticed."

"Now, Curtis, I was real patient yesterday when you couldn't talk to me, I even stayed with my cousin Mary and her family last night. Hell, Alan here had to sleep on the couch," he lamented, pointing to his deputy. "You know family, Curtis, they'll always be there for ya'. Kinda like you and your cousin ol' Artie Swanson. You uh...seen him lately, Curtis? Hmm? Talked to him recently, maybe? Or maybe his buddy there, Mike the Marine?"

Exasperated, Anderson looked up from his desk at the sheriff and then to the deputy. "Why don't you make yourself useful and make us up another pot of coffee. Go on now," he gestured to the offended deputy.

"Be nice," Sinclair softly chided. "Now look, Curtis, I have got to talk to you about an SBI agent you have investigating a murder around here."

"Fuck you Boyle. I do not have an SBI agent investigating a murder. There is a piece of shit Raleigh pain in the ass who thinks she is working on a case independent of this office. Her whereabouts are unknown, but she is wanted for – ah, screw it. She's just wanted, that's all you need to know, ass-wipe."

"Why so salty?" Sinclair held out a hand to calm the chief as Deputy Marshall brought in two cups of coffee. He gave one to the sheriff and, while Anderson waited for him to hand the other one to him, Marshall began to drink it and sat down next to Sinclair.

Anderson laughed.

"You two asswipes listen here. I don't care who you are, or where you're from or what you're here for. I'm in the middle of evacuating the entire freaking beach in a matter of hours and I do not have time for this shit. You want that bitch from Raleigh? You got her. When my boys bring her in you'll be the first one I call. Until then, get the hell out of my office!" He stood and planted both hands on hips, emphasizing the last part of his diatribe.

Almost immediately, the deputy got up and clumsily made his way to the door. He looked back at Sinclair, who was still sitting, smiling, his cup of coffee raised almost to his lips. He sighed and got up out of his chair, walking slowly to the door.

Turning to face Anderson, he said, "You sure you don't know why we're here, Curtis?"

Anderson just glared.

"We'll uh, catch you later then," Sinclair teased, closing the door behind him.

"You think he knows we wanna ask him about his cousin?" Deputy Marshall asked.

"Yeah, I do Alan. I'm not sure if he had anything to do with getting his cousin to try and take out Agent Francis, but I'm damn well sure I want to find her before Anderson does."

◆ ◆ ◆

Bart Taylor's cell phone rang in the middle of explaining to his boss about how the storm about to hit the Outer Banks would actually help garner votes for more projects like the Peterson project in order to spur economic recovery. "It's a Raleigh number, let me see who this is. This is Taylor," he answered, looking out the window of the fast-moving Town Car.

The distinct, southern voice on the other end of the line said, "Hi there, Mr. Taylor. Robbie Cartwright here. Got a minute?"

Taylor felt naked, adrenaline rushing through his veins. "I've, uh, got to take this. Can you hang on?" he asked Pennington, who nodded and leaned back to study paperwork on the project. Taylor crawled to the other side of the wide rear seat of the Lincoln. "What've you got?"

"Can't talk, huh? That's okay, you need to listen more than talk now. Now, I went out on a line here, spoke to some people I think you'd rather I didn't. Lots of interesting information on that shooter at the Francis home, you know?"

Taylor's heart was pounding. He could feel blood rushing to his face. "Look, I don't have a lot of time. What's the bottom line here?"

Robbie spoke slowly, calmly, clearly. "I want you to focus, Mr. Taylor. Focus on the future. The future can be bright, or it can be, well, not so bright. You're a sharp fella. Went to Carolina, right? Well, be a good Tar Heel and focus on the future."

Taylor was quiet for a minute, contemplating what to say next. "I'll think about it, okay?"

"No thinking about it, Mr. Taylor. If I have to spell it out for you, I will. You call off the dogs, you get my girl back here safe, then you come see me and I'll see what kind of deal I can work out for you."

Taylor angrily replied in a low growl, "You don't work out a deal for me. I'm the one who deals." He paused and looked over at Pennington to make sure he was still engrossed in his paperwork.

"I want a good deal without any liability."

"Son, there's always liability. You can cut your losses only so much."

Taylor wanted to throw the phone through the window. He composed himself before answering, "I'll get back to you."

Back in his deserted Raleigh office, Robby Cartwright held his phone out in front of him and stared at it. "Shit," he said, then hung up and dialed another number. After quite a few rings, Harry McCairn picked up. "Yeah," he shouted into his cellphone.

"McCairn, where are ya?"

"I'm at RDU International, about to jump into a chopper to get out east," McCairn yelled back, adding, "What happened with the deal?"

"Didn't go through as I hoped, apparently Mr. Taylor's not as spineless as he seemed. I think he's in this deep, and I didn't like the tone of his voice. We've got to get Michael out of there ASAP. What's your ETA once you're in the air?"

"No idea 'til we get up."

♦♦♦

The Lincoln Town Car swung across a busy lane of traffic, incurring the wrath of several horn-happy motorists trying to cross the bridge into Manteo on their way to the mainland. The vehicle swung again into the parking lot at the Pennington family restaurant, pulling up to a lone dark blue SUV in the far lot. Taylor swung open his door before the Town Car was at a complete stop, popping out shortly thereafter.

"Bartholemew, what about meeting with Paulsen tomorrow morning? Are you still going to make it?" Skip Pennington asked calmly, climbing across the car seat and following Taylor outside.

"Yessir, don't worry about it," Taylor said, walking quickly to the SUV against a stiff wind as he dug a set a keys out of his pocket.

"Well, where will you be staying tonight?" Pennington yelled after him, following close behind.

Taylor kept walking, answering over his shoulder, "I'll be back in Raleigh, sir. I've just got to run a quick couple of errands, see some people before I get back. Don't you worry about a thing, everything's under control."

"Hey!" Pennington shouted, stopping Taylor in his tracks. "If everything's under control, why are you running off with your tail between your legs?" Pennington asked, walking up to Taylor, crossing his arms and waiting for an answer.

Taylor stumbled over his words, nervously looking at the ground, his heart racing, half-wanting to pound his incredulous employer for the sheer lack of appreciation for what his most dedicated staffer was doing for him. "Sir, I, everything is fine, I assure you. The deal with Peterson is fine, the deal with Paulsen is fine, I just have some loose ends to tie up."

"Loose ends?" Pennington repeated sharply, twisting his neck and raising his eyebrows, mocking Taylor. "Loose ends? Dammit, son, you know there's no loose ends with me. What needs to get done, gets done." He was now up in Taylor's face, hands on hips, scowling down at him from over his bifocals.

"You know the stakes here. I don't want to have to spell it out for you."

Taylor threw up his hands as if to wave off his boss' doubts. "Sir, you don't have to explain anything."

"Just so you don't forget. This deal with Peterson is a career maker. It can also be a career breaker. Now, I'm headed up the ladder in Washington. I'm going to the show. And I want you to come with me. And you damn well know you can't get there without me; I can see to that. Now, I told you what I need. I need a squeaky-clean district, with a booming economy, growth, staunch environmentalism, and no crime," he pounded his fist into his hand, making a point with each word, leaning in and quietly saying into Taylor's ear, "Especially no damn murders of my own damn staffers. Now, you've been working great on everything so far, and this meeting tomorrow with Paulsen is going to go smoothly, you hear?

No damn blow off the Atlantic is going to mess this up, and you better put a lid on every little bad piece of news coming out of here for the next three months, you got that? I can't have any news about any controversy coming out of here. You got that? Now, I don't know what you've been doing, but I do know that you better make damn sure that there aren't any loose ends, you got that?"

Taylor felt as if he was going to throw-up, he was so angry. "Don't worry about it, sir," he mumbled.

Pennington smiled and straightened-out Taylor's collar and tie. "Alright. Bartholemew, I'll see you tomorrow morning at my office, nine sharp for a briefing. Meeting's at 11:00. Don't stick around here too long."

With that, Skip Pennington flashed his winning smile, winked, then turned and walked determinedly back to his car and waiting driver. Taylor watched him close the door and head out toward the road out of town.

In the Town Car, Pennington dug around in his pocket for Julianna's cell number. He needed to make sure that loose end was tied-up, for the time being.

♦♦♦

Julianna's cell phone rang. "When? What do you need?" She looked over to Michael then away quickly. "You already asked me to do that, I'm getting around to it. I understand, okay. No, no, okay fine. Yeah I'm at the lighthouse. Bodie. Yeah. Okay. Okay!" She hung up and got out of the Jeep.

Michael watched her for a moment then followed. The two women walked to the front door of the lighthouse welcome center.

Michael tried the front door. "Locked."

"He must be in the light. Follow me," Julianna said, leading Michael across the wrap-around porch to the back of the center, 50 yards across an open field from the lighthouse.

Michael looked up at its horizontal black-and-white stripes. "This thing made out of wood or what?"

"Brick. It's painted. Been here since the 1800s if you were wondering," Julianna said as the two walked towards it.

"Still working?" Michael asked.

"Wouldn't be much use if it wasn't," Julianna said, bounding up the front concrete steps to the door, which was half-way open. "What'd you say this guy's name was?"

The two ducked inside the cavernous structure which was cluttered with construction materials. Michael looked up the imposing cast iron spiral staircase enveloped in scaffolding and yelled, "Mister Lane!" Her voice echoed. There was no answer. She looked over at Julianna. "What's with all this scaffolding?" The two women looked up at metal pipes weaving their way up one side of the lighthouse wall toward the top. What looked like several makeshift landings held piles of wood and drywall. "They're refurbishing this, wanna open it to the public like Hatteras," Julianna said.

"Lane!" Michael gave one more call, her voice reverberating off the brick walls.

"He could be on the parapet outside the lens, checking out the storm," Julianna suggested. Michael nodded, and Julianna headed up the steps. Michael tapped her on the shoulder. "Wait," she said, stepping in front of Julianna.

"This is my deal. You're only along for the ride. I'm going first."

It took the women a good ten minutes to climb the 200 or so feet up to a small landing surrounding the lens and its ten-foot glass panels, with a huge lamp encased in thick glass in the center. They stepped off the stairs onto the landing, and Julianna pointed across the room. "There, outside. That your man?"

Chris Lane turned and saw the two women, smiling with relief as he saw Michael but frowning when he saw Julianna. The women walked around the lamp to a door on the other side of the landing, then through it and outside onto the wind-swept parapet. The sky was ominously dark for an afternoon, and they could hear waves breaking 200 yards away across the marsh, Route 12, and dunes.

Everyone grabbed onto the large black iron railing to steady themselves in the howling wind. Chris looked at Julianna nervously. "I thought you were coming alone?" he asked.

"A good agent always brings backup," Michael said, then turning to Julianna asked, "Mind waiting inside?"

The parapet was exposed to the full force of the gusts coming off the open ocean to their left. To the right was the Oregon Inlet, and as Michael quickly glanced around to make sure the coroner was the only other person up there, she caught sight of the marina and Coast Guard station in the distance. When she glanced at the sea, all she could see was whitecaps and black clouds moving in to overtake dark charcoal-grey ones.

Chris saw the look of concern on her face, and turned to look over his shoulder at the impending storm. He laughed, "Yeah, gonna be a blow. Probably gonna start raining any minute now, soon as those black clouds get here. We don't have much time to get off the island, really."

"Extenuating circumstances," Michael smiled back. Taking on a serious look, she nodded at Chris and asked, "So you got me up here in the middle of nowhere. What, couldn't you meet me in a diner?"

"Sorry for the theatrics. It's just that, well, Anderson kind-of..." Chris voice trailed off, then he composed himself and continued. "Threatened me."

"What? With violence?"

Chris nodded. "I'm afraid I've stumbled across something very serious about Kathy Kirkland, something that's a worst-case scenario for someone wanting to just keep on keeping-on, living his life. You know, I just wanted a normal life. I have a wife, kids. Kathy...she reminded me soooo much of my girl Anna. You have kids, Agent Francis?"

"Yes. Daughters."

Chris smiled. "You a religious person, Agent Francis?"

"Lifelong Catholic."

Chris wiped his eyes. "That's too funny, me too. Everyone I meet around here is Baptist or Methodist. My family was one of the only Catholic families on the island back in the day. I guess I'm used to standing out. I just wish now I didn't have to. So I have this girl, my daughter's age, give or take two years, looking like my daughter, murdered, and I start to feel for her, okay? Like I have to take care of her. I feel, I don't know…responsible. Like I have to do everything in my power to find out who did this to her, to make things right. You ever feel like that, Agent Francis? Like you're on some kind of ethereal mission that your whole life depended on?"

Michael felt butterflies in her stomach. Her exhaustion, and Lane's diatribe, were distracting her. She started to think about Brian, and her girls.

"Your daughter," she blurted out. "Where is she now?"

Chris straightened up and bit his lip, composing himself. The wind was gusting harder now, and his thinning grey hair blowing wildly gave him the look of a mad scientist. "She's dead."

That didn't surprise Michael, but the next words out of Chris' mouth did.

"She fell from this lighthouse, just over there," he mumbled, pointing a few feet behind Michael.

She turned to look and said, "I'm so, so sorry, Mr. Lane. I can't imagine how that must have hurt you. How did it happen?"

"I had to do the autopsy. There's not another qualified M.E. for miles, and we wanted to take care of all the burial details quickly. I couldn't bear the thought of her body filling up one of those terminals a few feet from my desk. Can you imagine the pain, Agent Francis? The pain of conducting an autopsy on your own child? I did blood tests, checked for alcohol, drugs, she was clean. But I did find..." his voice trailed off again. "She was pregnant. Three months, and I didn't know. My wife and I, we didn't realize, she hid it."

"I'm so very sorry," Michael said, moving forward and placing her free hand on his shoulder.

Chris nodded in appreciation and seemed to draw a little strength from the gesture. "We raised my daughter Mary Margaret very Catholic. All of us Catholics on the island were tight, and Maggie took it seriously, she loved The Church, it was her second family. She had a scholarship to go to Notre Dame, for crying out loud. She would never even think of aborting it, you know? She was a great girl, beautiful girl, reminded me so much of her mother when we were younger and dating. She helped me deal with troubles her mom and I were having. We were very close, up until a few months before she died. She became distant, reclusive. Hard to reach. Anyways, I wanted to find out who the father was, I tested the blood of the baby, harassed her old boyfriends, pulled their records, none matched. She wasn't dating when she died, not for months, and I never found out who the father was, although I have an idea."

Chris reached into his back pocket and pulled out a small spiral-bound notebook. He leaned hard against the glass window of the lens chamber, propping himself up so he could thumb through the pages without being blown over the outside railing. "It's funny, the things that fall into place. Almost like God is reaching down and saying, 'Look here dummy.' One night at the morgue I was looking at the Kirkland girl's report. I started thinking about my daughter. I got a sick feeling in my stomach, it was like I was being pulled in some kind of riptide, you know? I almost didn't know what I was doing. When I first got her, ah, body, I saw some blood under three of her fingernails on her right hand. I took a sample and used my testing kit to determine the blood type, then drew some blood from Kathy and determined hers. There was no match between the two. I pulled up my daughter's file on the computer, and her, um…" Chris' voice trailed off. "Her baby's blood type. Her baby's blood, it's the same type of the blood under Kathy's fingernails."

Michael's head began swimming and she felt an adrenaline surge as she connected the dots.

"Mister Lane, we can't assume that matching blood types mean the same person who killed Kathy Kirkland raped and killed your daughter."

Chris began crying.

"Suicide is a major no-no in the Catholic Church. And my Maggie was a good girl. She would never kill herself. At the same time, you would've thought that if she was raped, she would've come to us? Unless she blamed herself for being raped."

Michael watched as Chris' complexion seemed to go even paler than it already was. His wind-blown hair gave him a crazy, almost lunatic look, unstable.

"You think she blamed herself, Agent Francis? You think she thought she brought that on herself?"

"No, no I do not."

"I called Chief Anderson the other day for the files on her case, but he wouldn't give them to me. I tried to remember, but everything was real sketchy. She hit the ground around 5:30 one Thursday afternoon in April, no tourists were around. The damn lighthouse was still open to visitors then, but everyone was down at Hatteras all the time. Anyway, a park ranger, old Mike St. Claire, stationed here called the police, but he's almost 70 years old. He leaves the damn key to this lighthouse under one of the pots at the rear of the welcome center, for God's sake, how do you think I got up here? So, old Mike, he doesn't secure the scene, Anderson, he doesn't give up the files on any witnesses, although at the time he said there were none. The story he was selling was that she jumped."

He took a few steps forward, with a faraway look in his eye. Suddenly, he turned his gaze back to Michael, his face curling up in what looked like growing anger.

"I'm sure she was pushed."

He took a few steps toward Michael.

Julianna popped out from the lighthouse turret onto the deck.

"Are we through? Storm's coming, you know," she said, arms crossed against her chest, eyeing wild-haired Chris cautiously.

Dark clouds were moving in rapidly from the horizon, overtaking charcoal-grey clouds that had made the mid-afternoon seem dark enough; now it was as if early nightfall was coming.

Chris Lane looked frustrated at the interruption. "I need...I need to talk to you more, before you leave OBX." He turned and walked into the turret.

Michael watched him leave. It all seemed surreal, she thought. The story Chris Lane had just told her, about his daughter, got her thinking about her own three daughters. What would she do if they fell victim to a similar fate as Maggie Lane? How far would Michael go to avenge their deaths? The mere thought of her daughters in trouble made Michael's head spin. She walked to the edge of the railing and, holding tight, looked over the edge to the grassy field below.

"You're not gonna jump now, are you?" Julianna teased from the doorway.

All Michael could think about was her girls. Her girls and, surprisingly, Brian.

She could feel her eye start to twitch, mixing with the onset of tears.

"Don't worry, I have a job to do," she said absent-mindedly in response to Julianna's taunt.

Julianna stepped up to the railing beside her. "Why?"

Michael turned to look at her. "Why?!" she said incredulously, fueled by a rush of adrenaline.

"Yes, why? Why are you still hunting down some murderer when you damn well know you should be getting back to your family and regrouping. All this, this beach, this bullshit. It isn't your affair. It's not. But you've made it your affair. Honest to God, I've never met anyone I couldn't figure out before. But you, sweetheart, I have no idea. I just don't understand why someone who has her shit so much together needs to risk throwing it all away for people she doesn't even know."

"I don't have shit together," Michael spewed. Tears began streaming down her face, and the steady demeanor of a seasoned investigator blew away like sand off the top of a dune. "My marriage is falling apart. I don't know my oldest daughter anymore. My career is just sitting around waiting for a paycheck. There was a shootout in my house. Someone tried to run me off the road coming out here. And everyone save for one grief-stricken father wants me to pack it up and head back home empty handed!"

Julianna leaned in a little closer. "You can't change anything here. Do yourself a favor, go home, go back to your life!"

"I can't go back to my life! I don't have a life to go back to!" Michael yelled, slamming her fist into her hip as she spoke. "I'm going to go back home, get a divorce, move out of my blood-stained house, and deal with my screwed-up daughter living in a broken home! And what, I'm supposed to just leave here empty-handed? Not having accomplished anything?! I can't do that! I've come too far; not you, not anybody, not anything anybody says is going to stop me from finding out who's killed this poor girl on the beach, in the prime of her life, before she's had the chance to screw it all up!"

Her head was pounding, and she was short on breath. Michael felt like she would faint. She stumbled a bit, and Julianna caught her. Michael sensed Julianna's face inches from hers. She turned up her tear-soaked eyes and found Julianna staring back at her, deeply.

Lovingly.

Michael brought up her hand from the railing and shoved Julianna away.

"What?" Julianna pleaded, stumbling, face painted with the unmistakable look of rejection. Her wide open mouth closed into a sneer and she scowled at Michael, spinning around and marching to the lighthouse door. Hand on the knob, she turned and took two steps back towards Michael. "We have something. Might not be what you might be used to but I know women, and we connected, here just now and a whole bunch of other times. Whether you want to admit it or not we have something," she screamed, voice cracking.

Michael leaned her back against the railing, grasping it with both hands, staring at her feet. "How well do you know Skip Pennington?" she shot back hatefully.

Julianna's face twisted up in pain. "No! We're not doing this."

"How well do you know him?" Michael asked again, digging into her pocket and retrieving the photo of Julianna and the senator she had taken off the Shoal Surfer. She held it out to Julianna, who stepped forward, took it, looked at it, then threw her head to the sky and spun around angrily.

"God-DAMMIT!" she shouted. Turning back to Michael, Julianna angrily waved the picture at her. "You wanna go there? Okay, I'll go there. You know that guy who knocked me up, ruined my life? Well, voila. I was young and naive, and sexually adventurous. I still am. You want more? I'm still having an affair with him. He comes out here, we meet, he pays the mortgage on my beach house. I run errands for him, smooth-over the business community for him in absentia. There, you satisfied?"

She threw the picture in Michael's direction but the wind whipped it off the lighthouse tower.

It started to rain hard.

Michael watched the photo blow away. She lost her

train of thought momentarily. She turned back to Julianna and shouted, "Run errands? Like what? Like break into a beach house to steal evidence?"

"Just go home!" Julianna screamed.

Michael took an aggressive step toward her. "I'll ask you one more time. Did you ever break into a crime scene? Recently?"

"I don't know who killed that girl!" Julianna cried.

Michael took another step closer. "I didn't ask you that," she said quickly, shaking her index finger accusingly. "No, no, no. I asked you if you've ever broken into a crime scene. Have you?"

Julianna turned and paced, running fingers through her wet hair. "You're a treat, you know that? A real treat." She tried brushing the hair out of her eyes, and wiped tears away. She glared at Michael. "I just wanna know, are you asking me all this as part of your investigation? Or are you jealous?"

"I'm investigating a murder."

"That's all this is?" Julianna yelled. She walked back to the door, yanking it open. Standing in the doorway, she turned back to Michael.

"You know, I thought I was falling for you. I thought you were smart enough to see that. Either I was wrong, or you just can't deal with it."

"How well do you know Skip Pennington's son, Bruce?" Michael shouted over the wind and rain.

Julianna huffed and disappeared into the lighthouse gazebo.

Michael began to cry, burying her face in her hands.

She stood there, in the wind and rain, sobbing.

She was alone.

Her mind raced back again to the night of June fifth, when Brian had come through the front door. The confrontation that followed. The heated words. It all started to race back into her head, minute by minute, almost frame-by-frame, replaying for the first time in a long time. Michael had tried so hard not to think about that night, to bury it, deal with the guilt. Now it was flooding back, and she couldn't stop thinking about it, helplessly getting pulled back under layer upon layer of emotion, vivid memories of the worst night of her life.

She started to think about an even worse night.

The night she had found out her father had been murdered.

Her mind drifted back to her youth, the officer coming to her living room, walking in with her aunt Suzy, who was in tears. Kneeling down. His steel blue eyes staring sadly into Michael's.

She could still feel his eyes now, piercing.

The lighthouse gazebo door slammed, snapping Michael out of her daydream. She felt soaked, must've been standing in the rain for a while without knowing it. She brushed her now soaked hair out of her eyes; through the steady rain, Michael could make-out the figure of a man in a business suit. She squinted and looked more closely.

A smarmy looking slickster with a painted on grin.

"Agent Francis!" Bart Taylor shouted. He stretched out an arm toward her, holding the door to the gazebo open with his back.

"How did you find me here?"

"I called our mutual, ah, friend, Ms. Gray, on her cell. She's a friend of the Senator's. I had to ask her a few things before everybody disappeared because of the storm. You must've heard her take the call; she was with you, she told me you two were headed out here. I just saw her downstairs, in the parking lot, heading out in her Jeep. She said you were up here; do you need a ride? Let's get you out of this gawd-awful weather!"

Michael watched him for a split-second. He looked pathetic. He still held the door for her. She cautiously walked toward it. "Well, you found me. What do you need?"

Taylor's smile grew larger, and he lightly touched her shoulder as he ushered her through the door. "Whew! That's coming down, isn't it?" he said, brushing the wet off of his suit coat, then bending down to brush the rain off his slacks. Michael walked to the top of the stairs.

In one motion, Taylor snapped upright and forward, slamming into Michael. She grunted as the force of his slightly larger body caught her off-guard, sending her tumbling down the first flight of stairs, maybe eight feet down to the metal grate floor. Taylor took the steps behind her quickly. "Just wanted to make sure I got to see you off before I left this wonderful paradise," Taylor said menacingly, reaching down and grabbing Michael by the left arm and lifting her up.

Momentarily disoriented and a little dizzy from the fall, Michael flailed desperately but Taylor grabbed onto the back of her shirt, lifted her up slightly and neatly deposited her over the railing.

All Michael could do was hold her hands in front of her head. It felt like she was falling forever; she landed with a thud, outstretched arms first, with her lower body and legs tumbling awkwardly behind her. She had hit the spiral staircase railing fifteen feet down, and bounced five feet over some scaffolding next to the stairs. Michael flipped over the top of the scaffolding and crashed through a stack of drywall, causing it to tumble down on her, burying her with about a half-dozen eight by twelve pieces. She wasn't crushed by the drywall but its weight caused the scaffolding to shift, and pieces of it, looking like a 150-foot-high jungle gym, broke off, sending the structure crashing in on itself for about 50 feet. In a matter of seconds, everything settled and dust filled the lighthouse.

Taylor covered his face and coughed until the dust settled a bit. Still, the interior of the lighthouse stairwell was almost pitch-black now, save for the small yellow lights on each metal landing. He walked quickly, coughing, halfway down the stairwell until he was directly across from the section containing Michael. He stopped, kept coughing, and looked around for a way to cross the five-foot divide to the scaffolding. Taylor desperately wanted to see if she was dead or not. The wind howled outside. Taylor coughed and coughed. The scaffolding groaned.

Figuring the entire scaffolding was about to collapse, he ruled-out climbing up the scaffolding from the bottom. There was no way to check if Michael was alive or not.

His mind racing, Taylor heard a loud thunderclap and had an idea. Smiling, he double-timed it down the rest of the stairs and burst through the door out into the rain.

Under the drywall, Michael gasped for air, breathed in sawdust in short, choking chunks. She felt dizzy, sick to her stomach.

Michael blacked out.

CHAPTER 18

Bart Taylor was driving about 70 miles per hour and weaving back and forth across the windswept expanse of Route 12 from the Bodie Island Lighthouse and the intersection with the main drag in Nags Head up at Whalebone Junction. His nerves had taken a hit. Throwing a law enforcement official down a flight of stairs in a lighthouse was far beyond anything he would have ever imagined himself doing, but these were extraordinary times. The Peterson deal had to go through; his boss had to get a boost into the U.S. Senate; and Taylor had to ride those coattails to his own appointed position in D.C. It was his dream, and Taylor had convinced himself it was his destiny. He had worked 12 years, eaten buckets of shit for his shot at the big time. Do or die.

Still, no amount of bravado could mask the nervous guilt that racked Taylor's brain as he peered through the driving rain, making out lights and movement in the road ahead. The sky was almost black, and the late afternoon looked more like 8:00 at night. As Route 12 dumped out of the Pea Island refuge into Whalebone Junction, Taylor saw a yellow trench coat-wearing trooper with light sticks waving people over the bridge to Manteo. There were no cars heading North anymore.

The trooper looked surprised to see Taylor's car weave around the closed gate, bumping over some low dunes. Still, he motioned with his light sticks for Taylor to enter traffic. Instead, the nervous legislative director steered around the trooper to the right, cutting across a KFC parking lot onto Beach Road. The trooper yelled something, but Taylor was too far gone.

Taylor stopped momentarily as he was about to head down Beach Road. He looked to his right, across a vacant lot. He could see spray jumping into the air beyond the dunes. Soon, he figured, the ocean would wash up onto the land and take-out Beach Road. He had never been in a hurricane or tropical storm before, but Taylor had heard that storm surge was the most dangerous element of a hurricane, at least to those on shore. Where they once thought they were safe, people soon found themselves knee-deep in fast moving flood waters, all with a current, knocking people over and pulling cars into the ocean. Taylor looked left at the tail lights of cars heading over to Manteo; he wondered if he should give it up, join them, and just run away.

He took a deep breath. Taylor looked down Beach Road, at the blinking traffic lights swaying in the wind. There was a gas station about seven miles down.

He started toward it.

The wind burst in strong gusts through the alleys between beach houses, intermittently blowing his car almost clear off the road. Taylor's hands tightened on the wheel, and he concentrated on the deserted road ahead. Soon enough, he came upon a combination Exxon station and general store. All the lights were off.

Jumping out of his car at the pump, Taylor rushed toward the front door, which was locked. He ran back to his car, popped the trunk, and grabbed the tire iron. The novice murderer tried his hand at breaking and entering, smashing in one of the glass doors while lights blinked all around him as a silent alarm sounded. He reached through and unlocked the door, opened it and burst inside.

Taylor jumped behind the counter, tossing items about, looking for a gas can. Finding none, he stood up and looked frantically around the store, water dripping down his face.

Camping supplies. Taylor ran out from behind the counter and over to the display.

Sure enough, he found a two-gallon red plastic gasoline can. He ran back outside through the stiffening winds and over to the pump. He flipped up the lever on one of the gas handles, but nothing happened. The pumps were turned off.

Bracing against a gust of wind and rain, Taylor ran back into the store and behind the counter. He searched feverishly, finally locating a bunch of buttons under the counter. He pushed every one, then ran back outside.

The lights on the pump were on.

Taylor began pumping gasoline into his two-gallon can until it was full, then switched-off the pump and placed the gas handle back in its slot. He was screwing on the gas tank top when a police car of some kind pulled up.

Sheriff Sinclair.

"Hey, bad time to stop for snacks and a smoke, no?" Sinclair yelled out his window. Taylor smiled and waved as he put the gas can into his trunk.

"What the hell happened here?" Sinclair yelled, gesturing toward the smashed door.

"Gotta get outta!" Taylor yelled back, motioning for the man in the truck to get to safety. He slipped behind the wheel and calmly pulled out south on Beach Road.

Watching Taylor drive away, Sinclair turned to look at the broken front door. He got out of his cruiser and headed over to the station to quickly check for anyone inside.

"Where's that fella off to in such a hurry?" he yelled

back to his Deputy, who was standing outside the passenger side.

"That don't seem right, does it?" the Deputy shouted back. He shot a concerned look to the Sherriff, then ran over to the edge of the parking lot by the road, peering south on Beach Road. He ran back, yelling, "I can still see tail lights; they're weak, but I can see 'em. You wanna roll?"

Sinclair nodded, climbing into his cruiser. As he did, his phone rang. "Sheriff Sinclair," he answered. On the other end, crackling from the storm, and the muffled voice of a frantic Chief Anderson.

"Boyle, you seen that Francis bitch?"

♦♦♦

Michael couldn't stop dreaming one long dream in what seemed like slow motion. She was sitting in her kitchen, cold coffee in hand, untouched, staring out the picture window at some finches eating from a feeder. Brian had come into the kitchen quietly to get some milk out of the fridge. He poured a glass and came to sit across the table from Michael.

"We need to talk about last night," he said.

Michael wasn't sure if it was a dream or a memory from the morning of June sixth, the day after her whole life changed. It was all very confusing to her now – it seemed familiar, yet not quite right.

Something was off. Something about the way Brian looked, he looked a little off, a little less like himself and more like someone else.

"You really hurt me," Brian said.

Michael looked away, back out to the feeder. The bird was gone. She looked back toward Brian, but he wasn't the person sitting across from her.

It was a grinning Julianna Gray.

Michael opened her eyes, back in reality. She blinked a

few times, adjusting to the darkness around her. There was a faint light overhead, about 20 feet up. It was the low-light of what was left of the gray day being driven away by the oncoming storm. Michael could make out part of the glass enclosure on the lighthouse gazebo. Suddenly, what had happened to her came flooding back: she had been tossed down the stairs by that prick Taylor. Michael laid quietly, her professional training taking over. She listened for any sounds, but heard only the howling wind and rain hitting the glass of the gazebo.

Suddenly, she was jolted by a loud clicking noise from above followed by what sounded like turning of gears and an engine coming to life. She saw bright light overhead flashing; the darkening skies had triggered the lighthouse light into action, Michael soon realized. The interior of the lighthouse alternated between night and day as waves of the light swept back and forth, illuminating the walls and stairs. She tried moving her legs and arms, and found everything functioning, although as she moved her head began to throb. Her entire body ached terribly, and she felt hungover. She reached and touched the back of her scalp, just below her hairline, and found it slightly damp.

Blood.

Michael moved some of the broken drywall she had fallen into and sat upright on the scaffolding. She looked down, but saw nothing but the iron spiral staircase winding down for what seemed like about a hundred feet or more. She looked at her watch.

It was almost 7 p.m.

A noise rushed up from below. Somebody was opening the door to the lighthouse.

Michael looked down.

In the shadows she was able to make out Taylor's squirrely profile. He was lumbering in through the door, pushing it closed with his shoulder as he carried something in his hand. It looked like a bucket or briefcase or something.

He looked up. Michael rolled behind some drywall and kept quiet. She heard Taylor put down what he was carrying, followed by a brief silence and then a familiar clicking echoing up the staircase. Michael looked down again.

Taylor had a gun and was trying to remove the safety and cock it.

"Agent Francis? You up yet?" Taylor yelled up the stairs.

Michael kept silent and still.

Taylor reached into his coat pocket and removed a flashlight, shining it up at the scaffolding, but its beam was blocked by a bunch of drywall that had fallen on some scaffolding below. The light switched off, and Michael moved around to look downstairs again.

In between the sweeping beam of the lighthouse she could make out Taylor putting his flashlight in his pocket, and grabbing whatever he had been carrying in one hand, the other holding the gun. He started up the stairs laboriously, as if whatever he was handling was cumbersome and fragile.

About fifty feet up the stairs, Taylor stopped, put down his load, and shined the light up toward Michael again. This time the light caught her, and Taylor saw her open eyes watching him.

"Hey there! Glad to see you're awake!" he taunted her. "You don't have one of these do you?" Taylor asked, waving his gun in the air.

"You're in it deep, Mister Taylor," Michael labored weakly. The pain was making her grit her teeth as she spoke. "You wanna think real hard before you do anything else you might regret."

"Ahhh, you won't need to worry about me soon enough," Taylor replied as he picked up his gas can and began his climb once again in earnest. Both he and Michael were silent until Taylor was at a landing about six feet below, about eight feet away from her section of scaffolding. She saw the gas can and got an idea as to what Taylor was thinking of doing.

"That won't work, asshole," she shouted, voice strained in pain. "What fire starts in a lighthouse made of brick?"

"The kind of fire that starts in a heap o'drywall, that burns pretty well. I figure a lightning strike could have started it, who knows? I don't have time to argue now," Taylor said. He put his flashlight on the stairs, pointing it in Michael's general direction. He placed the gun down next to it, then picked up the gas can and unscrewed the top. Taylor pulled the can far away from his right side, set his feet, and then flung it in Michael's direction. A small amount of gasoline hit the bottom of Michael's level of scaffolding, but most of the toss fell harmlessly to the floor below.

"Fucking gravity," Taylor cursed, realizing he had to climb yet another flight of stairs to the next landing.

Michael tried to stall for time as she contemplated her next move. "Why not just shoot me you big pussy?"

"Agent Francis, I just don't have it in me. Besides, then people might find your body and the bullet and it wouldn't be an accident, would it?"

Taylor had left the gun by the flashlight on the landing below; he was almost at the next landing some four feet above Michael's head. She drew her legs up beneath her and got ready to launch herself over the scaffolding and grabbing on for dear life to avoid being burned.

Suddenly, the door downstairs flung open and Sheriff Sinclair and Deputy Marshall burst in, scrambling to shut the door quickly against the wind and rain from the storm outside. They looked around the ground floor, then Deputy Marshall glanced up just as Taylor realized he had company, vaulting down a flight of stairs in a panic to get his weapon, absent-mindedly carrying the gas can, banging it against the metal railing as he hustled down the steps, spilling gasoline on his shoes and pant legs.

"Gun!" Michael shouted in warning, rolling over to

take cover behind the drywall.

Below her, Marshall and Sinclair hesitated for a half-second, then pulled their weapons and began to seek out a target above them on the stairs. Neither could spot Taylor in the mix of dark and sweeping lighthouse beam. "Freeeeeze!" Sinclair shouted aimlessly. Taylor kept scrambling down the six feet of stairs to the landing with the flashlight and gun. "I said freeeeze!" Sinclair shouted again, barely making-out Taylor's dark form moving down the metal staircase.

Taylor, still holding the gas can in his left hand, reached down clumsily with his right hand to grab the gun. Deputy Marshall fired a warning shot down to the right of the staircase. Taylor ducked from the noise, knelt down and picked up the gun. Leaning over the edge of the railing and squeezing off a shot, he miraculously hit the deputy in his right shoulder, sending him crumpling to the floor.

The recoil of the gun sent Taylor sprawling backwards onto his ass, the gas can falling into his lap, spilling more gasoline all over his pants and waist as he lost his grip. He kept hold of the gun, bringing it down to bear on the intruders below from his prone position and squeezing off another shot, between the spacing in the metal stairs. The shot ricocheted harmlessly off the railing.

Sinclair stood still and straight, focused, and fired off three shots; the first went sailing wide of Taylor, the second caught his left thigh, and the third hit the metal stair grating between Taylor's legs, sparking as it hit.

The spark hit some of the gasoline that had spilled, catching Taylor's pants on fire.

Taylor began shrieking, first from the gunshot wound to the thigh, and then in horror as flames crawled quickly up his pant legs. The fire engulfed his lower extremities, causing him to stand up despite the pain in his thigh. Flames flew into the open mouth of the gas can just as it slipped from its resting place on his lap, causing it to explode in a fireball which seemed to envelope the man's upper torso.

Taylor clawed at his face and spun around madly, falling over the railing and plummeting down to where the Sheriff and Deputy were.

"Jesus!" Sinclair yelled, grabbing his deputy under one arm and dragging him out of the way just as Taylor hit the ground in front of them.

The Sheriff rushed over to a firebox and smashed the glass, yanking-out a fire extinguisher and putting out the flames on Taylor's unmoving body, then quickly turned his attention to his deputy.

"Ain't that bad," Marshall said.

"Malarkey," Sinclair said, yanking off his deputy's jacket. There was a lot of blood, and it was pouring out of the wound pretty quickly. Sinclair tore off the sleeve of his shirt and shoved it as best he could into the hole in Deputy Marshall's chest.

"Agent Francis? Are you up there somewhere?"

Michael, stunned by what she had witnessed, heart hammering, breathing heavily, kneeled and leaned over the railing of the scaffolding.

"I'm here, but I can't get down," she yelled in a sullen tone.

Sinclair cussed under his breath, then looked around the entry way. He scurried over to a pile of equipment and grabbed some thick, heavy electrical cable, the strong kind used for heavy duty loads.

"I've gotta get my Deputy back to town; there's gotta be an ambulance or something set up at the hospital. I'm gonna throw you this cable, you're going to catch it, right? You get one shot."

Before Michael could reply, Sinclair twirled the end of the cable around like a rodeo star and flung the heavy end up to her, almost smashing her in the face. She ducked and grabbed at the same time, clasping the cable with both hands.

"You're on your own now, girl," Sinclair shouted

angrily.

Michael smiled. "Nothing new there," she yelled down. "Sheriff, you get your man out of here, but I'm gonna need to talk to you in another day or so," Michael yelled.

Sinclair scowled. "Your case is over, Francis. Anderson's handling it, he just called me on my way over here, he's at that crime scene y'all are arguing about, looking for you, bitched at me to detain you on sight. Stay out of his way. Just get your ass to safety, this storm's just about on us."

Michael closed her eyes and clenched her fists. That prick Anderson was at the beach house? Now?

Sinclair lifted up his deputy and helped him to the door. Just before going out into the storm, Sinclair paused ever so briefly and yelled up the stairs once more. "Agent Francis, you're nothin' but trouble to me. You get outta here and stay away."

Michael closed her eyes and breathed to calm her nerves as she heard the Sheriff leave through the lighthouse door. She tied a knot securely around her waist, then wrapped the cable twice around her right arm, gripping the cable with both hands. She pulled up the rest of the cable, tossing the other end around some stairs and jiggling it until she could grab the slack and tie a knot.

Thunder boomed overhead and lightning flashes illuminated the gazebo windows above. The lighthouse seemed to shake in fright. Michael stopped momentarily and gazed upwards, closing her eyes and taking a deep breath to calm her nerves.

Without warning, the damaged scaffolding gave way. Michael fell free with it as it crashed down toward the floor a hundred-plus feet below. Her quick descent and weight tore the cable through her makeshift loop around the railing and burned her hands as it zipped by. Before she knew it, Michael was swaying freely below the stairs, suspended in space, dust and pieces of drywall floating down over her head.

The pain from her injured leg was excruciating. She was going to black out.

◆ ◆ ◆

When she came to, Michael was still swinging slowly back and forth in the dark lighthouse, intermittent lightning flashes illuminating her plight.

Gathering all the nerve she has left, Michael began to jerk her body around, swinging to the stairs as thunder boomed again, like a bomb exploding.

She heard the cable squeak and groan as her weight yanked on it, and felt the cable knot trying to slip away. She closed her eyes and tried to block the pain.

One more jerk.

She hit the stairs, twisting her ankle and holding on with the toe of her sneaker. Gritting against the pain, Michael Francis forced herself over onto the stairs, carefully climbed over the railing, and in time made her way downstairs, stepped over Taylor's burned, lifeless body and out the door of the lighthouse.

Standing in the rain and win, she looked over at the dead man's vehicle, then back over her shoulder through the door at his body once again.

She'd have to fish-out his keys to get back to town.

◆ ◆ ◆

Half-awake, clinging desperately to consciousness, Amy Miller moved her head from side to side. She heard noises above her upturned face, on the floor above her basement tomb. Feet shuffled, someone seemed to be pushing something across the floor. Amy heard clicking, and suddenly her black hole was filled with light.

Someone threw open the trap door leading to the crawlspace so quickly that the light from the room above blinded Amy. She felt something heavy slide down and land with a thump beside her; it felt cold and wet, like a plastic bag. Facing away from the light and forcing her eyelids shut with all her might, Amy heard someone mumble in surprise from above, and suddenly the searing white-hot light was gone.

She opened her eyes.

Amy saw spots, which slowly but surely dissipated, and she soon could make out some shapes in a semi-darkness, some faded light filtering down through the still open trap door. To her left she saw some short stairs, about three feet high, leading up to a room bathed in ethereal light, as if it was dusk. Amy heard more mumbling and feet shuffling, followed by harried clicking, like someone trying a light switch.

The electricity must have gone out upstairs.

Whoever was up there was trying to turn some on. In their haste to do so, they had left the trap door open.

Amy swung her head around to the left and saw a crumpled mass of something inside some large black plastic garbage bags.

She knew what was in there without thinking.

Her gaze swung back up to the door. She could make out something shimmering like a bunch of wind chimes. They were clinking in a slight wind; they made a nice crystalline type of noise, not like metal, but more like glass.

The light was suddenly wiped away as the trap door slammed shut.

Amy felt her heart begin to race. *No, no, no,* she thought. *This isn't happening.* Listening intently she heard footsteps running from the trap door and another door faraway opening and slamming shut.

Then nothing.

Think, Amy, think, she yelled inside her head. Her captor had dumped a full body bag into the basement, the electricity went out upstairs, they slammed the door and left. But why?

Amy thought about what she'd just said to herself.

Slammed the door and left.

There was a clicking noise when the door was first opened, but not when it was closed. Was it unlocked?

Slammed the door. But didn't lock it.

Amy could feel her heart racing faster. Closing her eyes and taking deep breaths, she tried to calm herself. Okay, let's work under the assumption that the door is unlocked, Amy thought. Better than working under the assumption it was still locked.

The door was over her head, just off to her left. Grimacing, Amy slowly, carefully bent her left knee and slid her heel up toward her ass. She gripped the floorboards with her nails as she slowly, carefully brought her knee up toward her chin and her left leg into the air, moving it up, up, up.

Something stopped her foot. Her toe was touching the door.

Amy grinned with satisfaction, then grimaced as her pain forced her to drop her leg to the ground. She straightened it out and breathed deeply to soothe the pain.

She would have to conserve her strength and try again.

◆ ◆ ◆

Sheriff Sinclair's cruiser dodged sand piles, puddles and logs, shimmying in the wind as its tires squealed against the forces of nature blowing across Route 12. Driving as fast as he could through the Pea Island Nature Preserve, Sinclair was sure he had climbed up on two wheels more than once.

Coming upon the wooden gates at the exit of the Preserve, the Sheriff floored the vehicle and crashed through the gates he had earlier gone around with a heavy jerk that sent his vehicle into a 180-degree skid. He gunned the engine, pulled out of the skid, and zig-zagged into the main intersection, and roared up the empty bypass for about a mile, underneath row after row of blinking stoplights blowing crazily in the wind, until he saw the lights of the Dare County Hospital. He floored the cruiser across the bypass, jumped the curb and flew through the front parking lot toward the emergency entrance, sliding to a stop just a few feet from a wide-eyed, rain-soaked Toby Jones, standing next to his Jeep, wave runner attached on its trailer, talking to some men in rain ponchos.

After it came to a complete halt, Toby ran over to the vehicle's driver's side. "What the hell you doin?" he yelled, then recognizing the driver, added, "Sheriff? What the hell's goin' on?"

"My boy's shot. This place still staffed?"

Toby looked grimly across the seat to the ashen-faced officer hunched over in pain, pressing a crumpled-up coat against his chest. "We got a skeleton crew here. Let's get him inside."

Sinclair jumped out of his seat and helped Jones and the other men carry his deputy inside the hospital. Once he was on a gurney and attended by orderlies, Sinclair stood back and let the medical professionals wheel him away.

He took a breath, then stood shaking himself dry. He turned and looked at Jones who was watching the gurney motor down the hallway.

"That boss of yours is messed up in this," he said, nodding toward where the gurney was. "Agent Francis knows it, too."

Sergeant Jones knitted his brow.

"I don't know about that."

"Well, why don't you go and ask him? He just called me a while ago, in the middle of a galdarn hurricane, from that beach house crime scene. Said he was grabbing some last-minute evidence before the storm took it."

He turned to face Jones and lowered his voice, talking very sternly.

"Now you know that ain't right. That just ain't right, Sergeant."

Jones looked at the ground.

Sinclair moved in closer.

"Sergeant Jones, what are you gonna do about it?"

Jones looked up, staring into the Sheriff's prying eyes.

"The beach house, huh?"

Sinclair nodded.

"You better get over there quick, Sergeant. If you're gonna beat Agent Francis to it."

◆◆◆

Brian Francis pulled up next to the abandoned ambulance in the gravel lot just outside Manteo. Rain and wind stinging his face, he made his way over to the driver's side window and peered inside. Nobody home. He tried the door. It opened.

Sticking his head inside the cab, he arched his neck around the steering wheel.

The keys were in the ignition.

"What the hell?" he mumbled, climbing inside and shutting the door. Brian crawled over the seat and looked into the back of the ambulance, which was full of supplies but unoccupied.

He slid back behind the wheel and turned the key. The engine started right up.

At the same time excited and concerned, Brian realized this was a gift that would get him past any roadblocks and into Nags Head. An ambulance meant there was a local hospital; a local hospital would have authorities who might know the whereabouts of his wife.

The same ambulance that had earlier carried the body of Kathy Kirkland out of OBX entered the highway leading right back where it had come from.

Behind, stashed in the weeds next to where the ambulance was just parked, lay the body of the ambulance driver, throat slashed.

◆◆◆

The wind was blowing hard against Michael's back as she staggered the fifteen feet to her vehicle parked at the motel. She fumbled with the keys, then opened the trunk and took out the shotgun. Heading back into the storm, Michael walked determinedly over to Taylor's vehicle, slid inside and shut the door. The vehicle shook from side-to-side from the wind as she backed out, and drove onto Beach Road.

She checked her watch; it had been about 20 minutes since she had left the lighthouse.

Eight more minutes passed as she dodged debris, driving awkwardly with her left leg working the brake and gas pedals, and drove through deep trenches of standing water to the beach house at mile marker nine.

She sat with her mouth wide-open as she pulled into the flooded driveway.

Ahead of her, by the front door, was Julianna's Jeep.

Michael absent-mindedly slammed the truck into park and sat staring at the Jeep. Was it Julianna's for sure? Hard to tell in the unnatural darkness, but it sure looked like it. Michael opened her door and limped out in the rain, ankle-deep in water, struggling to carry the shotgun. The wind almost knocked her off her feet, and the roar of the ocean just beyond the dunes was deafening.

That's when the wave took her.

The dunes between the beach house and the ocean had failed, and now a tall wall of water had crashed over the ruins of the natural buffer. The weight of the water collapsed what was left, and water had rushed forward unmolested, with force, crashing into Michael and taking her feet out from underneath her, sending her down onto her side, struggling to keep hold of the shotgun. Another wave abruptly followed, washing over her, rolling her out of the driveway and into the street. Seconds later, Michael felt herself stop tumbling forward and settle, as the water receded back toward the ocean. She tried to sit upright, but the wind knocked her back down on her side. She coughed and gasped for air, all the while clutching the shotgun tightly.

An arm reached down and grabbed her shoulder, rudely yanking her forcefully to her feet.

Chief Anderson stood above her, dripping wet, grinning malevolently.

"Well look who it is!" Anderson seethed above the wind through clenched teeth. Michael stood limply, coughing-up water, unable to answer. Anderson grabbed her with his other arm and yanked her along up the driveway against stiffening wind to the back of the truck, knocking the shotgun out of her hands. She saw stars as her right leg repeatedly slammed into the ground in her forced march.

"I kinda knew that shithead Taylor would screw things up," Anderson growled. Michael gathered herself and tried to break away from his grip. The much larger Anderson struggled, and held on tight to her. Suddenly he released Michael with his left hand, and brought it down hard on her right cheek with a clenched fist. The force of the blow knocked Michael into the side of her truck, and she fell the rest of the way to the ground as Anderson let go with his right hand.

Rain pouring down on her upturned face, Michael tried to see what Anderson was doing, where he would come at her next. She looked up to see the giant pointing his handgun down at her.

He took careful aim, using his left hand to steady his right arm with the gun from wiggling in the wind. He shook rain out of his eyes, focusing on his target.

That's when the wave hit him.

More storm surge had burst under the pilings of the beach house, flooding everything in sight, up almost to Anderson's shoulders like someone had turned on a giant fire hose. The waves had shot straight across the other side of the truck, sparing Michael most of the force of it, hidden down on the ground behind the left rear tire, but tackling Anderson and slamming him down. As the wave passed, Michael clamored to her feet, steadying herself knee-deep in water, staring through the darkness down the driveway. Anderson was struggling in the surf which now led to the street. The water receded; as it did, it dragged Anderson's prone body back with it, almost all the way back up the driveway to within five feet of the rear of Michael's truck.

Anderson pushed himself onto his knees, and started to stand upright when another, larger wave rushed past the side of her vehicle and hit him straight on. Michael thought she heard him scream as the wave knocked him back a good ten feet, throwing him to the ground with great force and rolling him clear across the street. As the wave receded, it rolled Anderson over and over back across the street. This time, Michael watched Anderson flailing in the deepening water, unable to get up. Michael noticed the water around her had risen to her thighs, and her truck was beginning to float. So was Anderson.

Another wave burst forth into the driveway, its power somewhat diminished due to the water already pooling in the street. It poured over Anderson's head, and he completely disappeared into the water. Michael felt her feet give way, and she turned her head and spotted the front door now almost at eye level due to the rising water.

Something bumped her leg.

Anderson's gun.

She reached down and grabbed it, shaking it to get water off.

Michael scrambled over to the front door, grabbing the stair rails to pull herself up to the door, pushing it open and spilling into the foyer with a rush of water behind her. She knelt on the wet floor, and turned to look out for Anderson. In the waning glow of lightning flashes, she saw something float by the rear of her car that looked like a pant leg and boot. It quickly disappeared under another wave.

Michael struggled with the door, throwing her body at it to push it shut against the surge. The lights in the house were off, and the blackness of the storm made it look like twilight outside. How the streetlights were still on amazed her; Michael looked up the stairs and saw light inside the house.

As quietly as she could, Michael swung open the cylinder of Anderson's gun and removed all six bullets, blowing into the empty cylinder and getting out as much water as she could. Reloading the gun, she made sure the safety was on and held the gun out in front of her as she limped slowly upstairs.

At the top of the stairs, she noticed some light reflecting off the wall leading into the living room. She looked around; the entire room glowed and stank with the strong smell of kerosene. Portable lamps and blue police glow sticks littered the room. She turned and saw Julianna, standing with a bucket of the foul-smelling liquid, sobbing, looking back at her by a brightly glowing lantern.

"You know, you had to push, push, push, didn't you?" Julianna screamed. "You couldn't leave well enough alone. Oh, no. Not the high and mighty special agent. Not you. You could leave me, though, couldn't you?"

"What," Michael pleaded, gasping for breath, "are you doing here?"

She brought up the gun and pointed it at Julianna.

Julianna straightened her posture, wiped her face with her forearm, and cleared her throat. "I'm sure you would've busted me sooner or later. I'm so bad, aren't I? I'm such a bad girl," she taunted over the wind and thunder clasps reverberating through the house.

Michael took a step forward into the area between the kitchen and living room, bringing her free hand up to her forehead, dumbfounded. "But...why this? Why are you here now?"

"I got a call. I got a call from my sugar daddy's little

buddy. He told me to come over here and meet Anderson, he told me to spread this stuff everywhere, to burn this freaking house down in case the storm doesn't take it whole, just to be sure it's clean. I tried coming over here two days ago but you and Deputy Do-Right showed up. Shit, I thought you were gonna shoot me."

"But why NOW?" Michael pleaded, stepping closer and dropping the gun to her side, a series of lightning flashes illuminating the inside of the house like a strobe light.

"Because Taylor thinks Pennington's son is gonna get tied to this murder. Why do you care?" Julianna screamed, throwing the kerosene bucket to the floor. The wind rattled the wall of windows behind her hard and the house seemed to creak and groan and start to sway.

"I dated the little bastard. After I started fucking his daddy, just for spite. He's the one who funded my charter business, kept me afloat when times were tough. Paid for my home. Took care of me. For a while I thought I loved the bastard. He's the one who got me pregnant, not his daddy. But his goddamn daddy talked me into getting an abortion so it wouldn't ruin his career."

"Where is Bruce now?" Michael demanded.

"Hell, he disappeared right after you talked to him in the bar. He hasn't answered his cell for days, probably hiding somewhere, the little pansy."

"I have to know where he is," Michael demanded.

Julianna laughed mockingly. "Puh-leeze, Bruce Pennington? You think he murdered that girl?"

"I think he murdered her and I think he killed Chris Lane's daughter before that. Threw her off the side of the Bodie Island Lighthouse."

Bending over and clapping her hands, Julianna laughed louder than before. "Now THAT'S a good one! Who told you that? Chris Lane?"

A bright flash of lightning and deafening thunder clasp made Julianna jump. She took a step forward, gesturing wildly, out of control. "Did lil' old Chris mention that his wife left him right before his daughter died, hmm? Rumor had it, she found out daddy was messin' around with his own daughter!"

Michael shook her head in disbelief. "That's disgusting! You're disgusting! Listen, you need to just leave, okay? You need to get out of here right now and forget about all this."

"It's fucking true! I live here, I know EVERYTHING that goes on! Did that asshole Lane tell you he actually went to school with Bruce Pennington? They were best friends, went to med school together. Lane graduated, Bruce failed out but they stayed buddies. They even co-own that piece of shit bar."

"Enough! Just tell me where Bruce is and get outta here before things get any worse."

Before Michael could finish her sentence, the beach house moved with a sudden jolt, knocking her and Julianna off their feet, the room pitching to one side at an angle. Furniture started to slide across the floor, over to Julianna's side. A lamp flew across the room and smashed through a window over her head while glow sticks scattered. The house kept sliding at an ever-increasing angle.

Neither woman screamed, but rather used their energy to scramble on the floor, trying to find a handhold.

"Grab onto something!" Michael yelled, bracing herself against the kitchen island. The gun slipped from her hands and slid across the living room floor into the bedroom. The glow sticks and the lanterns were swept together by water pouring in through the broken window at the bottom of the sloping floor as the side of the house sank. The force of the water broke the remainder of the wall of windows behind Juliana in a domino effect.

Michael tried to get a better grip on the kitchen island, her feet now dangling as the house turned completely on its end at a 90-degree angle. Michael caught a glimpse of

Julianna struggling toward the submerged portion of the house, in the water flooding the room. The lanterns all sank underwater and the room went dark, silhouetted against the constant lightning flashes outside. There was a loud boom, everything seemed to fall and then hit something hard, and the entire side of the house with the wall of windows imploded all around Julianna. Glass and wood flew everywhere through the room. Michael ducked her head and hung onto the kitchen island with all her might.

She turned back and saw the floor disintegrate and the entire other half of the house simply dissolve into the water. She heard Julianna yell something intangible, and saw her silhouette being pulled by the ocean out into the black night.

"NO!" Michael screamed. Her side of the house flipped back to its normal position, throwing her roughly onto the kitchen floor. The sounds of the storm were overwhelming, with thunder booming and wind howling, and rain and sea water rushing into the kitchen. Lightning was flashing everywhere, wind howling at her, hitting her in the face with cold blasts. Michael scrambled onto all fours and spun around.

She was on the remains of the house like a penguin on a patch of an iceberg. Michael was about 20 yards out into the ocean, with the empty lot where the house once stood slowly moving away from her. The houses and condos on the other side of Beach Road, illuminated by the streetlights, mocked Michael, standing like sentinels, watching her float away.

Suddenly the streetlights went out.

Total darkness broken by intense lightning. Wind. Rain. Thunder.

A wave pushed Michael forward, off of the kitchen floor. She tumbled into the water and the rest of the beach house disappeared under black waves.

Michael kicked hard with her bum leg and swam to

where she thought was up. Soon her head broke the surface, and she gasped for air. Rough waves were throwing her this way and that, and water was constantly smashing into her mouth and nose while her head kept bobbing below the water line.

Suddenly, just as a wave had knocked her out of the kitchen, another picked Michael up and sent her sprawling toward the shore. The lightning illuminated the tips of the dunes rushing at Michael as she felt herself hurled forward, eventually hitting some kind of sand and being rolled over and over and over. Her hand rubbed against something hard.

Gravel. The driveway.

Frantic, Michael flailed for positioning. She knew the wave would soon recede, and take her with it. She turned to face the road, and got her head above water. She was almost at the end of the driveway, toward the street, in deep water. Michael felt herself stop moving. She started swimming forward, maintaining her strokes as the surge pulled her back into the sea.

Michael noticed the tide was moving her at an alarming rate. She was 25 yards out before she knew it, and struggling to keep her head above water as she did her best Australian crawl.

Another wave hit her, forcing her down into the surf and forward, although not as far as before.

Michael held her breath as long as she could, then kicked and clawed for the surface, taking in a little sea water as her lungs gasped for air.

She broke the surface. She spun around. The dark outlines of the condos lay farther away. Maybe 30 yards.

She was losing ground. Her leg was numb; she couldn't tell if it was bending as Michael tried to kick at the water around her.

Lightning flashed and thunder boomed as the front edge of the hurricane bore down on Nags Head. Michael stopped kicking so hard, half-expecting the next wave to hit, half-wanting to take in the sights that may be her last. She felt peaceful, as if she had taken the worst Mother Nature had thrown at her and was simply waiting for the inevitable. She thought about her three daughters and felt sad for them. She thought about Brian, and surprised herself with feelings of longing to see him again. Michael felt as if she would cry.

Another wave hit.

Michael tumbled, but did not swim. She let herself float within the wave. She caught a break and surfaced long enough to take a breath, then another wave picked her up and threw her through the air into more water. Michael had no idea where she was, had completely lost her bearings. She felt as if she would pass out.

Then Michael felt her back bounce against something hard, and her right hand fell down to feel it too. Pavement.

The street.

Michael snapped back to life, and tumbled around in the dying tide to position herself with feet under her. She pushed up hard off the street and broke surface. She popped her head up and was looking south down Beach Road.

A single headlight was roaring toward her in the surf. She heard an engine roar, from some kind of boat.

Michael grimaced against the light as the surge started to turn and take her slowly back out to sea. The engine raced higher, and the boat raced toward her.

Toby Jones opened up the throttle on his wave runner. He roared up to Michael, and with his left arm reached down and grabbed a handful of her hair. "Hold on!" he screamed over the roar of the waves and thunder, turning the wave runner toward shore as the tide took both him and Michael out to sea.

She was screaming from the pain of Toby yanking on her hair; it seemed as if her scalp would rip off. Another wave came in hard, lifting Michael and the wave runner and pushing both in to shore. The wave runner turned and twisted as Toby kept his tight grip on Michael' hair, shifting his body to balance. When they got in far enough toward the street and the surge began to die down, Toby set the idle and reached down quickly with both arms, grabbing Michael and throwing her over the back seat on her belly.

"Hang on!" he yelled, cranking the engine and turning the wave runner north on Beach Road, fighting the tide as he careened past cars and furniture, speeding down a makeshift Venetian Canal. The two-seater responded, and Toby quickly got it positioned behind some houses that had not yet fallen, beating the surge.

"We've got to get someplace high and dry for a minute!" he screamed over the storm. His headlight illuminated an area where the flooding had died down to maybe three or four feet deep.

He pulled up to the front deck of the Purple Turtle, which was now at water level.

◆◆◆

Water was dripping more rapidly from the ceiling above Amy Miller's head. Off just to the side of the trap door, Amy could hear a steady stream falling like a wall between her and the large plastic bag to her left. Some water must be falling on the other side of the door as well, Amy thought, since she could hear it hitting the plastic bag.

Amy summoned-up all her strength and brought her left knee up toward her chin. She then pointed her lower leg toward the door, and extended it upward until her leg touched it. When it did, she rested. After a few more breaths, Amy pushed, but the door seemed to weigh a bit more than it had before.

The water, she thought. If there was water seeping in through the door, it must mean there was flooding up above, and that the water was covering the door. How much water was up there, and where was it coming from, Amy wondered, her heart quickening.

Was her captor running a hose to flood the place?

Before her thought process could continue, Amy suddenly realized she smelled seawater. The water pouring down into her area was seawater.

Flooding. Storm surge?

Amy's heart sank. Storm surge meant a hurricane. She was trapped in a basement God-knows-where that was quickly filling up with water, and outside there's a hurricane.

The water started pouring more quickly, and Amy heard the door above creak under the weight. She felt the water rising up around her face; it was touching her ears. It wouldn't be long before the basement flooded.

◆ ◆ ◆

Standing up straight on his personal watercraft, Toby turned to look behind him at the sea rushing in over the dunes and between the beach houses. There was a nasty storm surge that had completely covered Beach Road, and the wind was pushing debris inward. He turned and looked at the bar, and the porch was completely flooded and the water had burst-in the front door and was rising to the windows. The wave runner rose with the water and drifted onto the front deck.

"Listen, in a couple more minutes the flood water's gonna be high enough that we can ride it another block, but then we have to ditch this thing and huff it on foot the last two blocks to Route 12, to the hospital."

Michael pulled herself up to a sitting position on the seat behind him, summoning the strength to yell, "My leg's all busted up. I can't run."

"I need you to run. The wind's picking-up, and we'll have a short window of time to get across the highway. I'd say the eye is just a little bit out, that's gonna push some real strong wind in front of it. We won't be able to walk in it."

"You're gonna have to carry me," Michael yelled back weakly as she sat hunched over, grabbing onto Toby's back, too tired to lift her body completely straight.

Toby looked over his shoulder, his face twisted in concern for the poor woman, and nodded in agreement. He looked to his right and saw the floodwater rising rapidly, so that it was above the Turtle's deck railings and pouring in through a broken front window. He gunned the wave runner and turned to the right, slowing and navigating across the deck and then around to the side of the bar.

Michael looked back helplessly to where 3042 Beach Road used to be, for any signs of life amidst the flashes of lightning.

All she saw was black water.

◆◆◆

The floodwater in the basement had lifted Amy up as she gasped for breath, struggling to keep her mouth above the waterline. Soon her toes touched the ceiling, and she started sobbing. The water cushioned her beaten muscles as she moved her arms up, digging her fingernails into the wet wood and maneuvering herself directly below the trap door.

She held her breath as the water filled the space between her and the door.

The pressure below her was more than whatever water was rushing in above; with painstaking slowness Amy was pushed against the door as it raised up, bit by bit, until there was about a six inch opening where Amy could grab another breath of air. Another few inches. A foot open. Amy slid her left arm out into the dark room above. She grabbed the side of the door and pushed her body out, upper body first, then legs, then feet until she was clear of the door. The water in the room was rising, so the door rose with it. Amy kept her head above water, doing a semi-backstroke in about two feet of water and looking around. She was behind some kind of bar. Above her, beer mugs jostled and chimed with wind whipping in from somewhere.

Something bumped her from behind. She turned her head; the trap door was opened about halfway, and the black plastic bag was pushing its way out against her. It was heavy.

Amy heard a crash somewhere else in the building, then felt wind and a rush of water pour over her. It knocked her against the trap door and bounced her around and swept her away, past the edge of the bar, through a small alley and out through an open rear door, its screen door flailing helplessly against the onslaught of water. It took her outside, and Amy careened down a makeshift waterfall over some back steps, into about three feet of water in what looked like a back parking lot.

Amy heard a commotion to her right. Still floating on her back, she shook her head and listened; *a boat engine?*

◆ ◆ ◆

Toby turned the wave runner around the corner of the bar and slowly made his way to the back. He didn't want to gun it and make a run for Route 12, because he wasn't sure how deep the water was or what debris was in it. He was just at the corner where the side met the back when he heard a rush of water and the noise of something being dumped to his left.

Michael turned as Toby did and saw water rushing out of the back of The Purple Turtle, cascading down the back steps into the back parking lot, illuminated in the almost constant lightning. A few chairs and other debris came tumbling down.

And then the body flew over the steps. It was moving.

It was Amy Miller.

"Amy!" Michael yelled in back of Toby, who steered over to where Amy landed. Michael felt a rush of adrenaline and leapt off the watercraft, tumbled into the water, then struggled to stand up in the chest-deep water and waded laboriously across to Amy. She grabbed her outstretched hands and pulled her to her, cradling Amy's head in her arms.

Amy shrieked in pain.

"You hurt bad?" Michael asked. Amy just cringed. "We've got to get her to the hospital!" Michael screamed to Toby, who was about six feet from them.

"Throw her over the back seat; hold onto the side, I guess, and float with me. I'll follow this water out to Route 12 and get her across to the hospital."

Michael pulled Amy over to the wave runner, and she and Toby struggled against the wind and tide to pull her onto the back seat. Michael's body was so tired, and her rush of adrenaline faded. She let go of Amy and let the tide pull her on her back to the stairs by the bar.

"Agent Francis! Come on! Grab on!" Toby yelled.

Michael just grabbed onto a piece of the stairs and floated. "Go on," she yelled back.

Toby hesitated, going through his options. He didn't have many.

"Alright, wait there," he yelled back. "Just hold onto those stairs. This will take me just a few minutes. I'll get her to the hospital, then I'll come back for you. You'll have to..."

Toby's voice trailed off as he watched a large black plastic bag flow over the makeshift waterfall next to Michael and catch on a piece of wood, tearing a bit before coming to rest five feet away. It flipped over in the waves, where the tear was.

The black plastic folded back in the water to reveal a weathered woman's face.

Toby watched, stunned, as more bags began flowing

out the back door, falling over each other and down into the rear lot. One floated over to Michael. Toby watched in horror, struggling to steady the wave runner in the surging water. Amy was dead weight, and he was doing everything he could not to capsize. Michael motioned for Toby to pull out.

Toby pulled away slowly, concentrating on his headlight and the debris in the floodwaters ahead of him. Michael waded toward the back door of The Purple Turtle, eyeing a route onto the roof to wait for Toby's return. Along the way she bumped into a body that had slipped out of its bag.

Michael reached down and lifted up the head by what hair was left. A decomposed skeleton with bits of withered flesh looked up at her. Michael dropped it and backed away quickly, half-falling into the dark water.

Realizing she had little light to work with, Michael began to wade toward the back of the bar. The floodwater was rising, up to her neck. She maneuvered through two, three, four more bodies flowing out of the back door. Their exit had been slowed due to the floodwater inside the bar reaching the levels of the water outside, draining the waterfall of its sucking power.

Michael waded up the back steps, and as more of her body emerged from the neck-deep water, she got to a point at the top where the water was only up to her knees. Lightning flashed and thunder boomed as Michael surveyed her surroundings. She dared not go into the bar for fear of becoming trapped by debris. The rear roof of the building was flat. She looked to her left and spotted a gutter, and made her way over to it. She used the metal braces holding the gutter against the building as foot plants and shimmied slowly and deliberately up the pipe to the roof, slinging her dead-weight right leg as she went. Michael threw herself against the three-foot-high wall that separated the front pitched roof from the rear flat roof. Crawling over against the wall, Michael folded her arms across her chest and sheltered herself from the wind and rain as best she could.

Below, she watched the body bags continue to come out from the bar, lightning eerily illuminating them as they floated aimlessly, bumping into each other.

◆◆◆

The rented old National Guard chopper touched down in the deserted side parking lot of the Dare County Memorial Hospital. Harry jumped out and ran toward the front doors.

The burly Marine heard a man's voice yelling, "Hey, over here! We need a gurney stat!"

It was Toby, carrying Amy.

Behind him, Harry saw an ambulance careen up to the front doors and slam to a stop. Almost as soon as it did, the driver jumped out and ran into the hospital.

"Holy shit," Harry said.

It was Brian Francis.

An orderly came out of nowhere, rushing past Harry and over to Toby, who dropped to one knee and lowered Amy onto the floor. Two other orderlies came outside with a gurney.

Harry was face-to-face with Brian. He opened his mouth to say something, but Brian quickly shook his head no. Brian looked down at the woman the orderlies were attending, half-expecting to see his wife.

Toby stood up and gave the orderlies some space, ripping off his poncho. Brian noticed his police uniform.

"You local?" he asked. Toby looked over and nodded, then turned his attention back to Amy, who was being lifted onto the gurney. The orderlies brushed everyone aside and hurried down the hallway, with a nurse nearby grabbing a phone and hollering commands. She then followed the rush through the swinging doors, and silence engulfed the waiting area.

Brian turned to Toby, who was making his way quickly to the front door. "Listen, my name is Brian Francis. My wife is an agent with the State Bureau of Investiga – "

"Francis?" Toby replied. "You're Michael Francis' husband?"

Brian nodded.

Toby half-laughed. "Alright, I guess that figures. We've gotta hurry," he pointed over his shoulder and started running for the front door.

"Whoa! Whoa!" Harry called after him. "I've got transport in the side lot. Where is she?"

Michael sat on the roof of The Purple Turtle with her knees drawn up to her chest, numb to the piercing cold, driving rain and wind which swirled over the roof from her backside and periodically smacked her in the face. She rocked back and forth, sobbing without tears, her body almost completely worn-out, trying to stay awake as she hung onto a venting pipe. She watched to her right as tiles at the sides of the roof flew off in the wind from the approaching edge of the storm; water was flying sideways in every direction, and lightning was flashing constantly.

Below her, Michael watched as the floating bodies – she had counted seven, but couldn't be too sure – floated up toward her with the rising water. The storm surge had pushed the level to within a foot of the flat roof in a matter of minutes, and the bar creaked and groaned under the intense pressure, the noise more noticeable now that the winds seemed to be dying down.

Michael groped around her neck, her finger grabbing onto a chain. She looked down and glimpsed the small gold crucifix Brian had given her a long time ago.

She was surprised she was still wearing it.

Michael closed her eyes, blotted out the turmoil around her, and remembered June fifth. It was Friday night, around 8 p.m., and Brian was out with people from the station yet again, said he'd be home close to 11. The girls were at friends' houses for overnights.

And Michael was in bed with a man she'd met not two weeks earlier at the gym.

The bed she shared with Brian.

After a couple hours of passion, Michael said goodbye to her lover at the side door to the garage, leaning into a passionate kiss as she flicked on the garage door opener.

As she did, the front door opened and Brian walked in.

The three adults stood there in shock, silently regarding one another.

Hours later, Michael was crying, detailing her tryst to her husband. Brian was stoic, telling her they would work things out, that he loved her regardless. He reached across the table and took her hands.

Michael pulled away.

As she played the scene over in her head, she remembered she had never felt so alone as she had the night of June 5th.

Michael sat on the roof of The Purple Turtle, eyes closed, feeling alone again once more. She could hear the sounds of the wind and thunder slightly off to the left as the storm hit the coast proper. Michael felt her body getting colder and number. She was shaking, more and more violently, from the cold and exhaustion.

Slipping away.

She saw her daughters' faces.

"So, so, sorry," Michael muttered through trembling lips. "So sorry."

She leaned over onto her side and lay down on the roof. The wind and rain sounds died down, becoming softer and softer. Thunder boomed, then reverberated. The thunder didn't slip away with the rest of the noises. Instead, it thumped-thumped-thumped in her head, growing slowly louder and louder. Michael started blinking her eyes, confused by the noises.

A light was drifting in the air straight toward her, from the general direction where Toby had sped off. The light was growing, growing, growing. Michael pushed herself back up to a sitting position, bringing her hand weakly up to her forehead to keep the rain out of her eyes. She could see the light was surrounded by smaller red and yellow blinking lights.

The lights of a helicopter.

Michael stared, emotionless, watching it approach. It swung to its side and hovered, about twenty feet in front of her. A man in an orange helmet was calling to her, but she couldn't hear him. He started gesturing up with his hands, and Michael watched as the helicopter raised up about twenty feet, then slowly maneuvered almost directly over her head.

"We've got to go above and drop down to get her. You've done this?" Harry yelled at Brian.

"No, but, I'm good to go," Brian yelled back, tightening the body harness and clipping himself onto the winch before anyone else in the chopper had the chance to do the same.

The chopper wiggled back and forth, violently at times, in response to an occasional wind gust as it repositioned itself almost directly above Michael. "We've got one shot at this!" the pilot shouted into his headset. "We're in the eye right now, but the wind is gonna get nasty again in a few minutes."

"Ready?" Harry yelled at Brian, who gave thumbs up, turned and rappelled out the open door of the chopper.

He was about five feet down when he noticed the white water rushing in from the sea toward the front of the bar. "Shit! Shit! Down! Down! Down now!" he started yelling into his headset. "No! No! Up, up, up!" Harry yelled, seeing the same wave.

Below, Michael craned her neck upward as she watched someone drop from the chopper, then hang in mid-air. Whoever it was kept turning his head to watch something at the front of The Purple Turtle, out of Michael's line of sight. She started to turn her head to peer over the roof when a giant wave that had glided silently over the broken dunes crashed dead-on into the front of the bar, jolting the structure and sending Michael rolling onto her back, tumbling across the roof. White water cascaded over the pitched roof section of the bar and along the sides, spraying frothy white everywhere.

Overhead, the chopper shot upward about ten feet, yanking Brian like a yo-yo.

Michael steadied herself on her belly, lifting her head up off the roof; she thought she could feel the bar starting to drift. With a sickening crack, a shudder tore through the structure. It spun about twenty degrees clockwise, then began to break apart. Within seconds, Michael's flat roof was flying off into the water below, as the rest of The Purple Turtle exploded into a thousand splintered pieces.

Michael started to fade, feeling like she was watching an IMAX movie. She began to close her eyes, to fall asleep. She lay her head back down on the roof.

"Down! Down!" Brian was screaming into his headset. Harry leapt across the rear compartment and slammed the winch lever to the down position. Caught off-guard, Brian momentarily let go of his cable but grabbed it again just as he splashed down into the water below.

In the water, Brian was splashing about, calling after his wife. "Michael! Michael!" The chopper above shone a spotlight down below in a sweeping motion. Moving right, the large beam suddenly jerked back and centered on Michael's figure on the roof, not thirty feet from Brian.

Brian saw and started swimming furiously toward her. Above in the chopper, the crew member next to Harry let out more cable and told the pilot to swing over and center-up on the victim.

Fading fast, Michael started to black out. Her eyes closed, and images of her wedding day started flashing in her mind. "Michael, Michael," she heard Brian saying to her, as he hugged her tightly outside the church.

Suddenly, somebody was shaking her. Michael opened her eyes and saw Brian's wet face. He was screaming at her.

"Hold on!" Brian yelled, wrapping his arms and legs tightly around her. He took his right arm from her momentarily and flashed a thumbs-up to the chopper overhead, which was weaving back and forth, trying to stay steady in the wind.

Michael felt Brian hold her tightly as they rose out of the water, slowly. Eyes closed, she started to drift-off, her memory flashing back once more to the night of June fifth.

After blurting out that she'd cheated on her husband she expected him to scream, or storm out of the house. Instead, he had come to her, thrown his arms around her, telling her that he loved her and needed her. She remembered wriggling out of his arms and slapping him in the face.

"You dragged me down here, away from all my friends and all my family back in Buffalo. Then you abandoned me for your goddamn job, left me to raise the girls on my own. I'm failing at my job, Brian, I'm fucking failing. And I'm failing as a mom. And you and I, well we're failing too. It's not gonna work between us, we've lost. Just accept it," she had screamed.

That was the last time she had felt Brian touch her.

Until now.

Looking up at the chopper, Brian felt Michael wriggling, almost as if she was trying to push out of his grip. "Michael?" he said. "Michael! Stop!" he yelled, as his wife gathered strength from somewhere and started pushing and kicking out of his life grip.

Brian's clothing was wet. Michael wasn't holding onto him. He lost her.

Michael slid out of his grip, and Brian grabbed at her hair with his left hand, which spun his body upside-down in the harness as Michael passed below out of his reach. He threw out his right arm and caught her left wrist as her hands flew up over her head. The jerk on the cable made the crew helicopter winch jam.

Brian looked down at his wife, and beyond her to the water ten feet below them. His grip on her wrist was slipping. Her hand slipped through his, but she grabbed his fingers, and they hung there, hands entwined. "Michael! Baby, don't leave," Brian pleaded.

Michael looked up at him weakly, closed her eyes, and let go, falling into the water below.

"Shit!" the chopper pilot yelled into his headset. Harry turned his head and looked toward the front of the chopper, toward the sea. He could make out a white crested wave rushing toward them, about thirty yards out.

It was almost as high as the chopper.

Harry watched helplessly at his friend below, bobbing up and down as the helicopter swung upward.

Michael dropped straight down deeper in the water, not trying to break her descent. On impulse, she had held her breath as she hit the water, but was too weak nor determined to hold it on her own. Her feet bumped something, breaking her fall and descent through the water, jostling her slightly and then forcing Michael to slowly drift upward, the obstruction floating with her, pushing her up.

Michael's head popped out of the water, and her survival instincts told her to move her head back and breathe, which she did. The object below was positioned almost directly below her, and it was big, almost her size, and it was floating. Michael was floating on something just below the surface, keeping her head and face just above the waterline.

Above, Brian felt the chopper start to move upward. He looked down, and spotted Michael float to the surface. With his right hand, Brian smacked at the release button at his waist, and with a jerk he sprung free of the rescue cable, plummeting into the water below, just to the right of Michael.

"Dammit!" Harry yelled into his headset. "Climb another ten and hold steady!"

Below, Brian broke the surface and grabbed onto Michael again. He spun her around and looked into her face, but her eyes were shut and she was coughing-up water. He looked past her at a wave, cresting about ten feet over their heads, bearing down on them. Brian wrapped his entire body around Michael, closed his eyes and held his breath.

The wave passed about fifteen feet below the chopper, completely covering the area where The Purple Turtle had been just moments ago. As soon as the crest passed underneath, Harry gestured over to Toby who was holding onto a strap by the door.

"Hand me that harness."

Under the wave, Brian and Michael tumbled over and over, and some debris Michael had been floating on tumbled with them. Brian felt it bang against them, smooth against his arms. He momentarily opened his eyes in the black water but couldn't make out what it was. They tumbled some more, then when the current died, Brian kicked up hard toward the surface, grabbing Michael in his arms. He broke the surface, took in a huge breath of water, and yanked Michael's head out of the water. The debris was tangled on their clothing, and Brian had a hard time keeping afloat. Suddenly, he felt someone grab him from behind.

Startled, Brian turned to see Harry in a harness. The chopper was overhead, and soon a second cable plopped down behind Harry. He hurriedly snapped the line onto Brian's harness, and gave the thumbs up. The cables started pulling all three into the air.

Once they were free of the water, Brian looked down to see what debris was still hanging on them. Michael's right foot was stuck inside one of the body bags. Brian started kicking at the bag, and finally hit something solid which shot it free, off of Michael's leg.

In the searchlight beam, Brian made out what looked like a young blonde woman's body sliding half out of the bag just before it plunged beneath the black water below.

Toby worked furiously to pull everyone aboard the pitching helo, with the pilot spinning it around and heading away from the ocean. Michael was flat on the floor of the chopper, by the open door. She bounced around and shook violently as the chopper fought the wind. Brian threw off his helmet, grabbed his wife, and pulled her to the back of the chopper, onto a row of seats.

Michael was coughing up water, but opened her eyes and gazed out a window by her face; she saw nothing but water reflected in the helicopter's search lights. Everywhere, water. Beach houses sticking up like nothing more than boulders in the ocean; Beach Road completely gone. The new shoreline was the block next to Route 12. Michael stared in amazement through glazed, tired eyes as the scene receded before her.

"Touch down at the hospital in five," Harry reassured Brian, who nodded. He had his arms around Michael, pulling her close.

Michael's head momentarily cleared, and in her brief moment of lucidity she looked up at her water-soaked husband.

Instead, she saw the face of Julianna Gray smiling down at her.

Michael just stared, blankly.

She pushed away weakly, coughing, glaring defiantly at the visage as she struggled to wipe water off of her face. Michael turned away and looked out the window of the chopper, staring groggily at nothing in particular. She leaned forward, her forehead resting against the window.

Out of pure exhaustion, her eyes slowly shut, and Michael Francis passed out.

Brian watched her for a moment, then leaned over and

carefully, gently, brought her back to him, propping her body against his side, her head in the crook of his arm. He held Michael tenderly, moving her wet hair out of her face, then stared out the window at the violent white and yellow flashes as they exploded across the endless black night.

◆◆◆

On Highway 64 West, a white SUV slowly made its way across the Alligator River, the last stretch of water separating the Outer Banks to the mainland, to a roadblock on the other side of the bridge. Sheets of water flew crazily side to side, illuminated by the headlights of several state trooper cars. One of the troopers came out of his car and frantically waved an orange light stick at the SUV to get it to stop.

"A little late gettin' out, wouldn't you say?" he shouted over the storm, walking over to the driver's side of the vehicle.

"Had some last minute business to tie-up," the driver yelled out from the darkened cabin as he lowered his window.

"Good deal sir, you keep it slow and safe, drive straight out, keep going West on 64. You're not going to stop anywhere soon, right?" he admonished, shining the light inside on the driver's face.

Chris Lane smiled weakly. "No sir. Not anytime soon."

Pulling away from the roadblock and closing his window, Chris fumbled around in a pile of papers in the passenger's seat, finding a small index card he'd written on earlier and holding it up close to the dashboard lights.

"Let's see, 120 Hidden Pine Way, Apex," Chris read out loud.

He'd made the decision to wipe out the Francis family when he was interrupted atop the lighthouse, just a few seconds before he was going to throw the pitbull agent over the side. She knew too much, no telling who she'd shared her info with. Just like that Amy Miller girl he'd killed and thrown into the basement of the Purple Turtle with the rest of his trophies, right under Bruce's nose. His beautiful, blonde trophies, like the Kirkland girl, who reminded him so much of his precious little girl who took her own life, along with their baby. He was hers, dammit. And she left him.

Deprived him of his pleasure.

That made Chris mad. Just like the thought of Michael Francis made him mad.

I wonder if either of her daughters is a blonde, he thought to himself.

The possibility gave Chris a tingle between his legs.

Pressing down heavier on the accelerator, he sped away from the storm behind him, forward into something much, much worse.

ABOUT THE AUTHOR

David Dean grew up loving the books of Dean Koontz and the films of John Carpenter. An avid fan of suspenseful thrillers, mysteries, science fiction, and horror, he enjoys writing novels, novellas, and short story anthologies that challenge each reader's perceived understanding of reality, science, and religion, and the role each plays in the ongoing struggle between good and evil in every human being.

David enjoys spending time with his wife, dogs, friends and family in the coastal paradise surrounding Topsail Island, North Carolina, while doing his best to make a positive impact in people's lives.

Made in USA - Crawfordsville, IN
14803_9798218008628
06.03.2022 0500